TOUCHED BY TIME

Mail-Order Brides/Time Travel Series, Book 1

Written by Zoe Matthews
And
Jade Jensen

Chapter 1

Kimberly woke up with the alarm ringing in her ears and she swung her hand to turn it off. She groaned and slit one of her eyes open to make sure it really was time to get up. She groaned again when she saw that it was indeed 7:30. She only had a few hours before she had to be at work.

She wasn't looking forward to work today. She worked as a trauma nurse in an ER hospital in Denver and she had gotten home late the evening before because she had covered a shift for another nurse. Kimberly remembered how excited she was when she first got the job. She had always wanted to work in a large emergency room since she graduated from college three years ago. She had been working in this ER for six months, but it hadn't turned out to be the job she thought it would be. Her manager, Angie, for some reason developed an intense dislike for Kimberly right from the first day on the job, and things had gone downhill from there.

Angie always made sure Kimberly did the jobs no one else wanted. She sometimes even assigned Kimberly jobs the CNAs or orderlies should have done. Even though she had been hired to work with trauma patients, she rarely got that opportunity. Today was supposed to be her day off, but another nurse had called in sick during her shift the day before. Just before Kimberly had left for the night, Angie had insisted she come in this morning to help out.

Kimberly dragged herself out of bed and headed to the shower. She quickly dressed in her green scrubs and pulled her dark brown hair into a ponytail to keep it out of the way at work. She always made sure it was long enough to fit into a ponytail easily; she hated it when her hair would tickle her face at work. She stared into the mirror at her tired green eyes. Even her fair skin was starting to look dull. She wasn't sure how much longer she could stick with this job. She went to the kitchen and prepared some oatmeal and toast. She knew her roommate, Nicky, had already left for the day to teach at a local elementary school.

She smiled as she thought of her best friend. Kimberly thought of Nicky as a sister. Her name was Nicole, but she felt the name was too stiff for her bouncy personality, and preferred to be called Nicky. When Kimberly was 15, her parents had been killed in a car accident by a drunk driver. Her mom and dad had gone out for their twentieth anniversary and had never come home. She missed her parents desperately and didn't like to remember how much her life had changed after their deaths.

Kimberly didn't have any other family, so she had been put in the foster care system by the State of Colorado. The first few families that took her in were awful. In one of the homes, their own children treated her almost like a servant with the parents' encouragement. In another one, the man had tried to abuse her, but luckily, her birth parents had insisted she learn the art of Kung Fu, and she had been able to defend herself. Nicky's family had been her third placement. Nicky had been her same age and Kimberly had been blessed to be able to stay in her home until she graduated from high school. In fact, Nicky's parents had let her stay until after graduation even though she had turned 18 four months earlier and the state had stopped paying for her care.

Nicky's family still treated her like she was part of their family. Kimberly stayed with Nicky during college breaks and went to some of the family parties. Nicky had an older brother, Justin, who treated her like a little sister. Kimberly enjoyed sharing a place with

Nicky. They rented a townhouse together. Justin lived in the same complex with his young son, Garrett.

Kimberly sat down and opened a newspaper to read while she ate her oatmeal. Nicky had been purchasing newspapers over the last few weeks because she liked to use them to help teach her fifth-grade students about current events, although she secretly only enjoyed the comics portion. Nicky wanted her class to learn how to research in many different ways to find current events, not just using their computers and tablets, but also using books at the library, encyclopedias, and current newspapers. Nicky had made arrangements for several different newspapers to be delivered to their townhouse from Denver and the surrounding area. Kimberly had opened up a small newspaper called *The Denver Rocky Mountain Gazette*.

Kimberly quickly found the classifieds and started to read them to see if there were any new openings for trauma nurses in the Denver area. She couldn't see any that she was interested in applying for. She paged through the rest of the ads while she finished her breakfast until she got to the personal section. A strange ad jumped out at her. It was very unusual.

The ad had a small black and white picture of a woman who wore a large fancy hat. The hat looked straight out of the late 1800s. Kimberly could tell that the hat was black and had various types of flowers on it. There was even what looked like a feather and some ribbon. Kimberly knew that during the 1890s, these types of hats were very popular. The woman's dress also looked like it was from that era. It was lighter in color and had puffed sleeves, although the bodice was plain looking. The picture was small, so it was hard to see many details, but it definitely looked like it had been taken in the 1890s.

The font in this ad was very different than the rest of the ads. It also looked like an ad someone might find in a newspaper in the 1890s. Kimberly had always been fascinated by that time period and she liked to read all the fiction novels she could about that era. She often would say that sometimes she felt she had been born in the wrong time period.

She was surprised to find that this ad was advertising for mail-order brides. This was one of the many subjects Kimberly enjoyed reading about. She always felt the women who answered these type of ads were very brave to do so. Most of them went to a part of the country they had never been to before, usually to a different life than they were used to. Some were orphans and others did have families but weren't happy with their lives. She knew that most of them immediately married the man they had been corresponding with as soon as they arrived.

Kimberly knew that not all of the marriages were happy ones, but she had read enough to feel a great admiration for these women who left the life they knew to marry a man they didn't know for a chance at a better life. Kimberly was curious and so she read the ad. It read:

Respectable hardworking men are looking for equally hardworking women who would be willing to travel to their homes in the west and marry. Many choices to choose from. If you are an unmarried woman who is between 18 and 30 years of age and are interested in a new life, please write to the following address for more information. Please address any letters to Mrs. Victoria Hilton.

Kimberly looked closely at the address that was provided. From what she could tell, it was located in the Denver area, probably in an older section of the city. She found it peculiar that a phone number, email address or website hadn't been provided. Most of the ads she saw in newspapers always had at least an email address or phone number.

Suddenly she became aware of the time and knew she would need to hurry if she wanted to make it to work on time. She grabbed a pair of scissors and carefully cut the ad out of the paper. She placed the ad in her cell phone case for safe keeping. She had made plans to meet Nicky for lunch at the hospital cafeteria and she wanted to show her friend the ad. She was curious to find out what Nicky thought of it.

****

Kimberly sighed with relief as she sat down at a table in the cafeteria to wait for Nicky. The morning had been rough and Angie had almost not allowed Kimberly to take her lunch when she was scheduled to, but in the end, Kimberly had been able to slip out before Angie gave her another job to do "really quick before you go for lunch."

She arranged the salad and fruit she had purchased and started to open the dressing packet. Nicky arrived in her normal bouncy manner. She was fairly tall and her hair was almost black, so she was easy to spot. She sat down with her packed lunch of a sandwich. Nicky worked at a nearby elementary school, so the two of them met for lunch at least once a week at the hospital cafeteria.

"How is your day going?" Kimberly asked as she took a bite of salad. She listened as Nicky told her a few things that had happened in her classroom. She always had some fun stories to tell. She had the unusual talent of talking so fast, Kimberly could miss an entire conversation unless she was listening closely. "You remember the troublemaker I told you about, Bryan? I think I finally got through to him. It just hit me in the middle of the night last night, I've really got to get on his level." She kept rambling for a while, while Kimberly's attention kept going back to the ad. She couldn't logically explain why an ad like that would be in a modern paper. Once Nicky hit a lag in the conversation, Kimberly jumped in.

"Look what I found in one of your papers this morning," Kimberly said as she pulled the ad out of her phone case. She passed the paper to her friend and finished her salad as Nicky read the ad.

"This is really weird," Nicky said, laughing. "Who would actually answer an ad like that? I bet it's a scam."

"That's what I think, too," Kimberly said. "But don't you think it is interesting that the ad looks like it came right out of a newspaper from the 1890s?"

"Yeah, especially the picture of the woman." Nicky was energetic, but she could always sense when Kimberly needed her to be more serious, and she looked more closely at the ad. "There's just an address. No email, phone number, nothing else."

"I thought that was strange, too." Kimberly pushed her salad plate away and started on her fruit.

"You know what you should do? You should answer this ad." Nicky's eyes shined, loving the challenge this ad had created.

"What?" Kimberly laughed, thinking Nicky must be joking. First Nicky thought it was a scam and now she was encouraging Kimberly to answer it?

"It says to write and ask for more information. It would be interesting to see if someone actually sends you something. Plus, who could better answer an ad for a woman like this? You would dress like this woman in the ad if you could, and you know it!" She playfully jabbed at Kimberly.

Kimberly thought about it for a moment. "You're right. It would be fun. I'd write just for a joke." She laughed, but also felt a thrill of excitement. She didn't do spontaneous things very often.

"You probably shouldn't use our address, though, just to be safe."

"Good suggestion. What address do you think I should use?" Kimberly wondered.

"Why don't you use my school address and have it delivered in care to my name."

"Are you sure? Then they will have your name also."

"Well, just use my first name then."

Nicky pulled a pad of paper out of her large flowery bag that she carried around with her all the time. Kimberly always teased her that it was a bottomless bag. Anything anyone ever needed could be found in Nicky's bag. Even though Kimberly thought it was a disorganized mess, Nicky always seemed to know just where she had placed things. Nicky added a pen, then an envelope and a stamp to the pad of paper.

Kimberly grinned at her friend. "What else do you have in there? Maybe a mailman?"

Nicky grinned back. "I gave my kids a new assignment this morning. I am teaching them how to write letters the old-fashioned way. They are to write to someone about something that is important to them. I will teach them how to address an envelope the proper way and then the kids can mail their letters. I am hoping whomever they write their letters to will be willing to write back to them. Although, Isabelle- you remember the girl with the long brown hair that goes clear down to her behind- wants to write to her favorite actress, and I don't expect any answer from her!"

Kimberly smiled and looked at her watch. She still had 20 minutes before she needed to be back to work. Kimberly wrote her letter, while Nicky interjected every couple lines to add a word here or there. Finally, the letter was deemed perfect:

Dear Mrs. Victoria Hilton,

I am writing in response to the ad placed in the Denver Rocky Mountain newspaper on April 25th. I would like some more information about being a mail-order bride. Please send it to this address.

Kimberly added Nicky's school address and then signed it.

"Well, I guess we will see if we get a response," Kimberly commented as she folded the paper and placed it in the envelope Nicky had provided. As she addressed the envelope, she wondered if she was being crazy. Who nowadays sends away for a mail-order bride? But then Kimberly didn't think she'd get a response. She figured that this letter would be returned to her, saying the address couldn't be found.

After telling Nicky goodbye, Kimberly walked by the mailbox that was just outside the hospital and dropped the letter inside. As she walked to the ER to finish her shift, she wondered if any other women would believe the ad was legitimate and also send away for information.

Chapter 2

Mrs. Victoria Hilton sat at what was her late husband's desk in her large Victorian home in Denver. Her butler, Collins, had just delivered a large stack of envelopes to her. She was thrilled that her carefully placed ad had created so many responses. A few of them were negative, of course, accusing her of taking a man's hard wages and leading innocent girls astray, but she just tossed those and didn't let them dampen her enthusiasm for her new business endeavor.

She picked up a metal letter opener and started to slit open the first letter in the stack. The letter opener had been placed by a picture of herself and her late husband, Charles. He had passed away a few years ago. She had spent 45 wonderful years with him. It had always been just the two of them since they were never blessed with children. She stretched her finger out and traced her husband's face in the picture frame. She missed him so much. She wondered what he would think about her new mail-order bride business if he were still alive.

She thought back to the day she first met Charles. They were both living in England at the time. The first time she ever saw him was on the day before their wedding. Both of their fathers had made arrangements that Charles and Victoria marry each other when they were both still young children. She remembered how scared and nervous she was. It was to be a match that would benefit both families financially. She had traveled with her parents to Charles' family home and had dinner with his family. She had sat next to her mother and Charles had sat across from her, but neither of them had even talked to each other beyond the expected greetings. Even then, she thought he was the most handsome man she had ever seen. A few days later after the wedding, they had moved into his family's home. Charles wasn't the oldest son, so he wasn't slated to inherit any property, although he did inherit quite a bit of money.

A year after they married, Charles decided he wanted to immigrate to America. He wanted to start his own business, one that wasn't connected to his family. He wanted to succeed on his own merit and not his family's name or money. They traveled to America and had settled in Boston. Collins, a man who had been Charles' valet, came with them and took on the role of their butler.

Charles started his own transporting business. It started out small; he transported goods from Boston to the surrounding cities, but eventually it grew, and he started to transport goods all over the Eastern United States. Then ten years ago, he decided he wanted to open an office in Colorado, so they moved to Denver. After he died, Collins helped Victoria sell the transporting business since they hadn't had any children, and there was no one to inherit the company. She received a large amount of money from the sale, enough to live very comfortably for the rest of her life.

But a few months ago, Victoria finally admitted to herself that she was bored. She had helped Charles with the bookkeeping end of things with their business and missed the thrill of helping to run a company. One day, she saw an ad in the newspaper from a man asking for a woman to travel to where he lived in Montana and marry him. Over the next few weeks, she searched all the newspapers she had access to and saw many ads advertising for women to marry men who lived in the west. She soon decided that she would start a mail-order bride business where she would help men and women get together and marry. She named the business *Mrs. Hilton's*

Matchmaking Services. She did her best to make sure that the men who were looking for a wife were good and hardworking and would treat a woman well. She also made sure the women who wanted to marry a man they hadn't met before were doing it for the right reasons and were honest women who would keep their promises. She made sure both the men and women had Christian values.

She did have one criteria for her business. She only helped men who lived in Colorado. She insisted on meeting each one of them and with Collins' help, she was able to screen the applicants, and make sure they were each matched to the best possible candidate. She couldn't expect to meet all the women since quite a few of them came from back east, but she corresponded with them a number of times before she matched them with a man. Collins had an uncanny ability to look a man in his eyes and be able to tell if he was being honest, if they were who they claimed to be, and if they were upstanding citizens. She had already turned two men away because Collins could tell they were just looking for a woman to cook and clean for them, and not to eventually form a good marriage.

She was grateful that Collins had agreed to stay on after Charles died. He had always kept to his role as butler even though they now lived in the United States. He was a very formal man and would rarely relax in her presence. She also had a woman who worked for her as a housekeeper, a maid, and a gardener, but she had let everyone else go after Charles' death. She had a difficult time having so many people around her.

There was one part of the business that only she and Collins knew about and that part they kept secret. Victoria picked up two gold keys that were about three inches long. Even though they were old and tarnished around the edges, she kept them shined so it was easy to see the intricate design of the handles. One showed just slightly more age than the other. She remembered when she found the first key. One of the activities she enjoyed was to hunt for old items in stores, and one day while she had traveled with Charles to a nearby city, she had spent part of her day shopping. In one store, she had found this key. She remembered when she picked it up, it vibrated in her hand, and she set it down again in shock. The storekeeper noticed and approached her.

"That is a beautiful key, isn't it?" he had asked her, as he looked directly into her eyes as if trying to read something in them. "I just found it a while ago and have been trying to find the right owner for it."

"I...I am not sure I am interested in buying a key," Victoria had said to him.

"It isn't for sale. A key like that can't be bought. It is a special key."

Victoria had started to walk away from him, but his words sparked her curiosity. "What do you mean, a special key?"

"The key picks its owner. I think it picked you."

"How can a key pick an owner?" Victoria had scoffed. "A key can't make decisions like that." She had started to think the storekeeper was crazy in the head.

"You felt it," was all he said.

Victoria started to deny it, but then slowly nodded her head. "I felt a vibration, a tingling sensation, when I held it. It was strange."

"You may take it if you wish, but remember..." the storekeeper hesitated and did not say anything until Victoria looked at him, letting him know she was listening.

"Remember that you can only use this key for good. It has powers that you cannot override. I am giving you this key to your safe keeping. Use it wisely and always keep it in a safe place that no one knows about when it isn't with you."

"Powers?" Victoria questioned. "What powers?"

The storekeeper ignored her question. "You may tell one trusted person about this key, but no more." He then turned away and went to help another customer who was looking at a rack of dresses.

Victoria remembered standing there, wondering what she should do. "What a strange man," she had thought. He didn't look like he even belonged in the 1890s. He was short and stocky. He had a bald head with a little bit of white hair that curled at the base of his neck. His clothes were almost what she would imagine a wizard would wear. He had on black pants with white shirt and a velvet purple vest. There were gold buttons on the vest. She could see he had a timepiece in his pocket, the chain hooked to a button. He wore strange looking black pointy shoes.

She watched him for a moment, wondering if he would come back to her when the customer left, but he ignored her and acted almost as if she wasn't even there. She turned her attention to the key. She wondered if she picked it up, would she feel the tingling sensation again? She slowly picked it up and sure enough, the sensation went from her hand through her entire body. The tingling was even stronger than before. She kept the key in her hand and looked at it very carefully. It was almost as if it was calling her name. She made an instant decision and slipped it into her dress pocket.

As she started towards the shop door, the little man turned and looked at her. He smiled as if he was telling her she made the right decision, and that he was happy she had taken the key. Then he turned away to straighten some goods on a shelf and she left the store.

When she returned to the hotel where she was staying with Charles, she decided to write down everything the man had said to her so she wouldn't forget any of the instructions. She remembered he told her she could tell one trusted person; so of course, she told her husband.

Charles had laughed when she told him her experience that evening, but when she showed him the key, he told her that she had acquired a pure gold key. When he held it, she could tell he hadn't felt the vibrating and tingling that she felt, so she felt reluctant to mention it to him. She had put the key away in a pocket of her dress bag and had not taken it out again. Even when they had returned home to Denver, she left it in the bag.

A few weeks after they returned, Charles again went on a business trip, but this time, Victoria had stayed home. She had been sick with a cold and hadn't felt good enough to travel. A few days after Charles had left she was feeling better and was sitting on the sofa in the sitting room reading a book when Collins had approached her.

"Ma'am, I was emptying your bag that you took with you on your last trip and found this." In his hand was the gold key.

"Oh, yes. I acquired that in Boulder at a shop. I will put it away." She held out her hand for it, but Collins kept a hold of it.

"There is something strange about this key," Collins told her in his formal voice.

"What do you mean?" Victoria had been curious. Had he felt the vibration and tingling she had felt?

Collins looked at the key that he held flat in his hand with his palm up. "I feel a tingling sensation when I hold it."

Victoria was surprised and tried not to show it. "So do I."

"What does it mean?" Collins had asked.

"I'm not sure," Victoria hesitated because she remembered that the little man had specifically said she should only share her information with one person and she had already told Charles. She held out her hand and Collins reluctantly gave her the key. She knew Collins wouldn't ask any more questions because he always did his best to respect her privacy.

Over the ensuing months and years, Victoria learned exactly what the key's power was. It was a time travel device. When clutched in a person's hand, that person traveled to a specific time or place that they were thinking of.

Victoria remembered when she first discovered its power. She had been holding the key in her hand when she received news that her father had passed away. She had cried and felt very sad that she no longer had the option of seeing him again in this life. She started to think about her childhood and some fond memories she had of her father, mother, and her older brother. She clutched the key in her hand as she cried and thought about her memories. She pictured her old childhood room and the vibration and tingling she always felt when she held the key grew stronger.

Suddenly she was there! Victoria was in her family home in England, in the bedroom she had when she was a girl. The room looked exactly like it did when she lived there. The bed was small, with a homemade quilt she had loved, spread out to reach the floor. Her desk was in a corner, where she remembered propping a mirror up to try different hairstyles.

She remembered hearing voices and something told her she shouldn't allow herself to be seen, so she quickly hid in the closet her clothes had been kept in. She closed the door, but kept it slightly open, and she saw her mother come into the room. Her mother looked much older than she had when Victoria had married Charles and moved to America. Victoria wanted to leave the closet and greet her mother, but again something told her not to, so she stayed hidden.

"We are going to need to remove the bed; it is much too old. The desk can stay, but you will need to sand and polish it so it looks nice. Now that my husband has passed, we need to liven up this house for my son and his family. It must look its best." A maid trailed behind her mother, taking notes about what needed to be done.

Victoria was amazed at what she was hearing. Had she really traveled to England? Did the key have something to do with it? She had put the key into her pocket when she had arrived in her old room and she pulled it out. She heard her mother instructing the maid to make sure the clothes closet was emptied out and she heard footsteps coming her way. She knew she couldn't let them see her, so she clutched the key and pictured her own house in Denver, and just that quickly she was back home.

Over the next few years, Victoria tested the key many times. She never used it when her husband was home. She only used it when he was gone on business trips and when she could not accompany him. She learned many things about the powers of the key. She could go back in time if she wished. She could also travel into the future. All she needed to do is pick a specific date, say the date out loud, and picture the location she wanted to be in her mind.

When she time traveled, she was always very careful to let as few people see her as possible and she never let the key out of her sight. She had a specific dress she always wore when she time traveled with a hidden pocket. This is where she kept the key. She never stayed long and no one in her own time ever knew she had left. There were a few times she suspected Collins knew something was going on, but he never asked, although he would mention that he had been looking for her for a certain reason, and wondered where she was.

She always kept the key in a secret compartment of her bureau when she wasn't using it. No one knew of the drawer and so it was safe.

Because Charles hadn't felt the power of the key, she never told him what she did and where she went when he was gone on his trips. She loved her husband dearly, but he was a practical man and would have never believed her. She sometimes wished she could confide in Collins, but didn't dare because the little man had specifically told her to only tell one person.

About five years before Charles had died, she had time traveled to Ireland. She had always been interested in that country because her mother's parents were from Ireland. She had never met them, but remembered receiving letters and small gifts from her grandparents, and she had always wanted to meet them. She decided to time travel to the early 1800s, to her grandparents' home, and meet them, even though she wouldn't be able to tell them who she really was.

One of the things she learned very quickly was she needed to dress of the time period she was traveling to. She started to collect various clothing from the time periods she traveled to and kept them in an old wardrobe in a spare room that she kept locked. She learned to not stay very long, no more than a few hours at a time. She had also done her best to gather small amounts of money of the different time periods she liked to visit, so she had a way of purchasing things if she needed to.

On this particular trip, she had been able to meet her grandparents and some of her cousins. She pretended she was on her way to a nearby village. Her grandfather owned a small general store and so it was easy enough to pretend to shop for supplies while she visited with her grandparents. Then she saw the second key. It had been tossed in a small basket of other odds and ends. There was a sign on the basket saying all the items were being sold for a penny.

The key looked exactly like the first key, except it was a bit smaller. The design and gold color were exactly the same. She had picked it up and felt the same tingling sensation she felt when she held the first key. She knew she had to somehow purchase that key. She remembered reaching into her pocket and felt relief when she pulled out a five cent piece. Her grandmother had looked at her strangely when she bought the key and she had left soon after, almost afraid that her grandmother would want the key back.

When she returned back to her own time, she compared the two keys. Sure enough, they did look the same. She took a piece of wire and twisted both keys together. When the two keys touched each other, a small spark would appear. When she had her next opportunity to test the new key to see if it had the same time travel powers, she discovered that it did indeed work exactly the same as the first key.

A month after Charles had died, she had a deep desire to go back to England again. She decided that now was the time to tell Collins her secret. She was never sure how time passed when she was gone. Sometimes when she returned, it was almost the exact time that she left, but other times it was a few hours later, and one time an entire day had passed. She wanted to see her beloved England again and she wanted to be gone longer than a few hours. She knew she needed to tell Collins so he wouldn't wonder where she disappeared to.

Collins accepted her story as truth right from the beginning, and she suspected it was because he knew that sometimes she would disappear and then suddenly be home again. Collins always knew what was going on in her home. He agreed to keep an eye on things while she was gone. This time, she took a suitcase with her. She wasn't sure if it was going to arrive with her, but she held onto the case in one hand while she clutched the key in the other. She arrived in England with the suitcase clutched in her hand. She had pictured herself arriving on her family's property, in a small house that she had played in as a girl. The house was still there, but it was falling down around her, and unsafe to stay in. She spent a glorious week in England seeing and exploring places she remembered from her childhood. She made sure no one saw her that would recognize her. She wanted to see her brother and talk to him but didn't dare. She did watch behind a large tree one evening while he played with a few children on the lawn. She knew they were his grandchildren because they called him grandpa.

When she returned, she told Collins all about her trip. Collins accepted all she told him and she felt relieved that someone else now knew about her secret. Collins had no desire to use the key himself, but he was the one who came up with the idea to advertise in a future newspaper for mail-order brides and see what happened. Victoria had told him about some of her trips into the future and how hard it was for some young women to find good men to marry.

Later, when Victoria had her business set up and running, Collins did agree to accompany her into the future every once in a while. Sometimes he would use the second key at the same time she did. They also discovered if they held hands while one of them held a key, they were both transported into the future together. This soon became the main way they traveled together, holding each other's hands.

****

Victoria took the letter out of the envelope she held and glanced briefly through it. She had organized the letters in certain piles. One pile was for potential men and one was for women. She also had a pile for the letters she didn't want to respond to because she could tell they weren't writing for the right reasons.

All of the letters were from her time period, except one. She could tell the letter was from the future because the envelope and stamp looked different. She slid the letter out and saw that it was brief and written on lined paper. She read:

Dear Mrs. Victoria Hilton,

I am writing in response to the ad placed in the Denver Rocky Mountain newspaper on April 25th. I would like some more information about being a mail-order bride. Please send it to this address.

Kimberly

Victoria smiled as she read the short note. "Collins," she called out, hoping her butler was nearby, and of course, he was.

"Yes, Ma'am," he came into the room and stood at attention like he always did. Victoria wished he would relax around her. After all, he had been working for her for almost 50 years. And because people didn't act like butlers did in the England she once knew anymore.

"I received an unusual response." She handed him the letter and indicated to him that he should sit on a chair that was in front of her desk. Collins hesitated, then sat down to read the letter.

"Interesting," was all he said when he finished.

"What do you think? It is definitely from the future. Are you sure this will work?

Should I really send her information like she requested?"

"I get the feeling she wants a different life. She isn't sure she believes this letter is real, but she wants it to be," Collins responded.

"Yes, I felt the same."

"Of course, you must follow your heart in this matter, but I think it wouldn't hurt to send her the information. You won't be telling her about the key, yet. That can wait until you know if she is really interested."

"You're right. I will send her the information."

Chapter 3

Patrick Callaghan forked some hay into the horse's stalls. It was almost evening and he was glad the day was almost over. He was looking forward to going into the large family cabin and eating a good meal his sister, Bridget, would have prepared. Patrick could hear his stomach growl and could almost taste his sister's cooking. Working with food was what Bridget was best at and she always made excellent meals with the small variety of foods that they had available on their small ranch.

He lived on land that his father had secured during the Homesteading Act in 1873. His two younger brothers and Bridget lived with him. They worked hard on the small ranch together, doing their best to carve a living off the hard mountain land.

Patrick had been satisfied with his life until the last few months. This last winter had been hard and even though he had his brothers, Shaun and Keegan, and Bridget to talk to, he still felt lonely. He had turned 30 years old that winter and he knew it was time he thought about starting a family. This ranch had been passed to him when his father had died five years before since he was the eldest son. That was how it was done in his family. He always felt that it wasn't fair that he inherited the land and not his two brothers, nor his sister for that matter, but he tried to be fair to all of them and never made any of them feel like they needed to leave. He knew he would need to make some changes legally in the future, but for now, the way things were set up worked for him and his siblings, and he was satisfied.

He loved this ranch, this land that his father and grandfather had sacrificed much for. His grandfather, Patrick Callaghan the first, had lived in Ireland with his wife and four children. They had worked land that another man owned. Most of what they grew and harvested went to the landowner and they had very little for themselves. Then there was the potato famine. It lasted for about five years and many of their neighbors and friends died, including three of their children. Patrick's father was ten years old and was the only child left alive when his father and mother decided they needed to leave Ireland. They wanted to immigrate to America. They were lucky to have an heirloom, a set of fine china dishes that had been passed to them by his maternal great-grandmother. They had hidden them so their landowner didn't know about them, or he would have insisted they give them to him as part of payment to live on his land. They had buried them in their garden in a small wooden box filled with sawdust. One night Patrick's grandfather dug them up, then the family snuck out of their village to a nearby city. They sold the china dishes and received enough money for the three of them to immigrate to America.

Patrick remembered when his father told this story, he would say that the three of them actually ate better on the ship to America than they had for years because of the potato famine, even though they had purchased the least expensive tickets. They settled in New York and his grandfather worked for the rest of his life in several factories to support his wife and son. They saved what they could so Patrick's father could go to college. He earned a degree in accounting and after graduation from college, he worked at a large prestigious company, but his real dream was that he wanted to live on his own land. He wanted to own land like his father always wanted to in Ireland. He spent his free time studying and learning how to farm, how to care for horses and cows, and how to grow hay and other crops.

Patrick's father married his mother and soon he was born. A few years later Shaun joined the family, and then Bridget. When Patrick was eleven years old, his father decided he wanted to take advantage of the Homesteading Act and moved his young family to the Rocky Mountains in Colorado. There, they were able to secure 160 acres of their own land. He spent the next five years improving it until he owned the land. Then Patrick's youngest brother, Keegan, was born.

When his father first came to this land, he had built a small one-room cabin for the family to live in. It was barely large enough for the five of them. The summer that the land officially became theirs, his father immediately built a large home a short distance away from the smaller cabin. Right now, Patrick slept in the small home his father had built, although he ate his meals in the large cabin. Even though the small cabin was tiny, he loved that first home that his father had built. His siblings lived in the larger cabin.

Patrick had learned to love this land and he never had a desire to leave it. He would stay on this ranch all the time if he could, but he still had to make trips to Denver every so often for supplies. Denver was a four-hour trip on horseback, the easiest and fastest way to get there. He was planning on going to Denver the next day with Bridget and Keegan, leaving Shaun to run the ranch while he was gone. They needed supplies now that winter was over.

When they went into Denver for supplies, they usually stayed over one night, especially if Bridget came with him. Sometimes he would make the trip on his own so would only be gone for the day. That is how he preferred to make the trip, but he knew Bridget was looking forward to going into Denver, and he didn't have the heart to suggest she stay behind.

His little brother, Keegan, also was looking forward to it. Keegan was 15 years old, but he was getting old enough to continue his education. Right now, Bridget helped him with his schoolwork. There wasn't a schoolhouse nearby, so Keegan did his learning on his own with Bridget's help. He loved learning and Bridget had confided to Patrick a few months ago that she didn't think she would be able to help him much longer as he was passing her own knowledge. Patrick knew that they would need to look into boarding Keegan in Denver, probably in the fall so he could continue his education.
 Keegan talked about wanting to be a doctor.

Patrick knew that Keegan would not be spending his life as a rancher.

He knew Bridget would marry someday and move away, even though she was already 24 years old and considered an old maid. Bridget hadn't dated much. There weren't very many single men who were willing to travel to their ranch to court her. When Patrick would bring up the subject of marriage with her, she would insist she enjoyed her life and didn't regret that she hadn't found anyone yet. A few years ago, Patrick had suggested that she move to Denver and find a job in a restaurant. Maybe then she would find a man to marry, but Bridget had gotten very angry. No one was going to make her leave her home. She was staying where she was, and if she was ever going to find someone to marry, he would have to come to her. Patrick didn't dare remind her that the likelihood of that happening was very low because of how isolated they were from any nearby towns or cities, but he backed off and didn't suggest it again.

Patrick finished up with the care of the horses and then closed the barn door. He headed to the house, his two faithful border collies following him. The female was lagging behind a little, and Patrick knew there would be a litter of puppies soon. The dogs curled up on their pile of blankets on the porch as he went inside.

Bridget was at the stove stirring something. Shaun was sitting at the table, his eight-year-old daughter, Colleen, sitting on his lap. Keegan was sitting by the fireplace whittling on a stick. Keegan was always carving or whittling something when he had time. He liked carving animals and was very good at it. Right now, Patrick could tell that he was working on a whistle that he most likely would give to Colleen. On the fireplace mantle sat a number of carved animals; a bear, some birds, various horses, and other animals that were found in the mountains.

"It smells good, Bridget," Patrick complimented her as he kissed her cheek in welcome.

"Dinner should be ready in a few minutes," Bridget replied with a smile. "You have just enough time to clean up."

Patrick looked down at his hands and softly chuckled at his sister's not-so-subtle hint. He headed to the table where warm water, soap, and clean towels were set up and ready for him.

"Do you have the horses bedded down for the night?" Shaun asked.

"Yep, I checked Apache's leg. It seems to be healing fine." Shaun took care of all the animal's medical needs.

Shaun nodded and settled Colleen firmer on his lap. "Are you ready to go to Denver tomorrow?"

"I am," Colleen piped up. "I can't wait." She was going to Denver for the first time without her father. "I get to ride my own horse and everything."

"Do you really think she is ready for that?" Patrick asked Shaun as he teased Colleen.

"Daddy said I can go. I'm old enough," Colleen stated matter-of-factly.

"Yes, you are, sweetheart. Uncle Patrick is just teasing. You get to go."

Colleen smiled her relief and settled back against her father's chest. Patrick was glad Bridget would be going with him to help care for Colleen.

Bridget quickly had the food on the table and the family sat down to eat. She had prepared fried chicken, mashed potatoes and the last jar of green beans that she had preserved the summer before. Patrick knew that she had made an apple pie for dessert because he could smell the scent of sugared apples.

After Shaun said the prayer over the food, it was quiet for a while as everyone filled their plates and started to eat. Colleen broke the silence.

"Why haven't you married, Uncle Patrick?" she asked innocently as she took a bite of the chicken.

Patrick was surprised at her question. What brought this up? "I guess I haven't found the right woman who wanted me," he finally said.

"Why are you asking that, sweetheart?" Shaun asked his daughter.

"Well, I want a mommy, but Uncle Patrick is the oldest, so he needs to marry first. After he gets married, then you can get married because you are the next oldest."

Patrick almost choked on his food, trying to keep the laughter in. He was always amazed the way Colleen's mind worked.

"Good plan, Colleen," Keegan said with a grin. "Then it will be Bridget's turn."

Bridget glared at Keegan. "I'm fine being a single woman."

"I'll see what I can do, how about that?" Patrick told Colleen. He knew he had surprised his siblings because they all looked at him with questions in their eyes.

"Do you have someone…?" Bridget started to ask, but Patrick interrupted her.

"We can talk about it later." He had actually been thinking about this subject, but he didn't want to tell his siblings his plans with Colleen around.

Later, after Colleen had gone to bed, Bridget brought up the subject again. They were all sitting around the fireplace in the living area, each doing their own thing. Bridget was mending some clothes. Keegan was again working on the whistle, and both Patrick and Shaun were reading a book.

"Do you have someone in mind to court, Patrick?" Bridget asked.

He shook his head. "No, but I am already thirty years old. I want to have a family. I think it is time to find someone."

"How are you going to do that?" Shaun asked. "You barely leave the ranch as it is."

"I am going to send for a mail-order bride," he announced.

"What?" Shaun had been leaning back on his chair and it slammed down on all four legs.

"What's a mail-order bride?" Keegan asked curiously.

"I guess there are a lot of women who haven't been able to find someone to marry, for various reasons. Last fall when I went to Denver, I saw that an older woman had started a mail-order bride business in her home. She helps match women and men together that want to marry."

"Really? That's interesting," Shaun commented.

"Why would a woman want to marry someone she doesn't even know?" Bridget asked skeptically. Patrick could tell by the tone of her voice that she thought the whole idea was dumb.

"Because they want a new start in life. This woman said she had matched quite a few couples already," Patrick explained to her.

"What do you need to do?" Keegan asked curiously.

"I wrote a letter explaining what I am looking for in a woman. Then Mrs. Hilton will find a woman who might be interested in me, and then we will write each other. When we go into Denver tomorrow, I am going to meet with her. She might have someone who is interested in writing."

"Are you sure this is legitimate?" Shaun asked suspiciously.

"Sure, it is," Bridget responded. "I have heard about mail-order brides, although I think…" she didn't finish her sentence, but Patrick knew what she was thinking. That he was desperate.

"I'm just going to give it a chance," he said, and then changed the subject. He didn't want to talk about it anymore.

****

Kimberly entered her house after yet another long day at work. Angie had made her work a few hours later than she was supposed to, and she was tired, physically and emotionally. The day before she had applied to a few jobs she had found on an online job search site, and she hoped something would come of it.

She heard voices coming from the kitchen and headed that direction. She found Nicky and her brother, Justin, sitting at the table, along with Justin's son, Garrett.

"Hi everyone," she greeted and sat down on a chair with a tired sigh. She smiled at Garrett and reached over to ruffle his hair. "Hey, bud." The boy smiled at her with a mouth full of cookies.

"Not doing too well, huh?" Justin greeted her with a grin. "What's going on?"

"Work is, well, let's just say, it's not an enjoyable experience," Kimberly told him. She was already starting to feel better just being with her friends. She loved being around Justin. He was like a brother to her and he treated her just like he treated Nicky. He was protective of her in a big brother way that sometimes was annoying, but he was fun to be around.

"You got a letter today," Nicky said as she handed her an envelope, then stared at her expectantly.

Kimberly accepted the letter and started to set it aside until she saw who it was from. She saw Mrs. Victoria Hilton's name and her address on the front, and she gasped.

"I almost forgot about this. I really didn't expect a response. It's been almost two weeks."

"What's this all about?" Justin asked with curiosity.

Kimberly shook her head at Nicky, trying to convey to her friend to not say anything to Justin, but Nicky either didn't see her or ignored her. She really didn't want Justin to know about this. She knew his protective side would kick in and she would never hear the end of it.

"Oh, Kimberly just answered an ad for a mail-order bride." Her cheeky grin towards Kimberly hinted she saw Kimberly shake her head.

Justin had just taken a drink of water and he immediately choked on it. "What?"

Nicky pounded her brother's back with her hand. "Take a breath, brother dear. You heard me."

"What's going on, you two? What did you get mixed up with now?"

"A few weeks ago, I saw an ad in one of those newspapers Nicky has been collecting." Kimberly reluctantly opened her cell phone case and pulled out the small ad she still kept there and handed it to Justin. She knew Justin would just hound her until she told him the full story.

"Kind of weird," Justin said after he glanced at it and then handed it back to her.

Kimberly started to fill her plate with the dinner that Nicky had prepared. They had a good system going. Nicky cooked all the meals and Kimberly cleaned up afterward. Nicky had a creative flair that kept their dinners interesting. She listened as Nicky proceeded to fill her brother in with what they had done with the ad.

"You guys are nuts, do you know that? What do you think is going to happen?"

"I just sent away for the information as a joke. I didn't think I'd receive a reply," Kimberly said defensively, feeling a blush creep up to her cheeks.

"Well, open it and see what it says," Nicky said, so Kimberly slowly slit the envelope open and pulled out a single sheet of paper. She started to read silently.

Dear Miss Nelson,

Thank you for your interest in becoming a mail-order bride. As you may know, there are many men who live in the western United States and who live in areas where there are few women who are seeking companionship.

I have included some guidelines to follow if you should choose to continue in becoming a mail-order bride. The first step is to fill out a questionnaire about your likes and dislikes. The men fill out the same questionnaire. Then I will match yours with a man to help you both have the same interests.

You should also write an introductory letter, which I will give to the man I think will best fit you. If you both like what you read about each other, then you can write each other.

I do have some guidelines that you must agree to follow.

1. If you start to write a man, and then change your mind, you must write to him and let him know of your decision immediately.
2. I advise that you both exchange at least two letters before you decide to meet each other.
3. The man should agree to pay for any expenses for you to travel to where he lives. Each man should agree to not expect reimbursement from the lady, even if the end result does not bring about marriage.
4. If you make any promises to the man you are writing in letters, you must keep them. Be honest. If you don't know how to cook or plant a garden, don't tell him you can.
5. If you have a child, make sure the man knows about him or her and agrees to provide for their care.
6. If you choose to meet, you must agree to not marry for at least 30 days. This time should be used to get to know each other. I do not approve of instant marriages.

7. If, after the 30 days are up, you choose to not marry, you should depart from each other with no hard feelings.

8. If you do choose to marry, it must be performed in a church of your choice, in front of a licensed minister.

9. All applicants should be living a good Christian life.

If you are willing to agree to these requirements, please fill out the questionnaire and write an introductory letter, then mail them both to me. If I am able to match you with a man, I will be in touch.

Sincerely,

Mrs. Victoria Hilton
Owner of Mrs. Hilton's Matchmaking Services
In the Denver Colorado area

Kimberly couldn't believe what she was reading. If she wasn't mistaken, she would be thinking she had just read a letter just out of the 1890s. It was written in beautiful calligraphy handwriting. In fact, it looked like it had been written with real India ink. It wasn't written on paper that she was familiar with. It was heavier than the typical paper she would have used to write a letter. In fact, she would have expected a typed letter, not a written one.

She looked up and noticed Nicky and Justin were watching her, so she wordlessly handed it to Nicky. She was no longer hungry but forced herself to finish her meal. She didn't know what to think of the letter.

Nicky read through it, her eyes widening more and more as she read the entire letter. She then handed it to Justin, who had silently held out his hand for it.

"This is a scam, Kimberly," Justin announced as he tossed the letter on the table. "Surely you know that."

"Maybe," Kimberly admitted. But why did she feel disappointed that it might be? Did she really want this to be real?

"I agree with Justin," Nicky said as she stood up and held out her hand to Garrett. "Come on, buddy. I just bought you a new video game you might like."

Garrett whooped out loud his excitement and left the room with his aunt. Kimberly could hear the TV turn on and soon could hear the sounds of the game.

"I hope you are going to throw this away," Justin sounded suspicious as if he suspected Kimberly's thoughts.

"Don't worry about what I am going to do," Kimberly glared at him. "I can make my own decisions." She jumped up and started to clean up the kitchen, refusing to look at him. She eventually heard him leave the kitchen muttering to himself.

She sighed with relief and continued her chore. She wished she could reread the letter, but knew that if she showed any interest in it, Justin would be right back to question her about it. She quickly slipped the letter and questionnaire back in the envelope and tucked it under a stack of papers that had been on the corner of the counter for weeks. She knew it would be safe there until she could retrieve it. It was one of those stacks where she and Nicky would put mail that looked important but really wasn't.

Kimberly enjoyed the rest of the evening with her friends. They watched Garrett play his new game and then they watched a new movie Nicky had rented from a nearby Red Box. Kimberly spent her time drawing with her colored pencils. She considered herself an amateur artist, but she loved to draw anything she could. She loved to draw people, but she also did landscapes and other nature scenes. Drawing soothed her and calmed her when she felt stressed. That evening, she enjoyed drawing Garrett as he learned how to play his new game. Nicky and Justin were used to Kimberly drawing whenever she had some free time.

She was glad neither Nicky or Justin brought up the letter again, although she knew Nicky thought that since she disapproved of it, that Kimberly would follow her lead and assume it was a scam. Nicky tended to expect everything to be done the way she wanted it to. When it was Garrett's bedtime, Justin left, and Nicky went to bed shortly after.

Kimberly waited for a few minutes until she was sure Nicky had retired for the night, finishing up her drawing of Garrett. Then she pulled the letter out from its hiding place, went into her room, and quietly locked the door. She settled herself on her bed and reread the letter. As she did, she suddenly realized she very much wanted this to be real. She couldn't explain why; who knew what kind of man she would end up with? She wasn't even in a big hurry to marry. But, she felt a pull towards this idea, and maybe, just maybe it would bring happiness to her life. She wanted to fill out the questionnaire and write the letter. But she knew if she did, Nicky and Justin would give her a hard time.

Could she just answer the letter quietly? *No*, she whispered to herself, vetoing that idea. She didn't want to do this behind their backs. She didn't care if they agreed with what she wanted to do. She just wanted them to support her.

Suddenly, she made up her mind. She sat at her desk and quickly filled out the questionnaire. It was just a basic one. Would she be willing to relocate to an area far away from where she lived? If not, how far was she willing to travel? Did she have any children? Did she want children? Would she be willing to live on a farm or ranch, and if so what skills did she have? Kimberly always had wanted to live in a rural part of the country. She had always hated living in the city. Sometimes she felt so closed in and she felt she didn't have space to breathe, to just be. But she didn't know what skills she had that would contribute to living in the country, so she left that question blank. The last question was, would she be willing to travel and live near the man she was considering to marry for at least 30 days? She answered in the affirmative to that question, even though she knew she would need to take a leave of absence or even quit her job.

After she finished the questionnaire, she wrote her introductory letter. She described herself and wrote that she was a nurse. She enjoyed being out in nature and drawing. She didn't have any immediate family and she wrote a small paragraph about Nicky and Justin.

When she had finished her letter, she put both papers into an envelope and sealed it, and then went to bed.

Chapter 4

The next morning, Kimberly woke up late. She could hear Nicky in the kitchen and remembered that it was Saturday, so there was no school. Kimberly also had the day off and she suddenly knew what she was going to do. She was going to drive and find the address of this mail-order bride company. She wanted to see if it was a real address. If it was, she was going to mail in her application.

One thing she didn't count on was that Nicky insisted she go with her. When Kimberly announced over a bowl of cereal what her plans were for the day, Nicky looked at her as if she was crazy.

"Why would you want to do that?" she questioned. "I thought we decided this was a scam and you were going to throw it away."

Kimberly shook her head warily. "No, you and Justin decided that it was a scam. If you remember, I didn't say a word."

"I don't understand you. Are you really thinking this could be real? Even if it is, why in the world would you want to be a mail-order bride?"

Kimberly decided to try to explain her feelings to her friend, although she didn't think she would understand. She had already made up her mind about it, and in her way of thinking, the discussion was over.

"I just have this feeling that I want to try it. It's not going to hurt anything. I haven't agreed to marry anyone yet."

Nicky stared at her for a long moment. "Well, I am going with you. There is no way I am going to let you drive to some obscure address by yourself."

"I think I'll be okay," Kimberly protested. She wasn't sure she wanted Nicky to come along. "I'll be fine on my own. I just want to make sure it's a real address."

"I want to go with you. Afterward, we can go to that new mall that just opened up."

Kimberly knew she wasn't going to be able to leave without Nicky, so she finally agreed. A few hours later, she used her GPS and pulled up to the address. It was a large old-fashioned Victorian home. It had been located in an old part of Denver, just like she had suspected. It was built with different colored gray stones, with a wraparound porch on the left. Separating the porch and the front door was what looked like an indoor gazebo. Kimberly's gaze followed the tall white windows up to the roof, which had white molding emphasizing all of the sharp edges. Tall trees bordered the house, showing the age of the home more than the house itself; someone must go to great lengths to ensure this house was well kept.

She sat in the car with Nicky beside her, staring at the home, and she made an instant decision. "I am going to see if anyone is home."

"Oh, no you don't," Nicole tried to argue with her as she grabbed Kimberly's arm. "You just agreed to see if it was a real address. Well, it is, but it's someone's home, not a business. You can't just go up there and…"

Kimberly pulled away and opened the door. "You can stay here if you want. I'll be right back." She grabbed her small purse which had her application in it and got out of the car.

"Kimberly, you are acting crazy," Nicky yelled as Kimberly shut her door.

Kimberly admitted to herself that she *was* acting a bit strange. She usually was very reserved and didn't make spur of the moment decisions like this. She usually took many days to make a decision, looking at all the angles, making sure the decision she wanted to make was the correct one. For some reason, she just knew she needed to pursue this. She just didn't know why. She felt as strongly about this as she had when she decided to go to college to be a nurse.

She walked up the beautiful sidewalk. The yard was impeccably groomed and there were many spring flowers all over, with a thick green lawn. She heard a car door slam and Nicky calling, "Wait for me! If you are going to follow through with this, I better come along."

Kimberly smiled to herself. She knew Nicky wouldn't be able to just sit in the car by herself, wondering what was going on. She always needed to be in the middle of things. She could see out of the corner of her eye that Nicky was more excited about this idea than she was willing to admit.

Kimberly stepped up on the smaller porch that framed the front door and searched for a doorbell, but couldn't find one, so she just knocked. After a few moments, she raised her hand to knock again, but the door opened.

"Yes? May I help you?" It was an older man dressed in a fancy suit. His hair and clothes were impeccably taken care of. He held himself stiffly like he had a board down his back, and looked at Kimberly without a smile, although his eyes looked kind. He had a strong English accent.

"I was wondering if this was where I can find Mrs. Victoria Hilton," Kimberly stammered. The man intimidated her a bit.

"Yes," was all the man said.

"Is there a way I could speak with her? I am Kimberly and this is my friend, Nicky." Kimberly introduced them to the man, trying to keep her voice steady. "I know I don't have an appointment, but I would like to meet her."

The man looked at her for a moment and then nodded his head. "Please come in, and I will see if she is available for visitors." He held the door open while Kimberly and Nicky entered the home.

What Kimberly saw amazed her. The main entry showcased a large, gorgeous staircase made of dark oak. The walls were painted a clean white, keeping the room light and spacious. There was a thick arch that wrapped around the ceiling and led halfway down the walls, framed by molding that looked hand carved and extremely intricate. What seemed to be old family pictures lined the walls. The man bowed to her slightly. "I am Collins. I will inform Mrs. Hilton you are here." He then left, walking stiffly down a hallway and into a room off to the left.

Kimberly heard a snicker from Nicole. "He acts like an old-fashioned butler. You know, the ones that are shown in old English movies?"

Kimberly smiled at her friend and nodded her head in agreement. "At least we know that there really is a Victoria Hilton."

"We haven't met her yet," Nicky whispered to her as she reached out to touch a large bouquet of spring flowers that sat on a nearby table. "Just be on your guard. Don't agree to anything until we can talk about this. I don't want you to make a big mistake."

Kimberly didn't say anything. She didn't want to agree to Nicky's terms until she met Mrs. Hilton. She heard footsteps and turned to see the stiff man returning. He stood at attention and said, "Mrs. Hilton has agreed to see you. This way, please." He walked away and Kimberly and Nicky followed him down the hallway and into the room he had first disappeared to.

As she stepped into the room, Kimberly saw an older lady sitting behind a large fancy desk. She guessed the woman was in her sixties. Her hair was done up in a sweeping bun and not a hair was out of place. She was dressed in a long-sleeved maroon dress that had a neckline all the way up to her neck. The collar came up about an inch above the neckline and was lined in gray lace that came all the way down to her belly. The same lace also lined the hems of the sleeves. Kimberly had seen dresses like she wore in her research of the 1890s. She smiled kindly at Kimberly and Nicky but did not say anything. The stiff man introduced them.

"Ma'am, may I present Miss Kimberly and Miss Nicky. They have requested to meet with you. Kimberly and Nicky, this is Mrs. Victoria Hilton."

"I am so pleased to meet you both," Mrs. Hilton stood and then indicated for them to sit down on some chairs in front of her desk, which they did. She turned to the man who was standing nearby. "Collins, would you be so kind to ask for some refreshments to be brought in?"

Kimberly thought she saw the man look disapprovingly at her and Nicky, but that expression quickly left his face as he turned to his employer. "As you wish, ma'am." He turned and left the room. Kimberly could hear his shoes on the hardwood floor until they faded in the distance.

"What can I do for you ladies?" Mrs. Hilton asked as she sat back down on her chair behind the desk.

"I saw the ad that you placed in the newspaper a few weeks ago. I sent for some information and received a letter yesterday," Kimberly explained.

"Yes, I do remember your letter and I was the one who sent you the information on becoming a mail-order bride," Mrs. Hilton confirmed. "I don't remember your last name, though."

Kimberly hesitated. She wasn't sure if she was ready to give out that information yet.

"We are here because we think this is a scam," Nicky blurted out.

"Nicky," Kimberly hissed. "Let me handle this."

"What do you mean, a scam?" Mrs. Hilton looked confused at the word.

"That you are just trying to collect people's money. There are no such thing as mail-order brides today," Nicky continued. "Unless they are from Russia."

Kimberly laid her hand on Nicky's arm to quiet her. "I just wanted to meet you." She felt good about the woman now that she had met her. She had kind eyes and had greeted her as if she was expecting her to come. She hadn't made Kimberly feel foolish for making sure she was real.

She reached into her bag and pulled out the envelope with the questionnaire and introductory letter and handed it to the older woman.

"I filled this out last night," Kimberly said. "Can I just leave it with you?"

"What?" It was Nicky's turn to hiss as she glared at Kimberly.

"Yes, you may," Mrs. Hilton accepted the envelope. "If you don't mind, I will look through this now. I have a man in mind for you, but I want to read what you have written before I make a final decision."

"That would be fine. We can wait," Kimberley agreed, ignoring Nicky's continued glare, accompanied by an eye roll.

Mrs. Hilton turned her attention to Nicky. "I can see you care deeply for Kimberly. Please know that nothing will happen to your friend."

"Can you promise that?" Nicky asked somewhat sarcastically.

Mrs. Hilton kept looking straight at Nicky and nodded. "Yes, I can make that promise."

Nicky seemed taken back at Mrs. Hilton's frankness and quieted down while the older woman read Kimberly's information. She spent quite a bit of time reading what Kimberly had written. She even read the introductory letter twice. Then she smiled.

"Just as I thought. I will give you Patrick's introductory letter." Mrs. Hilton opened a drawer and took out a sealed envelope. Again the letter seemed to be in an old-fashioned envelope that was sealed with wax. "Please read this when you are alone, at your leisure. I will give your letter to Patrick. If you are interested in corresponding with Patrick, write a letter directly to him, but mail it to this address."

Kimberly gave a nervous sigh as she accepted the envelope. "Okay."

"Remember that you should exchange at least two letters. If at any time you change your mind, feel free to do so. You have not made a commitment as of yet. If you feel you want to write for a longer time period; that is fine. You must feel comfortable about every step of this procedure. I will be telling Patrick the same thing."

"Have you met him?" Kimberly asked curiously.

Mrs. Hilton smiled. "Yes, I have. He is a fine man. I won't say anything else. You should learn about him through his letters on your own."

Kimberly had all sorts of questions, but she knew Mrs. Hilton would not answer them, so she kept quiet. Collins came into the room holding a silver tray. "Here are your refreshments, Ma'am."

Mrs. Hilton nodded her approval as Collins set the tray on a small table nearby. He then stood at attention as if waiting for his next orders. "There is no need to wait, Collins. I will let you know when the ladies are ready to leave."

"As you wish, Ma'am." He bowed slightly to Mrs. Hilton and then turned to leave again. This time, as he passed Kimberly, she could have sworn that he winked at her, but she couldn't be sure. *What a strange man*, she thought.

"Is Collins an actual butler?" Kimberly asked as she accepted a cup of tea.

"Why yes," Mrs. Hilton seemed surprised at her question. "He has been with us since I married my dear Charles almost 50 years ago. He came to America with us when Charles and I moved from England."

"You've been married for 50 years?" Nicky asked as if she was amazed a couple had been together for so long.

"We were married 45 years. He died a few years ago."

"I'm sorry. You must miss him," Kimberly responded with sympathy.

"I do miss him very much." Mrs. Hilton smiled at Nicky, then stood to fix a cup of tea for each of them while she talked. "But I have this nice home to live in and wonderful people who work for me. And I have this new mail-order bride business to keep me busy."

"Do you mean this mail-order bride business is new?" Nicky asked with suspicion in her voice.

Kimberly laid a hand on Nicky's arm again to quiet her and smiled apologetically at Mrs. Hilton, who graciously let the remark slide while serving the tea. Each plate had a small pastry as well.

"Tell us how you met Charles," Kimberly invited and listened with rapt attention at what sounded like a fairytale story. Even though Mrs. Hilton had married Charles almost 50 years ago, she was amazed that there were still families who made arrangements for their children to marry. Even so, Mrs. Hilton sounded as if she loved her husband deeply and had been very happy.

She greatly enjoyed the next 30 minutes as she listened to Mrs. Hilton reminisce about her life with Charles. Some of the things she talked about sounded strange. For example, she talked about coming to America on a crowded ship. She mentioned riding in stages as she traveled around with her husband. When they moved from Boston to Denver, she mentioned that it had taken almost six months to move all of their belongings.

As Kimberly listened to Mrs. Hilton's stories, she looked around the room. It looked like an office, but she couldn't see any modern appliances like a copy or fax machine, or a phone for that matter. She found this very strange. There also was no computer. Once she started looking more closely, even the lamps didn't have a cord, as if there was no electrical outlet to connect it to. They looked like they needed oil to light them.

Either Mrs. Hilton must feel strongly about keeping the integrity of this home true to the year it was built, or she must be one of those older people who didn't understand technology and got along fine doing everything the old fashioned way, although Kimberly did find it strange that there wasn't at least a telephone with a landline in the office.

When the conversation wound down about Mrs. Hilton's husband, Kimberly held up the letter. "Would it be okay if I read this letter right now? Then I could answer him back and won't need to mail it."

Mrs. Hilton seemed to hesitate as if she wasn't sure this was a good idea, but then she nodded her head. "You should read it alone, so you may go into our library. I will have Collins direct you." The older woman rang a small bell and the butler immediately appeared at the doorway.

"Please show Kimberly to the library," Victoria instructed the man. She stood as Kimberly did. "There are paper and ink in the library if you wish to use it," Victoria said to her.

"I think I should go with you," Nicky said.

Kimberly shook her head. "I will be fine."
As Nicky looked like she was going to insist, Victoria broke in. "You may wait for your friend outside in the garden."

Kimberly held her breath, hoping that Nicky wasn't going to make a scene, and sighed with relief when Nicky finally nodded her head at Victoria, glared at Kimberly, and then left the room.

"Come with me," Collins told her in his stiff voice. Kimberly followed the butler as he led her out of the office, down the hallway, into another room. Kimberly immediately could tell it was the library for it had wall to wall shelves full of books. Collins kept walking until they arrived at a long table that sat in the middle of the room. It had a stack of paper, envelopes, and a bottle of ink with an old fashioned pen sitting next to it.

"I will return when you are finished," Collins told her and left the room.

Kimberly spent a few minutes just looking around the room. She was amazed at the number of books that were on the shelves. She stood up and walked to the nearest shelf. All the books looked old. She pulled one of the books from the shelf to look through. The cover was leather and the book was titled "A Study in Scarlet." She could tell the book had been read often because some of the pages were wrinkled and there were a few scratches on the binding. She flipped past the first few pages for the copywriter information and gasped when she saw the date 1887. She put the book back and pulled out another one which looked equally as old. She quickly found the copy-write page and saw 1856. Were all of these books in the library collector items? She knew there were people who loved to collect old books. Maybe Mrs. Hilton liked to do that.

She wanted to spend more time exploring the library, but knew she didn't have time for that. She reluctantly sat back down at the table and looked at the sealed envelope. Her heart skipped a beat as she contemplated what was inside. Did she really want to go through with this? She knew if she did, she was totally putting her trust in Mrs. Hilton.

She carefully opened the letter and withdrew a single sheet of paper. Again, the paper the letter had been written on was heavier than what she was used to, with no lines. It was handwritten in black ink in block letters. She could tell the letter had been carefully written.

To Whom It May Concern:

My name is Patrick Callaghan. I am 30 years old and have never been married. I live deep in the Rocky Mountains and run a small ranch that has been in my family for a number of years. I live about a four-hour horseback ride from Denver.

I am the oldest of two brothers and a sister. We live together on our ranch, along with a niece. I am not rich, but we live comfortably enough and I will be able to provide for your needs.

I am interested in marrying and would invite you to write and tell me about yourself. I am looking forward to your letter.

Sincerely,

Patrick Callaghan

Kimberly read through the letter twice and then set it down. The information Patrick gave wasn't very much. She would have liked to hear about his family and more about the ranch. And what did he mean, "Denver is a four-hour horseback ride away?"

I guess I am going to have to write and ask him these questions, Kimberly whispered to herself. She took a piece of paper off the stack nearby and looked around for a pen. All she could see was a bottle of ink, with the old fashioned pen, the kind that needed to be dipped into ink to write. Did Mrs. Hilton expect her to write the letter the old-fashioned way? She looked around the library for another writing tool, but couldn't see one. She finally sighed and sat back down at the table. She took the lid off of the ink, being careful not to spill any. She picked up the pen and dipped the tip into the ink.

She carefully set the pen on the paper to write her letter, only to find she dripped ink spots along the way, and had left a pool of ink where she had touched the paper with the pen. She sighed as she realized she needed to practice before she wrote her letter. She spent the next few minutes practicing, and she had used up two sheets of paper before she felt comfortable starting her letter.

She carefully told Patrick that Mrs. Hilton had given her his letter and that she was interested in learning more about him. She asked about what his brothers and sister did on their ranch and how old they were. She wanted to know how old his niece was and which sibling she belonged to. She asked him to describe his ranch and what animals he had. She admitted she didn't know much about ranch life, but was willing to learn. Finally, she asked why he went to Denver on a horse.

As she folded and sealed the letter, she made herself step back mentally from this possibility of being a mail-order bride to

Patrick. Very likely, many other women were also writing him, although Mrs. Hilton had not indicated that. Why would he want someone like her, who didn't know a thing about ranch life? Who had been a city girl her entire life?

Chapter 5

Over the next month, Kimberly drove almost weekly to Mrs. Hilton's home. She would give the older woman a letter and get a new one from Patrick. Sometimes there wasn't a letter from him and Mrs. Hilton explained that it was because Patrick lived so far away and couldn't get to Denver regularly, which puzzled Kimberly. Why couldn't he just mail the letters from where he lived? But what he wrote to her made her want to get to know him better. Each time she received a letter, she always wanted to know more about him. His letters were short, but she had learned quite a bit.

She learned his father had been born in Ireland and had come to the United States for a better life. She learned that his sister, Bridget, was 25 years old. His brother Shaun was 28 and Keegan was 15. His niece was Shaun's daughter and had a story all her own as to why she was part of the family, but he didn't tell her what that story was.

He described the ranch and its surroundings and it sounded idealistic to Kimberly. She wanted to meet Patrick just to see his ranch.

In his last letter, he confessed to her that he enjoyed writing to her and wanted to know if she would be willing to come to Denver and meet him. He was willing to marry her if she wished. She knew that he was saying, if she wasn't interested, she should let him know now, and not continue writing any more letters.

Kimberly took two days to make her decision. She read over each letter of Patrick's carefully. She really wanted to meet him. She knew from the guidelines that she had first received from Mrs. Hilton, she would not be expected to marry him for at least 30 days. That was a comfort but it also scared her. *In 30 days I could be married.* She tested the sentence out to see how it felt. She liked the idea more than she thought she would. In one of his letters, Patrick had informed her that there was a small log house a short distance yards away on his ranch where she could live until they had gotten to know each other better and made the decision to marry. She would be able to eat her meals with the family in the larger ranch house nearby, but she would have her own small home to live in for a while.

Kimberly hadn't told Nicky that she had been writing Patrick. She hadn't taken her friend with her the other times she visited Mrs. Hilton. She knew Nicky thought she had given up on the idea of becoming a mail-order bride because Kimberly hadn't talked to her about it since their first visit. She knew she should tell Nicky what she was doing, but she hesitated. She wanted Nicky's support and something inside her told her Nicky wouldn't encourage her to try this new endeavor. In fact, she very likely would do everything she could to stop it.

Finally, one evening, while she sat on the couch beside Justin as they watched another children's movie with Garrett, she knew she wanted more out of life. Her life had been stagnant since her parents' death at 15. All of the decisions she had made since then were only decisions that were safe. She hadn't dated very much, mainly because she hadn't met anyone she wanted to go out with more than a few times. There was one man who had wanted to take things further during college, but she hadn't been interested in him, and had broken things off when she realized the man was more serious than she was.

That evening, she silently made the decision to meet Patrick, and to live in the small home he offered while they got to know each other better. She already knew she would need to quit her job since she knew Angie wouldn't agree to hold her job for 30 days, but she felt confident she would be able to find another job if she needed to. Maybe there was a hospital or a doctor's office nearby Patrick's ranch and she could continue to work if she married Patrick. She had enough money in the bank to pay for her share of expenses for the month while she was gone, so her leaving shouldn't put Nicky in a financial burden.

Once she made the decision, she felt a peace fill her soul until it spread throughout her body. She knew this was the right thing to do.

****

Kimberly drove her car onto Victoria's driveway. She drew a deep breath and realized she was a bit shaky. Now that she had made the decision to meet Patrick and get to know him better, with the plan to marry him in the near future, she was feeling a bit nervous.

She got out of the car and walked to the front door of the large Victorian home. Before she even had a chance to knock, the door opened. It was Collins on the other side with his usual slight smile on his face. He held the door open for her.

"Mrs. Hilton is expecting you," he told her in his stiff way.

This comment confused Kimberly a little bit. How did Victoria know she was planning on coming today? She had just decided the night before.

Kimberly stepped into the cool house and followed Collins to Victoria's office where the older woman was sitting behind the desk, just as she had been when she visited before.

"I am so glad you came," Victoria told her with a smile. This time, she walked around the desk and gave Kimberly a hug. "Please sit down."

Kimberly sat gingerly on the edge of the flowery cushioned chair. "I came to give you my final letter to Patrick," she spoke in a rush. "I have decided I would like to meet him."

Victoria peered at Kimberly and then smiled again. "I know Patrick will be good for you."

Kimberly gave Victoria the envelope. "What happens next?"

"First, I must tell you a story," Victoria told her after she accepted the envelope and set it aside. "I must ask you to listen until I am finished."

"Okay...." Kimberly said, feeling confused. She really wanted to ask some questions about Patrick. Victoria seemed to like to tell stories.

"A number of years ago, I went with Charles on a business trip. He traveled quite a bit and I would go with him when I was able to. While he was in his meetings, I would often wander around whatever city we were in and look around in their stores. One day, I found myself in a small store that looked quite old. This store seemed to have many old items for sale. One of the items was this."

Victoria opened a drawer and took out a small wooden box. She opened it and picked up one of two golden keys. It was old and had a knot designed into the end, reminding Kimberly of the Irish knots.

"I was very intrigued by this key. The store owner noticed and asked me a few questions. I must have answered them to his satisfaction because he told me the key was mine if I desired."

"So he just gave it to you?" Kimberly questioned. From what she could tell, the key might be pure gold. It had to be worth quite a bit of money.

"Yes," Victoria confirmed. "He told me the key picked its owner and I was to have it next."

Kimberly watched as Victoria fingered the two keys in her hand and seemed to be brought back to the memories of her past.

"A number of years later, I found the second key in a store in Ireland and was able to purchase it, so that is how I own both of them.

"To make a long story short, when holding one of these keys in your hand, they will take that person back into the past, or into the future."

Victoria stopped talking and looked directly at Kimberly as if waiting for a reaction.

Kimberly was dumbfounded. Maybe this Mrs. Hilton wasn't as legitimate as she thought and she felt a distinct disappointment.

"Wait, do you mean, like time travel?" Kimberly asked. She had heard of time travel before, but it was always in movies or books. From what she knew of the subject, it was impossible to travel between times at will.

"Yes," Victoria nodded her head. She held up the larger key. "I have practiced extensively with the keys. They both work the same. I have traveled back to England to see my childhood home. I don't know if you realize this, but I am actually from 1892. I have used these keys and traveled into the future, to your time, to 2005."

"I don't understand," Kimberly told her. Was this why Victoria dressed as she did? Why didn't she use modern technology like a phone? Why the house they were sitting in looked so out of date?

"What about Collins?" Kimberly asked.

"He is also from 1892. At first, I only told Charles about the keys. The man who gave them to me told me only one person could know, so naturally, I told my husband, but he didn't believe me. He was a very logical man. I never told him that I had discovered I could time travel with them. After his death, I told Collins who did believe me."

Kimberly shook her head as if to clear it. "What does this have to do with me?"

"Because Patrick is from my time. If you want to meet him, you will need to use one of these keys and time travel to 1892."

Kimberly didn't know what to say. Time travel to 1892? Was Victoria serious? She could tell the woman really believed that the keys did take people back and forth between time periods. Maybe Nicky had been right all along. Maybe this had been a scam. Maybe she shouldn't trust her own feelings.

"I am not sure…" Kimberly started to say, but Victoria interrupted her.

"Are you interested in more information?"

Kimberly hesitated, but curiosity got the better of her, and after a few moments nodded her head. She was curious about what Victoria was going to say.

"If you are still interested in meeting Patrick, I will give you one of these keys. When you are ready to travel back in time, you will need to clutch the key in your hand like this." Kimberly watched as Mrs. Hilton held the key in the palm of her right hand and then moved her fingers and thumb until her entire hand covered the key so she could barely see any of it. "Then you will need to think of the time period you want to travel to, along with the place. You need to picture it in your head if you can and say it out loud." Mrs. Hilton closed her eyes while clutching the key. "1892, Denver, Colorado, my house."

Kimberly watched in amazement as Mrs. Hilton started to look hazy and then she disappeared! She was no longer sitting in front of her! Where did she go? Did she really travel back in time to 1892? Then just as quickly, Mrs. Hilton was sitting in front of her again.

"I just traveled back to my time, to my house, which is actually this house, located in Denver," Mrs. Hilton explained.

Kimberly didn't know what to say. Her heart pounded loudly in her chest. She knew she hadn't imagined the woman disappearing before her eyes. She watched as Mrs. Hilton held out one of the keys. "Hold this, and tell me what you feel."

Kimberly hesitated, and then reached out to grasp the key. She immediately felt a tingling sensation that spread throughout her entire body, and she dropped the key on the wooden desk in shock. She looked at Mrs. Hilton in amazement.

"You felt it." Mrs. Hilton commented as she nodded her head. "That tingling sensation is what moves you back and forth in time, somehow. I have never been able to figure out exactly how it works, but it does."

Kimberly picked the key back up very carefully and studied it. Now that she looked closer, she could tell the design wasn't a knot, but the gold did twist around in a delicate design with a long slender cylinder leading to three notches, one small, the others slightly larger. The entire time she held the key, she felt a slight tingling sensation. She gave it back to Mrs. Hilton who was watching her carefully as if making sure Kimberly wasn't going to faint or run out of the room screaming in shock.

"So, you can come and go when you please between your time period, which is 1892, and my time period, 2005?" Kimberly asked.

"Yes, my dear," Mrs. Hilton assured her. "I actually can go back in whatever time I want. I can also travel to a different part of the world, but stay in my same time period. These keys have an amazing gift."

Okay," Kimberly took a deep breath to calm herself. "So you have magic keys. I am still not sure what this has to do with me." She was a bit confused about the information Victoria was giving her.

"Like I just explained, if you want to meet Patrick and get to know him, with the option of marrying him, you will need to travel back to my time, to 1892, using one of these keys."

"Oh," Kimberly breathed, still in shock that all of this was even happening.

"Let me give you the rest of the information, and then you can make your decision," Mrs. Hilton told her to which Kimberly just nodded her head. "Once you arrive in 1892, you will meet Patrick at the Denver Train Station and he will take you to his ranch. You will need to be willing to stay there for 30 days. You will need to put this key in a safe place once you arrive at his ranch. If you decide you do not want to stay in 1892, you will need it to come back to your time.

"You are not to tell anyone about this key, including Patrick. If you make the decision to stay, then you may tell him. If and when you make that decision, I will come and collect the key. Or you can return it on one of your trips to Denver from Patrick's ranch.

"You need to promise me that you will not bring anything with you from this time, 2005, into 1892. Everything must stay here. It is not good to mix things that belong in the future in the past. You also need to promise that you will not use the key to go to any other time period. Can you agree to these things?"

"Ummm...." Kimberly stuttered. Her brain was still stuck on the possibility of traveling back in time to 1892. She didn't know what to think of what Mrs. Hilton was telling her.

The older woman looked at her kindly and with sympathy. "Why don't you take some time to think about it? If you decide you want to travel back to my time and meet Patrick, come back, and I will help you get there."

"So Patrick doesn't know I am from the future?" She was still trying to understand what she had just heard.

Mrs. Hilton shook her head. "No, dear. The only people who will know this is myself and Collins, and now you."

"Have you done this before with other women from my time?"

Mrs. Hilton shook her head. "Actually, I have not. You are the first one."

"What if it doesn't work? What if I end up somewhere else besides where Patrick is? What if I can't come back to my time?" She felt panic at the thought.

"If you follow my instructions, I can promise you that that will not happen. Collins and I have tested both of these keys extensively. There is no possible way to travel somewhere you don't want to go by mistake. And as long as you don't lose the key, you will be able to travel back to your time when you wish."

"I need to think about this," Kimberly finally told her. "When do I have to decide by?

"I am not going to give you a time limit," Mrs. Hilton told her firmly. "You must feel comfortable about your decision. I do ask that if you decide you do not want to go through with this, that you write Patrick one last letter to let him know of your decision. It is only proper that he learn of your decision through you, not myself."

Kimberly nodded her head in agreement and soon she was back in her car. For a moment, she sat there thinking about all she had heard and learned in the last few minutes. For the first time in a long time, she wished she could talk to her mother, and she missed both of her parents desperately. What would her mother advise her to do?

She instinctively knew she shouldn't tell Nicky or Justin about this, at least until she had made her decision. She hated that she couldn't confide in them, but she wanted to be able to make her choice without feeling like her friends thought she was crazy for even considering something like being a mail-order bride, and then adding time travel into the situation, she knew that her friends wouldn't understand.

Chapter 6

Over the next few days, Kimberly went about her days like usual. She went to work and met Nicky for lunch. She went to watch Garrett play a soccer game in a nearby park. On Sunday, she went with Nicky to her parents' home to celebrate her father's birthday. But always in the back of her mind, she was thinking about what she had learned from Mrs. Hilton. Sometimes she would make the decision to not go back in time and meet Patrick. Other times, she would make the decision to go for it, to meet Patrick and see what happens. She knew it would be difficult to suddenly be required to live like people did in the 1890s. She would be giving up many luxuries that weren't available back then, but she also felt she knew enough about that time period, that she would be able to accustom herself to it.

She also kept thinking about Patrick. She found it odd that she felt the beginnings of a bond with him, even though the only contact she had had with him was through letters. Now that she knew he was from the past, a lot of what he described made sense, including the four-hour horseback ride to

Denver from his ranch. He sounded wonderful in his letters. Did she really want to give up the chance to meet him?

Finally, on Monday of the next week, she left work early. It had been a terrible day, and her boss had been quite verbally abusive to her. She had been accused of making many mistakes she hadn't made, and impulsively she had quit on the spot. She knew she couldn't keep working in the environment she was in. It was draining her emotionally. At the moment she quit and walked out of the ER for the last time, she also knew she had instantly made the choice to meet Patrick. She was going to go back in time.

****

Patrick had just made the trip to Denver and back in one day. He had been very anxious to see if he had another letter from Kimberly, the woman Mrs. Hilton had matched with him. In his last letter, he had invited her to come to stay on his ranch so they could meet and get to know each other better.

They had only exchanged a few letters, but he liked what he had read. He learned that she didn't have any family and that she was a nurse. He liked that she had educated herself so that she could support herself if she needed to. She seemed kind and inquisitive. He enjoyed the thought of teaching her how to help him run his ranch, and from what it sounded like, she was just as interested in it as he was.

He had gone into Denver to pick up some supplies for the coming roundup. He and Shaun would be moving their small herd of cattle deeper into the mountains for the summer as soon as he arrived back to the ranch. He felt excitement at the thought that Mrs. Hilton had another letter from Kimberly and she had encouraged him to read it right then, almost as if she knew what Kimberly had written him.

After he accepted the letter, he took a few moments to himself in her gardens and opened the envelope. He quickly learned that she did indeed want to come to meet him. She indicated that they would need to work out a day and time for her to come, but she was agreeable to meet him and live on his ranch in the small cabin he promised her for 30 days. As he read her letter of acceptance, he found himself breathing a sigh of relief. He hadn't been sure she would want to come when no promises had been officially made between them, and he felt excited at the thought that maybe, within a short amount of time, he would soon have a wife.

When he returned to the Victorian house, he informed Mrs. Hilton of Kimberly's decision, and watched as the woman smiled in delight. Between the two of them, they agreed on the date she would come, which would be in two weeks from then since he needed to get the cattle moved before he could come to Denver again.

When he arrived at the ranch, he jumped off his horse, and saw Bridget hanging wet clothing on a rope. He ran to her and swung her around. "Kimberly has decided to come," he told her.

Bridget squealed and hugged him back. Out of all three of his siblings, she had been the most supportive in the decision to take a mail-order bride. Shaun was skeptical, but then he had always been bitter about women ever since the woman he wanted to marry a little over a year ago had basically left him at the altar when she found out the real history about his daughter, Colleen. His youngest brother, Keegan, was a typical 15-year-old boy who could care less about his eldest brother's desire to start a family.

"Give me the details," Bridget demanded with a grin. "When will she be here?"

"I am to pick her up from the Denver train station in two weeks from today. That will give us time to move the cattle and move my stuff out of the old cabin into the family home. The old cabin also will need to be cleaned up."

"Leave the cabin to me," Bridget offered. "I will have it ready for her by the time you and Shaun get back from moving the cattle."

Patrick was grateful for Bridget's offer and immediately accepted her help. He knew she would do a better job than he ever could. The cabin had been built sturdy. It was snug and warm. The roof had just been replaced a few years ago, but the inside needed a good cleaning, and a woman's touch.

Chapter 7

Kimberly was again at Mrs. Hilton's home. She had arrived a few hours before, letting the woman know of her decision. She was surprised how happy Mrs. Hilton seemed about her choice.

"I have a good feeling about this," Mrs. Hilton told her as she gave Kimberly a hug. "Patrick is a good man and I really do think you will both be good for each other."

"I hope so," Kimberly replied. She still wasn't sure how this time travel issue was going to work, especially since she wasn't allowed to tell him about where she was from unless she made the decision to stay.

"Now, we need to get you ready. Come with me, dear." Mrs. Hilton led Kimberly up a long flight of stairs and into a room that was filled with various items. "This room is where I keep everything that I have collected from the different time periods I have traveled in," Mrs. Hilton explained.

Kimberly was instantly curious and wanted to look around. She saw many items, mostly clothes and coins. Everything was organized into different sections depending on the time period, with different pieces of luggage to carry everything in. Hats were hung on the walls, all feminine. On a table in the far corner was a collection of collectibles, like an old Polaroid camera, and some spectacles that looked like one of the first ever made. Mrs. Hilton had even collected a few paintings from different eras.

Mrs. Hilton opened a small wardrobe labeled "1890s" and started to pull out a few dresses.

"You will need to dress as if you are from the 1890s," Mrs. Hilton explained as she laid a few of the dresses on a nearby bed. "You may choose a few dresses. I will also make sure you have anything else you might need."

Kimberly fell in love with the dresses. Most of them seemed to be for everyday use, with plain colors and aprons. There was one that seemed more formal, with satin fabric and slightly puffy sleeves. She loved the high necklines and the lace, and itched to see what they looked like on her. She instantly chose two of them and Mrs. Hilton encouraged her to try them on. Surprisingly, or unsurprisingly depending on how she wanted to look at it, they both fit her perfectly.

"These dresses are meant to wear for every day," Mrs. Hilton explained. "You should choose one more dress, a nice one that you will want to get married in. How about this one?"

Mrs. Hilton held up another dress and Kimberly instantly agreed. It was ivory, with a small train. Ruffles lined the bottom hem and the short sleeves. There was a beautiful design embroidered into the bodice, which ended in a steep "V" shape at her hips. It didn't look like the fancy wedding dresses that were worn in 2005, but she knew it would be perfect for her wedding, if she chose to marry Patrick, and then she would also be able to always have a nice dress to wear for more fancy functions.

Mrs. Hilton added some underclothing, stockings, and shoes. She showed Kimberly how to do her hair. Luckily, Kimberly's hair was long, almost to her mid back, so it wasn't going to be hard to arrange her hair like the women wore in the 1890s. Mrs. Hilton gave her a large cloth bag, which she called a carpet bag, and helped her fold and arrange all the clothing she had given her into the bag.

The last thing she gave Kimberly was the key.

"Now remember, keep this with you all the time. Once you arrive at Patrick's ranch, find a safe place to hide it. If you lose it, you will not be able to return to your time if you decide not to stay."

Kimberly nodded. She understood the importance of not losing the key.

Mrs. Hilton gave her a piece of paper with detailed instructions. A few days from now, a day that had been agreed upon by Mrs. Hilton, Patrick and herself, she was to clutch the key in her right hand, say the date out loud, June 5, 1892, and picture in her mind the Denver train station. If she did it right, she should immediately be transported back in time to the train station in Denver, the way it was in 1892. Patrick should be there to greet her.

"Good luck, my dear," Mrs. Hilton told Kimberly as she walked her to the door. "I will be living at my home in Denver during your 30 days with Patrick. It will look much like this one, only much newer. If there are any problems, don't hesitate to come find me."

****

Over the next few days, Kimberly did everything she could to prepare for her spontaneous trip back in time. She researched the time era and tried to learn how the day to day life would be like living on a ranch. She didn't want to seem stupid if she didn't know basic day to day habits. In the privacy of her room late one night, she tried on each article of clothing so she knew how to put them on. After she folded each of the clothing and put them all back in the carpetbag, leaving one dress out that she had decided to wear for her trip back in time, she looked around her room. There were two things she wished she could take with her. She had a small first aid kit that she had put together in nursing school and that she kept with her all the time. The nurse in her had a hard time leaving first aid supplies behind. What if she might need them while she was gone? She also wanted to take her sketch pad and colored pencils. Drawing was as much a part of her as being a nurse. She drew when she needed to relax, think, or make a major decision.

Quickly, without thinking about the consequences, she put the first aid kit on the bottom of the carpetbag, along with her small sketch pad, colored pencils, and a battery-operated pencil sharpener. When she arrived at Patrick's ranch, she would make sure she hid both of the items well so no one would ever see them.

Kimberly also withdrew a large amount of cash to give to Nicky for expenses for rent. She didn't want her being gone to be a financial burden to her friend. She withdrew enough for expenses for two months which she placed in an envelope. She also included instructions on how to access the rest of her money should she not return. She wasn't going to need her money if she chose to stay in the 1890s.

The last thing she did the night before she was to leave was to write Nicky and Justin a letter. She knew Nicky thought something was up, but Kimberly knew her friend didn't suspect that she had actually decided to become a mail-order bride because she hadn't talked about it to Nicky since they visited Mrs. Hilton that second time. She knew Nicky had assumed Kimberly agreed with her that it was a scam.

Kimberly knew she couldn't tell Nicky and Justin about the time travel, but she felt she couldn't leave without letting them know she had decided to become a mail-order bride. She quickly pulled out a sheet of paper, the kind of heavy paper she had written on to Patrick, and started to write.

Dear Nicky and Justin,

When you find this letter, you will know that I am no longer here. I have made the decision to go visit Patrick and get to know him better. If in 30 days, we both feel it is right, we will marry.

I am going to ask you both something important. Please do not try to find me. You will not be able to. I cannot tell you exactly where I am, but I know that if you go to Mrs. Victoria Hilton's home, she will know how to get a message to me if it is important.

I am sorry about the way I am leaving. You both have been like a brother and sister to me, ever since my parents were killed, and I will be forever grateful. I can't really explain to you why I feel I should embark on this new life, but please know that I do feel it is the right decision for me.

Nicky, I am enclosing enough money to cover my expenses for the next two months. If I do not return, you are welcome to use the rest of the funds in my account as you see fit.

Love you both always,

Kimberly

Kimberly placed the letter along with the cash into an envelope and left it on her bed. She knew Nicky would find it when she got curious enough to wonder why Kimberly wasn't up for the day.

Then, it was time. Kimberly was finally ready to start a new chapter of her life. She clutched the carpetbag in her left hand and held the key in the right. She pictured the Denver train station while she whispered out loud, "June 5, 1892," just like Victoria had instructed.

Instantly the tingling and vibration she always felt when she held the key grew stronger. The sensation grew to remind her of the pins and needles she would feel if her foot fell asleep. Her heart pounded as, for a moment, she realized she could see two different scenes at once. Then she was at the train station, with people walking, not even realizing she had just appeared in front of them. She took a deep breath and started looking around, searching for what could be her future husband. Without second guessing herself, she was swept into her new life.

Chapter 8

Patrick quickly finished feeding the last of the barn animals and then sighed with relief. He had wanted to get an early start this morning, but a few things had slowed him down. He was heading to Denver to pick up Kimberly at the train station, and he had a long ride ahead of him. When he had arrived in the barn a few hours ago, he found a horse lame and a cow that seemed to be sick. He was glad he had his younger brother, Shaun, helping him. Shaun had a gift with animals and always seemed to know how to help them when they were sick or injured.

"I guess that's it," Patrick told Shaun as he put the pitchfork away in its place. "I need to get going."

"Go ahead and eat breakfast," Shaun told him. "I'll get Keegan out here to finish up the rest of the chores. I'm sure Bridget will have something for you to eat."

Patrick nodded at his brother's words. He was anxious to leave. He knew he was going to barely meet the train as it was. He hoped Bridget would be ready to go. He was leaving Shaun and Keegan at the ranch to take care of things while he was gone, but he wanted Bridget to come with him. He hoped having his sister along would help his new bride be more comfortable with her new situation.

He also knew Bridget was planning to do some shopping while they were in Denver. She wanted to purchase some new fabric for dresses for her and also for Shaun's young daughter, Colleen. Keegan needed some new school books. He also wanted Bridget to make sure Kimberly had what she would need in order to live on the ranch.

Their ranch was located in the middle of the Rocky Mountains and they didn't have any neighbors that lived nearby, although every once in a while, they would see Indians that lived deeper in the mountains.

Patrick entered the small ranch house and was relieved to see a plate of food sitting on the table. He quickly washed up with a basin of water that had been set aside for that specific use and sat down to eat. Bridget was washing up the last of the breakfast dishes.

Bridget smiled at him as he took his first bite. "I'm glad you were able to come in and eat." She placed a few slices of buttered bread next to him. "I just need to finish these dishes and pack up some food. We can leave whenever you are ready."

"Why can't I go with you?" a small voice asked. Patrick turned his attention to Colleen. She had her bottom lip sticking out in a pout. "Pa said I did fine on the last trip to Denver."

"That you did," Patrick agreed. "But this trip is just for Bridget and me. We won't be staying the night like we did last time. I want to be back this evening."

"Why are you going to Denver?" Colleen asked curiously.

"Remember? I am picking up my new bride today," Patrick answered her, feeling slightly more anxious as he said the words out loud.

Colleen nodded her head, her dark hair bouncing as she did. "I remember. Pa said it will be a miracle if she stays."

Patrick felt frustrated at her words. He knew Shaun didn't approve of what he was doing, but he wished he would keep his opinion to himself.

"Colleen, sometimes it is best to not repeat everything you hear," Bridget gently chastised her. "Will you please come and dry these dishes?"

Colleen obeyed, picked up a nearby towel, and started her chore.

Patrick quickly ate the last of his breakfast and stood to take his dishes to Bridget. "Good as usual, sis," he told her as she quickly started to wash his plate. "I'm going to get our horses saddled."

"Which one are you going to have Kimberly ride?" Bridget asked. "I wonder how much experience she has had with horses."

This was the only concern he had with Kimberly. He had enjoyed her letters, although some of what she had written had puzzled him. It was almost as if she had never left a city in her life. He desperately hoped she would be able to adjust to living on his ranch, especially since it was located so far away from the nearest city. In her last letter, she had assured him she didn't like living in the city and felt she would enjoy living on a ranch. He hoped she wouldn't change her mind.

He knew they wouldn't be able to marry until she had been at the ranch for 30 days. Mrs. Hilton was very firm on this rule. She didn't think it was wise for a man and a woman who first met each other to immediately marry. Patrick understood this guideline, but almost wished they could ignore it. He was anxious to have a wife and start his family. But he could also see the wisdom in Mrs. Hilton's request. If Kimberly couldn't adjust to their way of life, it would be better if they didn't marry instead of both of them ending up with an unhappy marriage.

He was glad that there was a small cabin on the ranch that Kimberly could sleep in for the required 30 days, but he also hoped she would want to spend most of her time with his family. Even though he would be marrying her, it was important that she would be able to get along with his siblings.

"I plan on bringing Honey for her," Patrick answered Bridget's question. She was the gentlest horse they had and a good one to ride if a person didn't have experience with horses. In fact, Colleen had learned to ride on her.

Bridget nodded her approval and turned back to her chore. Patrick jogged back to the barn. He smiled his thanks as he saw that Shaun had saddled his favorite riding horse, Apache. They worked together to get Bridget's horse and Honey saddled and ready to go.

Soon he and Bridget were on their way towards Denver. He sighed to himself as he listened to his sister talk about what she wanted to purchase. His life was about to change and he said a prayer that everything would go well over the next 30 days. He was traveling to Denver to get a wife. As he pondered this, he knew in his heart he was already committed to her.

****

Kimberly was suddenly thrust into a new world. She had just arrived at the Denver train station and she looked around in awe. The key worked! Just like Mrs. Hilton had said it would! She had actually traveled back in time to 1892.

Her eyes scanned her surroundings, thrilled to be taking in a new time period. She could tell by the slight chill in the air that it was spring time, just like it had been in her time period. People were going about their days as normal, going into one of the few shops that were located along the street, or shouting greetings to each other. Some people did look at her with mild curiosity; they must know just about everyone in the city, and she wondered if they were curious about who she was. She smiled shyly at those she made eye contact with. She could tell by the layer of dust covering the wood floors, she was going to have to get used to being dirty. She saw two boys throwing a small red ball back and forth to each other until an older woman yelled out for them to stop when the ball almost hit a store window.

She glanced down at her hand to make sure she still had the key. Seeing that she did, she slipped the key into the pocket of her dress for safe keeping. The pocket was quite deep and she knew there was little danger of losing it. She was still clutching the carpet bag that held her belongings in her other hand and she gripped it tighter when an older man inadvertently bumped into her.

"Sorry, miss," the man told her tipping his hat as he hurried past her to some important destination only he knew of. Kimberly didn't have a chance to say anything because he was soon gone.

Kimberly looked around at the people around her. What if she didn't find Patrick? He had briefly described himself in one of his letters, saying only that he was tall and had dark red hair. She started focusing on tall men with red hair and soon she spotted one. He was standing in the street near the train tracks, helping a woman down off of a horse. She almost dismissed this man because of the woman who was with him, but he did have red, almost auburn hair, so she kept an eye on him. He had three horses with him and she noticed that the woman also had equally red hair.

The man looked around and almost instantly looked directly at her. He seemed to know who she was, for he strode towards her, leaving the woman to follow him if she wished.

"Miss Kimberly Nelson?" the man questioned as he stood in front of her. She almost didn't answer as she looked into his sea green eyes. He was the most handsome man she had ever seen. He was indeed tall, with her head coming to the top of his shoulder. His auburn hair had a slight curl to it and was long enough to touch the tip of his shirt collar. He smiled slightly at her as he waited for her response.

"Yes, I am Kimberly," she was finally able to reply. She mentally shook herself. She couldn't afford to be attracted to him this early in the relationship. She had promised herself the night before as she was packing for her time travel trip, that she would not allow herself to fall in love with Patrick until she knew without a shadow of a doubt that she would want to stay in 1892. She didn't want to lose another person because of fate, like she had lost her parents.

"It's good to meet you," Patrick was saying as he stepped aside and pulled the woman Kimberly had seen with him towards them. "This is my sister, Bridget."

"Hello," Kimberly turned her attention to the woman beside him. She had equally auburn red hair like Patrick did and Kimberly thought it was the most beautiful color she had ever seen. Even though Bridget's hair was pulled back in a loose bun, Kimberly could tell that it was tight with natural curls, while Patrick's was more wavy than curly. Bridget's eyes were also different, a beautiful sky blue color.

Bridget smiled at her. "It's nice to meet you. Did you have a nice trip?"

Kimberly froze for a second and then reminded herself that Bridget was talking about the train trip, not the time travel trip. "Yes, I did," she said, trying not to stutter.

Patrick held out his hand to shake hers and Kimberly hesitantly placed hers in his and for a brief moment, the world seemed to stop. Kimberly felt something in her heart that had been asleep for so long. It was as if her soul was recognizing another whom she might have known before. But how was that possible?

Kimberly saw Patrick's eyes widen as if he felt the same thing she had felt. Kimberly pulled her hand away in confusion.

"I think we should go to the Denver Hotel and eat some lunch," Bridget suggested. "Then I need to do some shopping. We want to be back to the ranch by dark and it is already 1:00."

Kimberly had many questions about how they were going to get to the ranch. She remembered Patrick writing that it was a four-hour horseback ride from Denver and all she saw was the three horses. She could see people driving wagons and horses in the Denver streets. Why wouldn't they use a wagon to get to their ranch? Was she going to be expected to ride one of those horses? She had never been on a horse in her life! Somehow, even with all her preparation and study she did before coming here, she didn't think about taking horseback riding lessons. She hoped there was a wagon somewhere.

Patrick took the carpetbag from Kimberly. He tied it securely to one of the horses and then made sure all three of the animals were tied to a post. She watched as he patted one of them with obvious affection and it nickered back at him.

"Let's go," Patrick said and led Kimberly and Bridget down the dusty walkway. Kimberly followed and tried not to stare at all the new sounds and sights that were before her. What was that saying? She sure wasn't in Kansas anymore.

The hotel was cool as they entered and Kimberly watched as Patrick greeted a man. They were quickly seated at a table by a large window. Patrick ordered for all of them which Kimberly found peculiar, but noticed that Bridget took it in stride. Kimberly decided she would watch Bridget carefully and take her cues from her.

Little was said while they waited for the meal to be served. Patrick and Bridget talked briefly about what items she wanted to purchase and Kimberly listened, trying to act like the situation she was in was normal. What she wanted to do was watch everything around her, but she knew that it was considered rude to stare, so she refrained, and tried to focus on the conversation between Patrick and Bridget.

When the food arrived Kimberly discovered how hungry she was. Patrick had ordered fried chicken with potatoes, gravy, and peas. In her time period, fried chicken was considered a food to avoid because of the high content of fat, but it was the best chicken she had ever tasted. She had been too nervous to eat breakfast in her apartment that morning, so she was very hungry.

While they ate, she caught Patrick watching her a few times and would smile at her when he caught her gaze with his own. Every time this happened, her heart seemed to skip a beat and it would steal her breath away. She realized she would need to be very, very careful with her heart, and his.

After the delicious meal, they walked to a nearby general store. Again, Kimberly did her best to act like she had always been in general stores like this one. The store was small, probably less than a fourth the size of the grocery stores at home. The counter was to the left, with a man behind it lifting a sack of flour down off the shelf for a customer. She could see a few aisles ahead of her with shelves that were stocked with basic fruits and vegetables, and other necessities. She realized, not for the first time, that all of the food she ate would need to be cooked from scratch.

"I need to get some new books for our younger brother, Keegan," Bridget explained to Kimberly as they walked to a shelf full of books. "We live so far away from Denver, Keegan hasn't been able to go to school."

"So who teaches him?" Kimberly asked as she picked up what looked to be a history book.

"I do, or at least I try to," Bridget explained. "But this will likely be the last year I will be able to. He has passed me in what he has learned. For the past few months, I have just been guiding and encouraging him."

"Does he want to continue his schooling?" Kimberly asked.

"He does. He loves to learn. Out of all four of us, he has enjoyed school the most. We will have to arrange to board him next fall in Denver."

Bridget pulled a few books off of the shelf and started to look through them. Kimberly glanced at her own and saw that it was a history of England.

"How old is Keegan?" Kimberly asked.

"He is 15."

"Would he like this book?" she handed Bridget the book she was looking through and watched as the woman looked through it.

"This would be perfect," Bridget nodded. "It looks a little above his level, but it would challenge him. Let's see if we can find some other books like this one."

Kimberly gladly helped, and soon between the two of them, they had found two science books and another history book. Kimberly wanted to ask about math, but didn't know if that subject was something that was important in the 1890s as it was in her time.

She felt a presence behind her and turned to see Patrick standing close to them.

"Did you find what you needed for Keegan?" he asked Bridget who nodded.

"Kimberly actually helped. We found a few books that should keep him busy for a few months. I really think we need to talk about boarding him next fall, Patrick," Bridget told her brother as she handed him the books that were chosen.

"Yes, I have some ideas along those lines, but we have to get through the summer first." Patrick turned to Kimberly. "Do you need anything while we are here? I would like you to get what you need."

Kimberly didn't know what to say. Victoria had provided her with a few dresses and other essentials. She didn't know what she would need, and she didn't want Patrick to spend money on her.

"I don't think…" Kimberly started to say, but Bridget interrupted her.

"I'll take care of it," Bridget declared. She looped her arm through Kimberly's and led her away towards some women's clothing.

"I really don't need anything," Kimberly started to say again.

"Kimberly, we live on a ranch. From what Patrick has told me from your letters, you have lived in a city your entire life. There are some things you will need."

Soon Bridget had gathered another dress, boots, a few aprons, a hat, and a pair of pants, or britches as Bridget called them, that could be used for riding. When Kimberly saw all the items that Bridget wanted to buy, Kimberly again tried to protest. After all, what if things didn't work out? But she knew she couldn't say anything, so she finally decided to stay quiet, especially when Patrick came up to pay the bill. He didn't even blink at the amount, and Kimberly felt relief. She hoped that if it was too much, he would have said something.

Soon, too soon in Kimberly's opinion, Patrick had the purchases tied to the three horses. Bridget swung into her saddle by herself. Kimberly wondered if she would be expected to do the same when Patrick guided her to one of the horses and looked at her expectantly.

When she continued to stand awkwardly next to the horse, he looked surprised. "Have you ever ridden before?" Patrick asked her.

When she shook her head, he continued. "This is Honey. She is one of our gentlest horses. She is good to learn on. Let me help you up." He bent his knee up and looked at her as if expecting her to know what she was to do. "Place your left foot here." He touched his leg. She did as he requested and almost immediately he placed his hands around her waist and hoisted her onto the horse as if she weighed nothing.

She took a few deep breaths. She hoped she would be able to make the trip to their ranch without embarrassing herself. She arranged her skirts around her the best she could.

Patrick quickly gave her a few instructions on how to control the horse, but then said, "You really won't need to worry about telling her what to do. She will just follow the other horses."

Kimberly hoped that was true. She prayed that Honey would do what was expected of her and not take off on her own. A scene from a movie she saw a couple weeks ago flashed through her mind. The horse a woman was riding was spooked and ran off wildly with no hope of calming it. Luckily, there was a handsome man nearby to save her. Kimberly had to suppress a panicked giggle as she looked at Patrick. At least she had her own handsome man nearby in case something went wrong. Patrick said something to his horse and they were soon on their way.

Chapter 9

Patrick kept his horse from going too fast as he guided Apache towards the woods at the edge of Denver and onto the path that would lead them to their ranch. He wanted to chuckle at Kimberly's face when he had swung her into Honey's saddle. It was very obvious she didn't have any experience with horses. He wondered why she would be interested in being a mail-order bride if she came from a family wealthy enough to ride carriages everywhere. He chuckled again as he glanced back at her. She clutched the saddle horn so hard her hands turned white. Well, that would be one of the first things he would help her with. If she was going to be his wife, she needed to be comfortable being on a horse.

Overall, he was pleased with Kimberly. She seemed quiet and a bit shy, and he hoped as she felt more comfortable with her new life, she would open up and talk more. He was glad to see that Bridget was able to get her to talk. It was obvious she had been educated because she was able to help Bridget choose some of the books for Keegan.

"That is something I'll need to ask her about," he muttered to himself. Why would a woman who had received education want to be a mail-order bride? That was a question he had not asked in his letters.

He had been instantly attracted to her the moment he saw her. Her dark brown hair seemed to have a light tint to it when the sunlight shown on it. Her hair had been pulled back into a style that he had seen other women wear, but some strands had gotten loose and he could tell her hair was shorter than most women. He liked the interest she had shown when they walked along the streets of Denver. She seemed in awe of the store and it was almost as if she had never seen a general store before. Patrick dismissed that thought as soon as he had it. Of course, she had seen stores before. It was the 1890s after all and she was from the city. He could tell she had a hard time with him buying her things she needed. Well, that was another thing she would need to get used to. He intended to provide for her. She was going to be his wife, after all.

Part of him wished the thirty days were up and he could marry her, but he somehow knew that she needed some encouragement before she would be ready to commit. He would use the next 30 days to get to know her, and allow her to get to know him. He felt excited that he would be able to spend time with her. It would be fun to teach her how to ride a horse, to show her his ranch and the surrounding mountains: the best place on earth to live.

****

Kimberly breathed a sigh of relief when Patrick announced that they were going to stop and rest the horses for a few minutes. Her bottom was starting to hurt and she desperately wanted to move around.

She had actually enjoyed the first hour. After she had gotten used to the movement of the horse, she started to look around at her surroundings. The mountains were beautiful, just like they were in her time, although quite a few homes and towns had been built. In Patrick's time, there was nothing but aspen and pine trees, meadows full of wildflowers, and small animals showing their faces every so often. Over the last half hour, they had started to follow a river, and Bridget had explained to her that they would continue to follow the river all the way to their ranch. Kimberly had always enjoyed the sound of running water, so she tried to concentrate on that as her body became stiffer.

Patrick came over and helped her off the horse, keeping his hands on her arms until he was sure she wasn't going to topple over.

"We will take a break for about 15 minutes," Patrick told her and Kimberly nodded her understanding. "Are you hungry?"

She shook her head. She was still full from the lunch they had eaten. "I am thirsty, though."

Patrick immediately provided a leather canteen and Kimberly enjoyed some cold clear water. "I would like to walk around a bit."

"Don't wander off too far from us," Patrick warned and Kimberly nodded her agreement. She needed to use some bathroom facilities and knew that there would be nothing around. Her choice was to wait until they arrived at the ranch or use a bush. She chose to wait.

She walked along the edge of the river, stopping every so often to enjoy the water. She saw some minnows swimming in a shallow pool and bent down to touch the water which she found was ice cold. She scooped up some water and splashed it on her face, not knowing that Patrick was watching her. She stood and lifted her face to the sun, enjoying the rays. It felt so peaceful here and she slowly found herself starting to relax. It was nice to know she didn't have to wake up the next morning and go to work at the hospital. She didn't realize how stressed that job had made her until she had gotten away from the situation.

"Time to go," Patrick called and she returned to her horse's side.

"How much farther is your ranch?" She was careful to keep her tone of voice light as if she was just curious and not because she couldn't wait to get off the horse for good.

"About another hour," Patrick replied. He helped her up in the saddle the same way as before and they were soon on their way. Sure enough, an hour later they arrived at the farm. A man came up to them to help with the horses.

"This is my brother, Shaun," Patrick introduced the man as he helped Kimberly down. She noticed that Shaun didn't have the dark red hair that Patrick or Bridget had. He had blond hair with blue eyes and was almost as handsome as Patrick was. These

O'Connor men were gorgeous and she wondered why they weren't married.

"It's nice to meet you," Kimberly told him, extending her hand which he shook.

"Pleased to meet you," Shaun drawled as he helped his sister down.

Kimberly gladly gave her horse up to Patrick and started to walk around, trying to get her stiff legs to move properly. As she walked, she looked around for an outhouse, trying to remember if the toilets were outside or inside in this time period. Bridget must have noticed, and pointed Kimberly to the outdoor latrine to the side of a large house, and Kimberly headed towards it. Her long dress swished as she moved and she wished she could remove it and put on some pants. She was starting to realize learning how to get used to long dresses was going to be a challenge. In her time, she rarely wore dresses, preferring jeans and shorts, and of course, she would wear scrubs to work.

She stepped into the latrine and was surprised by the stink. She didn't think about the little details, like using the bathroom, would change so drastically. After she finished, she looked around for toilet paper, which she couldn't find. She did find a pile of old store catalogs in a basket on the floor and remembered reading that was what people used to use for toilet paper. Then she looked slightly more panicked for a sink to wash her hands in, which was also absent. She took a deep breath. She had a lot to get used to. She already felt covered in dirt, and realized she probably wouldn't have the opportunity to bathe as often as she had in her apartment either. She made a mental note to visit the river to rinse off as often as she could.

"I will have dinner ready as soon as I can," Bridget said when Kimberly had returned. "I know you are tired."

Kimberly nodded agreement at Bridget's words. She wished she could just go to bed right then. She had never been as tired as she felt at that moment. Obviously, traveling through time was an exhausting experience. She almost felt as if she was going to topple over. She watched as Bridget left, walking towards what looked to be a large cabin. Kimberly slowly turned a full circle, noticing the buildings around her. There was the large cabin that Bridget had disappeared into. A short distance away there was a smaller cabin. She could see a large building that she figured was the barn since Patrick was leading the horses towards it. There were fenced fields surrounding them. Some of them had a few cattle and horses in them and others were empty. She also noticed a large fenced area that had been totally cleared of plants and she wondered if that was a garden.

She wondered what she should do and finally decided to follow Bridget. Once inside the large cabin she quickly looked around. It was decorated simply, but she instantly felt like she had come home. There was only one level. She had walked into what looked to be the living room since there were a few sofas and chairs that were placed around a small table. There was a fireplace with a shelf above it filled with small animals carved out of wood and she wondered who carved them. She saw a large colorful braided rug on the floor. She could see the kitchen through an open door and could hear Bridget talking to someone, so she decided to head in that direction.

When she entered, she immediately noticed Bridget at an old-fashioned wood stove, stirring something in a large pot. There was a large wooden table in the middle of the room with benches and wooden chairs surrounding it. A young girl was walking around it setting plates and silverware down.

She looked up as Kimberly entered and smiled shyly at her.

"Hello," Kimberly greeted the girl. Bridget turned from the stove with a smile.

"I'm glad you came in," Bridget said as she continued to stir whatever was in the large pot. "I'm sorry for leaving you out there in the yard, but I wanted to make sure this stew was cooking properly."

"It smells delicious," Kimberly commented. She wanted to ask how Bridget had gotten a pot of stew cooking so quickly, but knew that question might likely be strange to Bridget. Luckily, Bridget answered her unspoken question.

"That is what's wonderful about stew. You can start it in the morning and let it simmer all day on the back of the stove. It's almost done." She turned, walked towards a nearby counter, and started to stir a flour mixture. "I just need to get these biscuits in the oven. By the time they are done, the men should be here and we can eat."

Kimberly didn't know what to say, so she just nodded. Suddenly she felt so tired she didn't think she could stand another minute and sank down onto a nearby bench. She knew she should offer to help prepare the meal, but she didn't think she had enough strength to even ask the question. She knew she wouldn't be much help anyway. She hardly cooked at all in her time and she knew cooking on a wood stove would be very different.

"I'm Colleen," the girl told her.

"That's right," Bridget said as she started to place spoonfuls of the biscuit mix onto a flat pan. "I should introduce you. This is Colleen, Shaun's daughter."

"Hello, Colleen," Kimberly said to the child. "I'm Kimberly Nelson."

"Are you the woman Patrick is going to marry?" Colleen asked curiously.

"I probably will marry him," Kimberly answered and instantly wished she could take back her words when Bridget looked at her sharply. She knew this entire family was most likely planning that the marriage between her and Patrick was going to happen when the 30 days were up. In their minds, the marriage was basically a done deal. She was glad when Bridget just frowned at her and turned back to the biscuits.

"I'm glad you came," Colleen told her. "Patrick needs a wife. He's getting too old."

Kimberly smiled at the child's words. She knew Patrick was 30 years old and in her time, that was the age most men decide to marry. In the 1890s, it was probably rare a man had not married by the time he was 30. Even at her age, 25, a woman was considered an old maid if not married.

"How old are you?" she asked Colleen.

"I'm eight," the child told her with a grin. "I turn nine in three months and ten days."

"Counting down, are you?" Kimberly asked her with a smile. She instantly felt a bond with this child. Colleen was a beautiful girl with long almost jet-black hair tied into a braid that hung down her back. She had equally black eyes and tan skin. She looked nothing like Patrick or Bridget with their red curly hair and fair skin, or Shaun with his blond hair and blue eyes.

Colleen nodded excitedly. "Pa told me I get my very own horse when I turn nine."

"That sounds like a great birthday present."

"I already have her picked out and Pa is training her."

"What is her name?" Kimberly asked.

"She doesn't have a name yet. I'm not going to name her until she is mine."

Kimberly thought that was a perfectly logical reason for not naming a horse.

"Shaun trains all of our horses," Bridget explained. "He also trains horses to sell."

Over the next few minutes, Kimberly enjoyed talking with Colleen about her horse. She learned more about life on the ranch just talking to the child than she had through Patrick's letters. Colleen talked about getting up early next morning to take care of chores and invited Kimberly to help her. She learned there were some chickens in the back, of which Colleen boasted about taking care of.

Kimberly heard the stomping of feet and then Patrick, Shaun, and a teenage boy came through a back door. All three of them went to a long table that was set up against one of the kitchen walls and started to wash their hands and faces, using some fresh water that was in a basin. For a few minutes, chaos reigned as the family sat down at the table for the meal.

Patrick said a blessing on the food and then everyone started to eat. Between bites, Patrick introduced her to his younger brother. "This is Keegan," he waved at him as he said his name, although Kimberly had already figured out who he was. Keegan had short dark brown hair. She found it interesting how different all three males looked from each other, given that they were brothers. She was also surprised that Colleen looked nothing like Shaun and so she figured the child took after her mother, and she briefly wondered where her mother was.

Kimberly didn't eat much. She started to feel more and more tired. She wished she could just go to bed, but didn't feel like it would be polite to say so. She could hear conversation around her, but couldn't focus on it. She felt a hand on her arm.

"You look very tired," Bridget told her with sympathy in her voice. "Why don't I show you where you will be sleeping? You can get to know everyone tomorrow."

Patrick stood when he heard Bridget talking. "Oh, Kimberly, I am sorry. I should have shown you where you will be sleeping earlier." He looked remorseful, so Kimberly smiled at him to let him know she had forgiven him.

"I can show her the cabin," Bridget told her brother.

"Thank you," Kimberly said, her voice shaking. She felt tears form in her eyes at Bridget's kindness. "I am quite tired." Kimberly rarely cried and knew the tears were likely from being exhausted.

"I have traveled before, and I know it can wear a person out," Bridget said as she led Kimberly outdoors.

Kimberly wondered what Bridget would say if she knew how far she had really traveled. Very quickly, Bridget opened the door to the small cabin that she had noticed when she first arrived and stepped inside. It was small, only one room, but Kimberly knew she would be comfortable here. She could see her bag sitting on a small bed.

"I will let you retire for the night," Bridget told her. "Sleep as long as you need to in the morning."

"Thank you so much," Kimberly told her and watched as Bridget left.

She hardly had enough strength to take off her dress. She did so, though she decided to just sleep in her underclothes and not bother with the nightgown Mrs. Hilton had given her. She laid down on the small bed and instantly fell asleep.

Chapter 10

Nicky came home from school that afternoon feeling exhausted. She absolutely loved to teach, but there were some days where she was glad the day was over. There had been a new student assigned to her schoolroom and he was having a hard time adjusting to his new class and surroundings, doing his best to be disruptive, and letting everyone know he wasn't happy with his new situation. She knew that his parents had just divorced and his mother had moved into some apartments that were located near the school.

"Kimberly!" she called as she entered the townhouse she shared with her friend. "Are you home?"

Silence answered her and she shrugged, thinking that Kimberly had gone out for some reason. Nicky knew Kimberly had quit her job and she wondered if she had received a job interview, even though it was late in the day for one. Kimberly was an excellent nurse and Nicky knew her friend would find a new job quickly.

But as the late afternoon became evening, Kimberly still hadn't shown up, and Nicky was starting to get worried. It wasn't like Kimberly to not let Nicky know what her plans were. She tried to call Kimberly's cell phone and she heard it ring in Kimberly's bedroom.

"Kimberly?" she knocked on the door. "Are you in there? Is everything okay?"

Again there was only silence and she hesitated a moment before opening the door. Maybe her friend was sick and needed some help.

But Kimberly wasn't in her room. Everything looked neat and clean, just like her friend liked to keep it. But something just felt different, not quite right. Then she saw the envelope on Kimberly's neatly made bed with her name on it.

Nicky picked up the envelope and for some reason, she was scared of opening it. There was something wrong, she just knew it. She slowly slit open the envelope and was surprised to see quite a bit of money fall out, along with a letter written in Kimberly's careful handwriting.

Dear Nicky and Justin,

When you find this letter, you will know that I am no longer here. I have made the decision to go visit Patrick and get to know him better. If in 30 days, we both feel it is right, we will marry.

I am going to ask you both something important. Please do not try to find me. You will not be able to. I cannot tell you exactly where I am, but I know that if you go to Mrs. Victoria Hilton's home, she will know how to get a message to me if it is important.

I am sorry about the way I am leaving. You both have been like a brother and sister to me, ever since my parents died, and I will be forever grateful. I can't really explain to you why I feel I should embark on this new life, but please know that I do feel it is the right decision for me.

Nicky, I am enclosing enough money to cover my expenses for the next two months. If I do not return, you are welcome to use the rest of the funds in my account as you see fit.

Love you both always,

Kimberly

Nicky sat on Kimberly's bed in shock. She couldn't believe what she had just read. Kimberly had just left to go meet a man she had never met before, without making plans ahead of time? This didn't sound like her friend, who usually took quite a bit of time thinking through things before she made any kind of decision. What was going on? She read through the letter again and then pulled her cell phone out of her pocket to call her brother, Justin. Maybe Kimberly had told him something that she hadn't shared in the letter.

When she reached Justin, she quickly told her brother what was going on. He told her he hadn't heard from her and had no idea where she was.

"I'll be over in a few minutes," Justin told her. "Let me finish feeding Garrett some dinner first."

Nicky knew it would be a while before Justin arrived because Garrett was a picky eater and didn't believe in eating quickly. She spent the next 30 minutes looking through all of Kimberly's belongings trying to find any hint where she might be, and where Patrick lived.

"Kimberly, I hope you didn't get yourself in some serious trouble," she whispered to herself. Why would she leave suddenly like this? It was so unlike her.

Nicky couldn't find anything that would tell them where Kimberly was. She noticed that all of her clothes were still in the closet and dresser drawers, including her favorite shirts and jeans. She did notice that her colored pencils were gone, along with her pad of paper she kept with her all the time, but other than that, everything that Kimberly owned was still in her room, including her cell phone. Why wouldn't she have at least taken her phone? And why wouldn't she need the extra money in her account?

There was a knock on the front door and Justin stepped inside, ushering Garrett in ahead of him. "Nicky?" he called and she walked into the living room.

Justin gave her a look. "Let me get Garrett settled with a game and then we can talk in the kitchen." Nicky nodded, glad that her brother was here. He would know what to do. She went into the kitchen, knowing that she was ready to break down in tears, and she didn't want to alarm Garrett.

"Okay, tell me what's going on," Justin said to her as he sat down beside her at the small kitchen table. Nicky quickly told him what she knew and gave him the letter Kimberly had left on her bed. She sat silently while he read it, watching as Justin's face looked surprised and then frustrated.

"Why would she just leave like this, without talking to us about it first?" Justin asked with frustration.

"I'm trying to figure that out myself," Nicky told him. "She has never made a decision like this without at least talking to me about it. I'm afraid something is wrong. What if she was forced to go?"

"So you don't have any idea where she is?"

Nicky shook her head. "She hadn't even talked to me about this since she wrote that first letter at Mrs. Hilton's home. I just assumed she decided it wasn't a good idea. I know I told her that a million times that day."

"Maybe that's why she didn't talk to you about it. She knew you weren't going to approve."

"Don't turn this on me," Nicky said defensively, folding her arms, and turning away.

Justin sighed and ran his fingers through his hair in frustration. "Sorry, but if you were that insistent this was a dumb idea, I'm not surprised she didn't tell you what she was doing."

Nicky waved her hand at him and changed the subject. "What are we going to do? I think we should call the police. I still think maybe she was forced to leave."

"Judging from this note, I don't think she was forced to leave." Justin picked up the letter and waved it at her. "She even left you money for her expenses."

Nicky ignored Justin's reasoning. "I think we should call the police, or at least go to Mrs. Hilton's home and see if she will tell us where Kimberly is."

Justin sighed again and pulled out his cell phone. Very quickly he was talking to police dispatch, and after being put on hold a few times, listening briefly to someone on the other end, he hung up.

"The police won't do anything about it until she is missing for 48 hours."

"Seriously!" Nicky screeched. "Something really bad could happen to her in 48 hours!"

"Just repeating what they said," Justin told her. Nicky felt a presence behind her and saw Garrett sliding into a chair beside his dad.

"Is something wrong?" Garrett asked in a small voice. Nicky felt remorse that she hadn't kept her emotions under control. The last thing she wanted was for Garrett to worry about Kimberly.

"Nothing, bud," Justin rubbed the top of Garrett's head with his hand, mussing his hair. "Kimberly isn't here right now and Nicky is worried about her."

"Oh," Garrett looked confused at his words. "Maybe you should just call her then."

Nicky turned her attention to Justin. "Can we drive out to Mrs. Hilton's house tomorrow if she hasn't come home by then?"

Justin hesitated and then nodded. "Yes, let's do that. I guess her house is a good as place as any to look for her." He looked at his son. "I really need to get Garrett home. He has some homework he needs to get done and it's almost his bedtime."

"Ah, dad, can't we stay for a while?" Garrett whined but stopped at Justin's look. Soon they both were gone, leaving Nicky alone in the townhouse. She was frustrated that the police weren't willing to help, and wanted to start looking for Kimberly that night. At least Justin was taking her concerns seriously and was willing to drive to Mrs. Hilton's home the next day. Hopefully, by tomorrow evening Kimberly would be back here where she belonged.

Chapter 11

Kimberly woke up the next morning feeling very rested, much better than she had the night before. She laid on the bed for a while and looked around the small cabin. It looked to be about 12 feet wide and maybe 10 feet long. There was little furniture in the cabin, just the bed she slept on, a small wood stove in a corner, and a large trunk that had been placed against a wall under a small window that had faded blue flowered curtains covering it. This cabin would definitely be only for sleeping in. There was a large colorful braided rug on the floor, much like the one that she saw in the larger cabin. The cabin had been made of logs that had what looked to be gray clay between each log.

She got up and looked carefully at the bed. A mattress had been placed on top of some ropes that had been strung up. She remembered reading about these types of beds in her novels. It didn't look very comfortable, but she had gotten a good night sleep. She put on the dress Patrick had purchased for her the day before. It was a simple but sturdy light blue dress, with long sleeves and a high neck. She tied an apron on as well, thinking she would probably get dirty throughout the day. She saw some pegs that lined the wall that the trunk was against so she used these to hang up the rest of the dresses. She opened the trunk and saw that there were a few folded quilts in it, along with some scraps of fabric. She took a piece of fabric and wrapped the key in it. Then she placed the key on the bottom of the trunk, under the quilts, along with her drawing supplies and medical kit. She hoped they would be safe there and no one would come in, look in there, and find them. She stored the carpetbag under the bed.

She noticed a small pail of water on the stove, although the stove wasn't lit. She used a towel that was nearby and washed her face and arms and then brushed and braided her hair. Soon she was ready for the day and what it would bring.

She wondered what time it was and hoped it wasn't too late in the day. She was starving and hoped she woke up in time for breakfast. She left the cabin and walked to the back door. She wasn't sure if she should just walk in or knock, so she decided to knock. The door opened and she saw the entire family at the table eating breakfast.

"Hello, Kimberly," Bridget greeted her as she opened the door. "You don't need to knock. Come in for breakfast."

Kimberly said hello and smiled at everyone as she sat down next to Patrick. Soon there was a plate full of food in front of her. There was bacon, biscuits, and scrambled eggs, along with a bowl of what looked to be oatmeal. There was so much food, she didn't know if she would be able to eat it all. In her time, all she ever ate was a bowl of cereal and maybe a piece of toast or fruit for breakfast.

"Did you sleep well?" Patrick asked her with a smile. She noticed him eyeing her dress and hair, and felt self-conscious. She worried she had put something on wrong, then she made eye contact with him. She saw a sparkle of fondness in his eyes and looked away with a blush on her cheeks.

"Yes, thank you," Kimberly responded as she ate a bite of eggs.

"Is the cabin to your liking?" Patrick asked.

"Of course," Kimberly nodded. "It is very comfortable." She looked around at all the family members. Colleen was still in her nightgown and she had her head leaning against one of her hands as she ate with the other. She looked like she was still half asleep. Kimberly chuckled softly as she compared this to the excitement Colleen had shown when she had met her the day before. Shaun and Keegan were talking about the plans for the day with Patrick and she quietly listened as she ate.

"Can you tell me what everyone does on the ranch?" Kimberly asked when there was a pause in the conversation.

"Sure," Patrick told her, looking pleased with her interest. "I'm over the cattle and the general running of this ranch. I also raise cattle dogs. Everyone actually helps wherever they are needed, but Shaun also works with the horses."

Kimberly nodded at his words. "Yes, Colleen told me yesterday that she gets a horse you're training." She looked at Shaun who glanced at her and then back at his food without answering her. Instantly, she got a definite impression Shaun didn't want her there.

"Keegan doesn't have a specific job. He just helps wherever we need him to," Patrick continued.

"I take care of the house and cooking, along with the garden and chickens. Colleen helps me. She is a great helper, aren't you dear?" Bridget said, addressing the child.

"Yep, I like to help with the chickens and with Uncle Patrick's puppies," Colleen said, looking more awake by the minute. "Keegan likes to read books. He reads and studies all the time," Colleen announced with a little disgust in her voice.

Kimberly glanced at the young man who blushed at Colleen's words. She could tell Colleen thought it strange that Keegan would want to willingly read.

"There's nothing wrong with wanting to learn," Bridget said as she glanced at her youngest brother. "I picked out some more books yesterday in Denver. In fact, Kimberly helped. I hope these will keep your interest for awhile."

"That's great, sis, thanks," Keegan told her, his voice breaking in the typical teenage fashion. "I'm glad you were able to find more books."

"What can I do to help?" Kimberly offered, hoping that whatever was suggested would be things she could actually help with.

Patrick looked a little surprised at her words, and then pleased. "Today, I would like to take you on a tour of the ranch. Maybe you can start helping tomorrow, if you want to."

"I would love a tour," Kimberly told him. She liked the idea of spending the day with him and getting to know him better.

"You can help me and Aunt Bridget," Colleen said eagerly. "We always have lots to do."

"Aunt Bridget and I," Bridget corrected her.

Colleen looked confused at her aunt's correction. "That's what I just said." Everyone chuckled at her words.

"I would love to help you and Bridget," Kimberly told the child who smiled widely at her.

"Great breakfast, Bridget," Patrick said as he put down a cloth napkin by his plate. He turned to Kimberly. "When you are ready for that tour, come out to the barn. I will be doing some things in there until then."

Kimberly nodded and watched him as he got up from the table and placed a small kiss on his sister's cheek. He then put on a cowboy hat that had been hanging on a peg by the door and left the cabin, letting the screen door shut behind him. Shaun and Keegan followed their older brother and soon Kimberly was left alone with Bridget and Colleen.

Kimberly ate as much as she could, but she only was able to finish about half of what had been put in front of her. She hoped Bridget wouldn't feel offended, but the woman just picked up her plate and scraped the remains into a bucket.

"Colleen, when you're done there, take this out to the pigs," Bridget instructed the girl.

"I can help with the dishes," Kimberly offered.

Bridget shook her head. "Patrick's waiting for you. If you want to help, you can start tomorrow."

Kimberly hesitated and then just nodded her head. She wondered if Bridget knew she wasn't going to be much help until she learned how they did things. She said goodbye and followed Colleen to the barn. There was a small building off to the side of the barn that housed the pigs and she watched as Colleen dumped the contents of the bucket into a trough over the fence. A large pig and several piglets grunted and snorted as they started to eat. Kimberly wrinkled her face at the smell the pigs made.

She watched as Colleen skipped towards another small building. This was enclosed with a wire fence and Kimberly could see a few chickens clucking and pecking the ground. Part of her wanted to follow Colleen and watch her take care of the chickens, but she decided to go find Patrick instead since he probably was waiting for her.

As she walked towards the large barn, she glanced up to the sky. It was bright blue and she loved the fresh air she smelled. She could see aspen and pine trees in the distance as well as close by. She knew it would take very little for her to fall in love with this place. Would it be just as easy to fall for Patrick?

She stepped into the barn and smelled the usual barn scents. She could see a few horses in their stalls and saw a gray and white cat run behind a small pile of hay. She spotted Patrick and Shaun near a long table, so she headed in that direction. As she got closer, she could tell they didn't know she was approaching, and that they were arguing about something, or someone.

"I think you're nuts bringing a woman you haven't even met to the ranch," Shaun said to Patrick. "What if it doesn't work out? What if she just leaves and doesn't follow through with her promise to marry you? You should have just visited Denver for a few days and picked a woman there."

"I didn't want a woman from Denver," Patrick told him with frustration in his voice. "I know you don't trust women, but not everyone is like Delia. Give Kimberly a chance."

"I still think…"

"Look, Shaun," Patrick interrupted him. "This is my decision. You have no say in it. I like her. I enjoyed her letters and Mrs. Hilton matched us. It will work out. Maybe you should let Mrs. Hilton match you with someone."

Shaun snorted. "That would be the day." They both noticed her at the same moment.

Patrick looked apologetic, but Shaun stomped out of the barn, glaring at her as he went.

"Sorry about that," Patrick told her as she approached him.

"That's okay," Kimberly told him. "I guess the way we met is a little strange."

"Shaun will come around after he gets to know you," Patrick promised.

Kimberly hoped so, but she also felt a little guilty and could understand Shaun's concern. She hadn't totally committed to Patrick and didn't want to until he knew the truth about her. Maybe Shaun could sense that there was something holding her back.

"Ready for the tour of the ranch?" Patrick asked her and Kimberly nodded. "Would you like to walk or ride horses?"

"Would it be okay if we walk?" Kimberly questioned. "I am still a bit sore from yesterday."

Patrick nodded. "We won't be able to see as much, but that will be fine. You should get back on a horse as soon as you can, though. It will help get your muscles used to riding."

The day was actually very enjoyable for Kimberly. It was obvious Patrick was very proud of the ranch. He showed her everything he could. Kimberly could only see a few cattle in a field and wondered where the rest of them were until Patrick explained how every spring they moved their cattle deeper into the mountains for the summer. In the fall, they would go get them and drive them to Denver to be shipped back east on the train. He talked about the cattle drive like she would be around to be part of it and Kimberly hoped he was right.

She met some of Shaun's horses and even watched him for a while as he worked with one of them. She could tell he was good at his job. Shaun ignored them while they watched and Kimberly knew that he was going to be the one that would be the hardest to convince of her intentions.

Patrick walked with her along the river that they had followed from Denver. He explained that this river was where they got all their water, for the family and for the animals. She could tell it was necessary for their livelihood. The river continued into the forest and Patrick had explained to her that it ran from a small lake a few miles away. He promised her that he'd take her there sometime when she was more comfortable riding a horse.

The last place he took her was to see his dogs. He had a small area fenced and there were two female dogs inside with numerous puppies running around and playing with each other. Kimberly could immediately tell they were Border Collies. She had always loved dogs even though she had never owned one since she was a girl. She had a dog when her parents were alive. He was a golden retriever, and he had been like another member of the family. After their deaths, Kimberly was sent to a foster care family, and she didn't know what happened to the dog. She assumed he had been put to sleep. She had wanted to get a dog after college. A few times, she had even gone to breeders to look at puppies, but something always stopped her from taking the last step in ownership.

Patrick allowed her to go into the enclosure to see the puppies. He explained that at the moment he had two female dogs who were mothers to the puppies that were running around. The father was Jack, a dog that had been following them around all day.

He was planning on keeping a few of the puppies to train for his own use, but he was going to sell the rest. All three adult dogs were excellent cattle dogs and so the puppies were in high demand at ranches and farms around Denver.

"They are so cute," Kimberly told him as she picked up one and cuddled it. "Do you name them?"

"Well, the female dogs are Summer and Autumn. I don't name the puppies unless I'm going to keep them."

Kimberly sank to the ground and giggled as all the puppies ran up and jumped on her for attention. Patrick bent down to stop the onslaught but backed off when he saw that she was smiling.

"I love dogs," she explained to him.

Patrick smiled back. "Have you ever had a dog before?"

Kimberly shook her head. "We owned one when I was a child, but I haven't had one since."

"Well, you are welcome to spend all the time here you wish," Patrick told her. "The more time spent with them, the better the puppies will be."

"I definitely will take you up on that," Kimberly said. She lifted her hand to him, asking him to help her to her feet.

****

Patrick grasped Kimberly's hand and pulled her up. He looked into her eyes as she stood. He had enjoyed his time with her. He loved showing her the ranch, but he loved, even more, getting to know her. After his conversation with Shaun, he had felt like maybe he had made a mistake. After all, he really didn't know Kimberly. He was totally trusting in the decision of Mrs. Hilton and the few letters they had written to each other. What if she really wasn't who she said she was?

But as he spent time with her, his concerns lessened. Kimberly seemed honest and genuine when she talked. Besides, he trusted Mrs. Hilton, and knew she had extensive questionnaires that weeded out people who weren't really interested in marriage. Kimberly seemed to love his ranch and the mountains. When they first started the tour, she didn't talk very much, but as the day went on, she opened up more and more.

She told him about her parents and how they were both killed when she was 16, although she was vague on how they were killed. She explained how she went to school to become a nurse and how much she enjoyed that job, although some of the words and descriptions she used were puzzling. She had said something about starting her degree with "online" classes, but he assumed that must be a different city he had never heard of. She talked about her best friend, her brother, and his son. She mentioned that the boy, Garrett, spent most of his time in front of a TV, and Patrick was going to ask what she meant, but she seemed uncomfortable, and changed the subject quickly.

Kimberly had also asked numerous questions about the ranch and how things were run and Patrick could tell that she was very interested in his answers. From the questions she had asked, he could tell she had been raised in the city, but that didn't bother him. He knew she would learn quickly how to live on a ranch.

As she stood in front of him, he admired how her brown hair reflected the sunlight, and the way her cheeks flushed when she caught him watching her. He reached out to touch her face. At first, she closed her eyes and leaned into his hand. His heart swelled, and he somehow knew that this woman was going to make his life infinitely better.

After a moment, she opened her eyes, and he could see she was still unsure of their relationship. Instead of pushing it, he dropped his hand to take hers, and started walking with her back to the cabin.

Chapter 12

The day after Nicky had discovered Kimberly was missing, she was able to talk Justin into driving to Mrs. Hilton's home with her. Justin wanted to wait a few more days, but Nicky was insistent.

On the way, Nicky prayed that they would find answers to where Kimberly was at. She decided she wasn't going to leave until Mrs. Hilton gave her the answers she was looking for.

When they arrived at the large Victorian home, Nicky felt unsettled. It looked different to her. The grounds looked the same, just like she remembered them before, well-groomed and cared for. But something was different. She left Justin's truck, leaving her brother to follow if he wished. She pounded on the door, waited for a moment, and then pounded again. But no one answered.

"Doesn't look like she's home," Justin said behind her dryly.

Nicky pounded again and then looked inside one of the front windows. She gasped in disbelief. From what she could see, it looked like no one had lived in this house for years. She could see sheets covering all the furniture. She couldn't see anything that would have indicated life was inside. She could see the marble table that had had a large flower bouquet sitting on it when she had come before with Kimberly. It was now empty and she could see a fine layer of dust on the top. What was going on?

Justin stood beside her and peered into the window. "Are you sure you have the right house?"

"Of course, I have the right house," Nicky snapped. "Something is strange. There are sheets draped over everything. There was a flower arrangement on that table the last time I was here. What is going on?"

Nicky felt fear clutch her chest. What if she never saw her friend again? She knew that Kimberly's disappearance had something to do with Mrs. Hilton and her strange English butler.

"Why don't we wait a few days, and then come back," Justin suggested diplomatically. Nicky felt frustrated that Justin wasn't as concerned about Kimberly as she was.

"I'm going to just sit here until someone shows up," she announced and plopped herself onto the porch stairs.

"You can't do that," Justin scoffed at her. "I need to leave. I've got work to do and Garrett has a soccer game today. I'm not leaving you here alone." He bent down to grab her arm and pulled her up.

"Okay," Nicky knew she didn't have a choice. "But promise me we will come back?"

"I promise. Let's go."

"I still think we should call the police when the 48 hours are up."

"We'll call the police," Justin agreed. As he helped his sister into the car, he turned and looked at the empty house. He, too, felt that something strange was going on. He just didn't want to admit it to Nicky and add to her worries. He promised himself that he would come back later and look around, alone.

****

Kimberly left Patrick and went into the family cabin. She wanted to offer to help with the evening meal, but Bridget was nowhere to be found. She saw Keegan sitting in a wooden chair near the fireplace. He had a pocket knife and a piece of wood in his hands. She was curious to what he was doing so she sat down next to him.

"Are you carving something?" she asked Keegan. He grunted his response.

"What are you making?"

"Hopefully, when I'm done it will be a squirrel." Keegan didn't look at her but kept his eyes on his work.

Kimberly watched him carve in silence for a few minutes and then stood to look around the living room. She gravitated towards a bookshelf filled with different books. Most were history books, with a few novels placed carefully at one end. She then noticed the carved wooden animals that were arranged on the shelf above the fireplace. She stood and looked at each of them. They were very well done. There were a few bears, along with a couple of cubs. She also saw birds, horses, deer, and small animals like a chipmunk and a mouse.

"Did you make all of these?" she asked Keegan.

"Yep."

"Have you sold any of them?"

Keegan looked at her, astonishment on his face. "Why would I want to sell them? I just do them for fun."

"I think you could make some money on them." Kimberly stopped talking as she remembered what time period she was in. In her time, people would definitely be interested in his talent; the carvings were that good. But maybe in this time period, people wouldn't buy them.

Keegan shook his head at her words. "I doubt people would want these. They aren't that good."

Kimberly sat next to him again and watched him silently for a while. "Can you tell me what you like to study?" she finally asked. "From what Bridget has told me, you love to learn. Those books she bought looked hard."

"I like to read just about anything," Keegan responded.

"Have you always done your schooling here on the ranch or is there a school nearby?" she asked even though she already knew the answer.

"No school. Bridget has been teaching me," Keegan looked at her with a mischievous grin. "Don't tell her, but I think I'm smarter than her already."

Kimberly wanted to ask him what his plans were for the future with school, but didn't dare. *Remember things are different in this time period*, she reminded herself silently. Keegan answered her question without her asking it.

"I might get to go to school in Denver in the fall if Patrick says there's enough money after the fall cattle drive. I'd have to board there somewhere. It would take too long to ride back and forth from the ranch every day."

"That sounds like a great idea." Kimberly was glad Patrick was willing to let Keegan continue his schooling.

"I want to be a doctor someday," Keegan told her, a blush creeping on his cheeks. He seemed embarrassed and didn't look at her.

"That's a great goal. Did you know I am a nurse?"

He looked directly at her eyes for the first time. "Really? Can you tell me what it was like? How did you learn? Did you go to school?"

Just then Bridget and Colleen came into the cabin. Bridget had a basket of green leafy plants in it. Kimberly knew that it was time to start dinner.

"We can talk about this later," Kimberly told Keegan. "I will tell you anything you want to know." *Within reason, of course*, she thought. She stood to follow Bridget to the kitchen when Keegan called her back. He stood, removed one of the carvings off the shelf and handed it to her.

"You can have this," he said almost shyly. She accepted the gift and saw it was one of the bears he had carved.

"Thank you, Keegan," Kimberly was touched he could give one of his carvings to her. "I will cherish this."

****

"I wanted to let everyone know I have seen signs of bears close by," Patrick announced to the family at dinner. "I'm pretty sure it's a mother with cubs."

Kimberly felt frightened at his words, but also a bit of excitement. Bears were nearby? She would love to see some cubs in the wild. She promised herself she'd keep her eye out for them, although she knew she would need to stay away from the mother bear. She had heard horror stories about what happens to people who get too close to a mother bear and her cubs.

"Do you hear that?" Shaun asked his daughter. "You stay close to the cabin and don't go wondering off until we know the bears have moved on."

Colleen nodded her agreement. "I don't go wondering off anyway, Pa."

Kimberly knew this was true. She rarely saw Bridget without Colleen by her side.

"Has it attacked any livestock?" Keegan asked.

Patrick shook his head. "Not yet. I've just seen their tracks along the river. Hopefully, they were moving on deeper into the mountains."

The conversation shifted to other things, but Kimberly was still secretly hoping she could catch a glimpse of the bear family.

****

Nicky slammed down the phone in frustration. This was the third time she had been on the phone with the police, and they still refused to start a search for Kimberly because it hadn't been long enough since she had been missing. They were starting to get frustrated that she kept calling. She could tell by the short curt answers they would give her. She didn't care.

Tears started streaming down her face. She was so scared for her friend. Kimberly could be somewhere hurt and cold right now, and no one but Nicky seemed to care. She walked dejectedly to Kimberly's room and stared at her bed.

Questions had been spinning through her head since she read Kimberly's note. *What were you thinking Kim?* And, one that made her heart ache: *Why did you want to leave so badly?* She knew Kimberly's job was stressing her out, but thought their time together watching movies, or playing games with Justin and Garrett, was enough to keep her happy. She must have been wrong. Nicky stumbled into Kimberly's bed and pulled up the covers. She focused on the one thing that would allow her to sleep at night.

I will bring you home safe, Kimberly. I will find you. I promise.

Chapter 13

The next morning Kimberly was helping Bridget with the noonday meal. She was feeling proud of herself for cutting the vegetables so well. She knew it wasn't much, but it was a lot more than she would do when she was in the city. She suddenly heard a loud cry of pain. Both women immediately ran outside to see what happened after Bridget told Colleen to stay put in the house.

They quickly located the source of the cry. Keegan was on the ground near the woodpile clutching his leg. Kimberly immediately saw that he had injured himself. As she approached the boy, she saw his pants had been cut and blood seeped through a large open wound.

"Oh, my heavens," Bridget breathed. Kimberly saw Bridget grow pale at the sight of the blood that was oozing from the wound and pooling to the ground. Keegan was still groaning in pain. Kimberly knew she needed to act quickly.

"Bridget, go get some cloth, and then get Patrick or Shaun," she ordered as she dropped down beside Keegan. "Hold as still as you can, Keegan. Can you tell me what happened?"

"I was cutting wood and the ax slipped," Keegan told her as he gritted his teeth. "Stupid."

Kimberly's training as a trauma nurse quickly kicked in and she immediately could tell that he hadn't cut a life-threatening artery. But he did have a severe wound. She could see almost to the bone in his leg. This was not good. For the first time since she had arrived, she wished she could act on her knowledge she knew from her time. She knew how to fix this type of wound, but would she be able to and continue to hide her secret at the same time?

Bridget thrust a handful of towels at her and then ran towards the barn, shouting for her brothers. Luckily, both of them were nearby and responded to her calls immediately.

"What happened?" Patrick shouted as he bent down beside his brother. He gasped as he saw the open wound. The look he gave Kimberly was of pure terror.

"He said the ax slipped," Kimberly tried to talk calmly like she would have if she was in the ER she had worked at. "We need to get him inside."

Patrick and Shaun lifted Keegan and very quickly he was settled in his bed in the cabin. Kimberly ordered them to bring her water and more cloth, as well as any alcohol they had on hand to clean the wound.

"What are you going to do?" Shaun asked suspiciously.

"I'm a nurse. I can help him," she responded firmly, not looking at him. Patrick had already left the room for the water.

"Are you sure?" Shaun questioned. "In my experience, nurses don't know how to handle this bad of a wound."

Kimberly opened her mouth to try to convince him, but Keegan was the one who answered.

"Let her help," he said weakly. "She's better than nothing, isn't she?" Shaun looked at Patrick, expecting him to interfere. When he didn't, his mouth opened in shock and anger.

Kimberly watched as Shaun whirled away and stormed out of the room. She breathed a sigh of relief when she heard the cabin door slam. It would be better if Shaun wasn't around while she worked on Keegan if he was that angry.

Patrick brought in some water and Kimberly went to work. Over the next hour, she cut the pants off and started to clean the wound. She cursed to herself when she realized she didn't have much to work with, not in 1892. Then she thought of her medical kit hidden in the bottom of the trunk in her cabin. Did she dare go and get it?

Kimberly decided to do what she could first with what they had. Bridget came in and instructed Keegan to drink some type of tea she had prepared, and Kimberly allowed it, although she didn't know what it was. The family had been living in these mountains, isolated for years. Surely they had ways to fix injuries and sickness she didn't know about.

She was able to get the wound to stop bleeding so heavily, but she was very concerned. As far as she could tell, no major arteries or tendons were cut, but it was a deep wound and it really needed to be stitched closed. Did she dare try? In the end, she decided to wait and see if the wound would heal on its own. She wrapped Keegan's leg tightly the best she could. Surprisingly, Keegan had drunk the tea and kept it down. Whatever was in it had made him groggy and he was soon asleep. Patrick had stayed with them the entire time, never once flinching when Kimberly ordered him to do something. She was glad he trusted her with his brother.

Kimberly cleaned up the mess she had made while she worked on Keegan and decided she would burn the bloody rags in the wood stove in the kitchen. When they entered the kitchen, she saw that Bridget was sitting at the table with Colleen leaning against her. Shaun was pacing the small length of the room.

"I think we need to take him to Denver to a doctor," Shaun told Patrick.

Patrick turned to Kimberly. "What do you think?"

"I don't think he should be moved," Kimberly responded. "If you will let me, I can care for him. If it looks like he isn't doing well in the next few days, then you can take him to a doctor." She said this, knowing that if that happened, she would get out her medical kit and do what needed to be done. It wouldn't matter what they saw. Keegan's life was more important than a secret that she had promised to keep.

Patrick turned to his brother. "I watched Kimberly as she helped Keegan. She knows what she's doing. I say we listen to her."

Shaun looked at Patrick in disbelief. He turned and stormed outside, muttering as he went.

"I'm sorry. Staying is just my opinion. If you feel you need to take him to Denver, then..."

Patrick shook his head. "It's too late in the day to go anywhere. We'd be traveling at night. I don't know how close that mama bear is. If we left and she smelled blood... no, we will stay like you suggested."

Kimberly breathed a sigh of relief. "I will do everything I can to help him."

"You already have," Bridget broke into the conversation. She stood up and started to make dinner. "I get so lightheaded when I see blood. I am grateful you were here. I don't think I could have..." She stopped talking and started to chop some vegetables.

"You could make him a broth with vegetables and beef or chicken," Kimberly suggested. "That would help Keegan."

Bridget smiled at her in relief. "Yes, I can do that." She went to work, glad that she could do something that would help her brother. "I do have a few packets of herbs we have gathered for medicinal purposes. Maybe some of them will help."

Kimberly agreed. "Show them to me, please. You probably will need to explain their uses. I haven't learned much about herbs." Bridget seemed surprised, and Kimberly realized that nurses at this time would have been taught about herb uses. She tried to backtrack. "I have learned about most, but need a reminder."

Over the next hour, Kimberly helped Bridget start the broth, and then looked over the herbs she had. She really wasn't sure if they would help Keegan or not. She had been trained to use drugs for healing, not herbs. But they didn't have any drugs available. One of the herbs was supposed to be for pain and another for inflammation. A third one sounded like it could be a natural antibiotic, but Kimberly wasn't sure. When she asked Bridget where she had gotten the herbs, she explained that they were found in the mountains. There was a tribe of Indians that lived about ten miles away from them during the summer months. One of the women who lived there had taught Bridget about the herbs. Most of the herbs were to be used as a tea, but the one that Kimberly suspected might be an antibiotic was supposed to be made into a paste and placed directly on a wound.

Did she dare put that particular herb right on Keegan's wound? It seemed very unclean to her. What if it made it worse? His wound was very deep. She decided to wait until morning to make that decision.

Dinner was a quiet affair. Shaun did come in and eat, but it was obvious he was still angry at everyone for listening to Kimberly. She was glad he didn't say anything. He just quickly ate and then left the cabin, this time taking Colleen with him.

Kimberly stayed the night in the family cabin. She sat next to Keegan, caring for him when he needed it. The tea Bridget had made for him earlier did seem to help his pain, so she asked Bridget to make it again. He was able to drink a few swallows of the broth his sister made. By morning, it was obvious the wound needed more attention than what she had given it the day before. When she unwrapped the wound, Keegan had cried out in pain, and it looked red and angry. Instinctively, she knew it was not going to heal on its own.

Patrick was standing by her when she exposed the wound and he gasped in disbelief. "It doesn't look good, does it?"

Kimberly made an instant decision. She had the training and the means to heal this wound and she was going to do it.

"Maybe we had better get him to Denver," Patrick continued.

"Patrick, I am going to ask you to trust me. I know you don't know me well. Shaun obviously doesn't believe I can help, but I can. I have had extensive training for these types of injuries. Please let me have today. If it looks worse tomorrow, then you can take him to Denver. I really don't think it will be a good idea to move him. It might make the wound worse being jostled around on a horse. He would lose a lot of blood in four hours."

"Do you really believe you can help him?" Patrick asked her.

"Yes, I can help him, although it won't be pleasant for him."

He looked intently into her eyes, then said, "Okay. Do what you need to do."

Kimberly was floored that Patrick trusted her so completely with his brother. She excused herself and ran to her cabin. She dashed inside and quickly located the medical kit. When she exited the cabin she ran straight into Shaun who grabbed her shoulders and shook her.

"Patrick told me he's not going to take Keegan to Denver today," he yelled at her. "If he dies, this will be your fault!"

Kimberly tried to speak calmly to Shaun. She knew people said things they really didn't mean when they were scared and hurting, and especially when someone they loved was injured and suffering. "I promise you, he will not die."

"How can you promise that? You know how bad the wound is! You're a nurse after all," he sneered.

"I can promise," Kimberly said and pulled away from him. She knew she had her work cut out for her this morning, but she felt a peace inside as she ran back to the cabin. She knew Keegan would be okay.

When she was back in Keegan's room, she set her medical kit down and ripped it open. She quickly laid out the supplies she would need. The gloves, the syringes, the thread, the needles. She gasped in delight when she saw a bottle of penicillin. When had she put that in her kit? She also saw a supply of ibuprofen.

"What are all those things?" Patrick asked her with curiosity.

Kimberly just shook her head. She didn't know what she was going to tell him after this was all over, but she didn't want to explain now. "Can you help me?"

Patrick nodded.

"Please tell Bridget to leave the cabin with Colleen." She waited until Patrick had left and then felt Keegan's head. She could tell he was starting to get a fever. The wound was infected. "Keegan, can you hear me?"

The boy nodded, his face wet with perspiration. "What are you going to do to me?"

"I am going to need to clean out the wound really good. Then I am going to stitch it up. It's going to hurt."

Keegan nodded his understanding and said bravely, "Do what you have to do."

Patrick was back at her side and waiting for her next instructions. After getting her all the water she needed, she told Patrick to do his best to keep Keegan from moving. In her time, the area around his wound would be numbed, or he would be put to sleep. She didn't have anything to help with that. She just hoped Patrick would be able to keep Keegan from moving a lot. She did have a small tube of numbing cream, but it wasn't enough for such a large wound. She would use it on top of the wound after she stitched it.

Using the Betadine, she did her best to clean the wound as best as possible. She took her time even though she knew Keegan was in a lot of pain; it was vital that the wound was cleaned thoroughly. When she was finally satisfied it was clean and she hadn't missed anything, she got the needle and thread ready.

"I'm going to stitch it up now," she told Patrick. Both Keegan and Patrick were sweating. "I'll work as fast as I can."

It took 20 stitches. When she put in the tenth one, Keegan passed out, and Kimberly was grateful. Never before had she been grateful for nature's anesthesia of fainting. She finished as quickly as she could before he woke up. When she was finally done, she inspected her work and was satisfied. It would take awhile, but she knew it would heal. He'd have a large scar, but there wasn't anything she could do about that.

She smeared some antibiotic cream and the numbing cream on the wound, and then wrapped it up tightly with an Ace wrap.

"He will need to be still for the next week or so, but I think he will be fine," she looked up at Patrick. "I have some medicine to give him that will…"

She stopped talking when he pulled her to his side and gathered her into his arms. "Thank you so much."

"You're welcome. I'm so glad I was here to help." Kimberly responded, relishing being in his arms. She hadn't felt this safe and loved since before her parents passed. She leaned into his chest and closed her eyes, feeling all of the stress from the last day seep out of her.

"I can tell you know more than any nurse I know of," Patrick said to her. "Are you sure you aren't a doctor? Is that what you're hiding?"

Kimberly shook her head. "I'm what is called a Registered Nurse." She instantly wished she could take her words back at his look of confusion. She had just let another hint of the future slip. He obviously knew she was hiding something.

"I can explain later," Kimberly told him. "I have some medicine to give him when he wakes up. This pill will help with pain and this pill will help with infection." She showed both pills to him. She hoped he wouldn't ask any more questions and breathed a sigh of relief when he just nodded.

"We need to talk, later," Patrick told her. He looked at her intently until Kimberly nodded her head and then went back to his brother. Kimberly watched as he tenderly placed a cool wet cloth on Keegan's forehead. She knew she had picked a good man.

Chapter 14

The next few days were a blur to Kimberly. She only left Keegan's side when Patrick forced her to. He always insisted she sleep at night in her cabin and he took over Keegan's care. But the penicillin was working and Keegan was coherent enough the next day to have a good conversation with Patrick.

"Did you sharpen the ax before you used it?" Patrick questioned Keegan when he was feeling better and he sighed when Keegan shook his head.

"I wanted to hurry and get the chopping done so I could read the history book Bridget brought back from Denver," Keegan admitted.

"That is one chore that you should never cut corners on," Patrick lectured his brother. "You know that."

Keegan nodded. "I'm sorry. I'm sure glad Kimberly was here."

"She saved your life," Patrick told him.

"I know," Keegan whispered. Then he looked at Kimberly. "I want to know what you did to fix me up."

"Maybe I'll tell you sometime," Kimberly said, but she knew she really didn't want to tell him. Things could have been so much worse. She was so glad she had brought the medical kit from the future and that it had the supplies and medication she had needed. She really didn't want to replay it in her mind.

A week after the accident happened, Keegan was sitting at the table again with the family, his leg propped up on a nearby chair. And Kimberly received a great surprise. Shaun had been avoiding her like the plague ever since the accident and she didn't know if he would ever forgive her for insisting they not take Keegan to Denver, even if he was healing and doing well. Shaun had been so angry with her for interfering.

On this night, Shaun had come into the cabin from working with the horses all day and stopped abruptly when he saw his younger brother at the table. Keegan was joking with Colleen and then gave the girl a small wooden fairy he had carved. Keegan had been carving quite a bit while he had been in bed all week. Shaun caught Kimberly's eyes and mouthed some words to her.

Thank you.

That was it, but it was enough.

****

The doorbell rang and Nicky hurried to answer it. It was a police officer coming to take a report of Kimberly's disappearance. Justin had also come over to talk to the police officer. The man introduced himself as Officer Pickering. After he was seated on her couch, he pulled a notebook out of his pocket to take notes.

"When did you first discover your friend was gone?" the police officer asked.

"A few days ago. I came home from teaching school and she wasn't here like she usually is." Nicky quickly explained that Kimberly had quit her nursing job and had been looking for a new position. She explained how she found the note and showed it to Officer Pickering when he asked to see it.

"It looks to me that your friend intended to leave, judging from this letter she wrote to you."

"But you don't understand. This is not like Kimberly. She would never do anything like this. She would have let me know she was leaving."

"I'm sorry, but there is nothing I can do. I will write up a report, but since she did write a letter, even giving you money for expenses, it is very obvious she left on her own free will."

"Is there anything we can do, officer?" Justin broke in.

"Let us know when you hear from her," Officer Pickering stood up as if he was anxious to be on his way. "You really shouldn't have even contacted the police, you know. The letter she wrote is proof she knew what she was doing. I am sure you will hear from her in a few days, if she wants to be found."

Nicky felt numb at the police officer's words. What was she going to do now? She barely noticed Justin walking the police officer to the door. Was the policeman right? Did Kimberly really leave on her own? If only she could just talk to Kimberly one more time.

She just knew if she could, she would be able to find out why Kimberly had left. And maybe, she would be able to talk Kimberly into returning to where she belonged.

Chapter 15

Patrick knocked on Mrs. Hilton's door. His trip to Denver had been spur of the moment. He hadn't been able to sleep since he saw Kimberly work on Keegan's leg. She had handled everything with so much skill and had tools and medicine that seemed so foreign to him. He remembered seeing different types of scissors and needles. Everything had been wrapped in weird packages. There were small cloths of various sizes that she called Band-Aids and they weren't anything he had ever seen before. It was impossible that she was only a nurse; there had to be more to the story than she was telling. She had been avoiding him, and he could tell she didn't want to talk about it. Out of respect for her and since she had saved Keegan's life, he let her have her space. Even still, he felt he needed to dig into Kimberly's life more before he married her.

So, he had finished his morning chores, and snuck off the ranch for the day to make a trip to see Mrs. Hilton. He knew that Mrs. Hilton knew Kimberly, and had done her research on her, so he was hoping she would shed some light on what he should do about his concerns with Kimberly. Mrs. Hilton's butler, Collins, opened the door formally, and invited him in without asking for an explanation.

"Mrs. Hilton is in her study," Collins announced, then led the way.

Patrick followed, suddenly nervous. What if he didn't like the answer Mrs. Hilton gave him? He had always planned on marrying Kimberly, but hadn't expected to develop feelings for her so soon. What if he learned something about Kimberly that would change his mind about marrying her?

"Patrick, what a lovely surprise. Please sit down." Mrs. Hilton greeted him, setting down the book she had been reading on a sofa next to her. Patrick sat in a stuffed chair across from Mrs. Hilton and watched Collins' gaze linger on Mrs. Hilton a moment before exiting the room. Patrick briefly was surprised; he had only seen Collins perform his duties with pure professionalism at his past visits. When Mrs. Hilton didn't seem to notice, he brushed it off, and focused on the issue at hand.

"Thank you for being willing to see me, Mrs. Hilton." Patrick began. "I have just a few questions."

"Oh? Isn't Kimberly such a lovely girl? I knew she would be perfect for you from the moment I saw her," the woman said as she smiled at him.

"Yes, she is. She has been great company, and very eager to learn about the ranch." Patrick hesitated, then let out a big gush of air. "Something happened about a week ago. My brother Keegan cut his leg with an ax. It was bad. I was scared he wouldn't make it. But, Kimberly saved him. She saved his leg. I know I grew up somewhat isolated in the city, but I know enough to be able to tell she has extensive knowledge as a nurse. More than most nurses do." He paused, not sure how to continue.

"It sounds like you were lucky to have her close by. What is troubling you about it?"

Patrick hated accusing Kimberly, but knew he had to figure out what she was hiding. He had to make sure his family would be safe.

"The way she healed Keegan, the things she did were unbelievable. It makes me think she is hiding something. Now, if I am to bring her into my family permanently, I need to know there is nothing from her past that may come back to affect us negatively."

Mrs. Hilton was quiet for a moment, then she stood. "I cannot tell you her secret. I can tell you that Kimberly is a wonderful, honest girl who would do nothing to hurt your family. It seems to me that you should address her about this, not me."

"So there is a secret?" Patrick's heart sank.

"Yes. Please, I cannot speak for Kimberly. It would seem she already cares for your family as much as you do if she was so intent on saving Keegan's life. Go back to your ranch, and talk to her. Consider it practice for when you are married." Mrs. Hilton smiled softly. "Do not condemn her for something you know nothing about."

"You're right, she has been nothing but warm and kind to all of us. Even to Shaun, who has been giving her a hard time. I will go talk to her."

Mrs. Hilton offered to have refreshments brought in, but Patrick declined. He wanted to get back to the ranch as soon as possible. He said his goodbyes and left.

Patrick jumped back on his horse, reassured. He didn't like that Kimberly was keeping secrets, but Mrs. Hilton had reminded him of the bigger picture. He would go talk to her, and he was sure Kimberly would be able to reassure him of her intentions.

****

When Kimberly had been at the ranch for two weeks, the whole family was sitting down for the noon meal. She and Patrick had spent little time together since Keegan had been injured. Kimberly knew she was avoiding him. She didn't want to put herself in a position to have to lie to him. She didn't like that she had to promise Victoria to not tell him about her past. But was she ready to commit to Patrick and stay in the 1890s? She wasn't sure yet.

She had been enjoying her time with this family. She sometimes felt more comfortable in this time period than she had in her own. There were quite a few adjustments. Wearing dresses for one. Some mornings she felt that if she had to put on another long dress, she was going to scream. Didn't these women know how hot and uncomfortable it was to wear a dress day after day? And to put on all the underclothing they did? Kimberly had stopped wearing most of the petticoats after a few days. She only hoped no one had noticed.

Cooking food took quite a bit of time. Bridget was patiently showing her how to use the stove and how to cook simple foods. Colleen seemed to know more about cooking than she did. Sometimes she wished she could just stick something in the microwave and be done with it. It seemed that it took forever just to boil water.

But she loved this land. She loved the mountains and being around so many animals. She loved the dogs. When Keegan was bedridden and Patrick kicked her out of the cabin for a break, she always found herself in the dog enclosure. There was one little puppy she had fallen in love with. She was smaller than all the others, probably a runt. Kimberly had secretly named her Daisy even though she knew Patrick probably wouldn't approve. The dogs were almost old enough to be taken to their new owners and she knew Daisy wasn't going to be around for long. But this puppy was so sweet and when she knew Kimberly had come into the enclosure, she would run to her as quickly as her little legs would let her.

Once everyone was done eating, Patrick approached her, looking nervous. He suggested they take a walk, she knew the time had come for their talk. He was going to want answers and she didn't know if she could give them to him, but she nodded her head in agreement. They started to walk towards the river. Patrick was silent for awhile and Kimberly was content to let him lead the conversation.

When they arrived at the river, he took her hand and guided her to a large rock to sit on.

"I feel like you are hiding something from me," Patrick stated. "Do you know where this relationship is going?"

Kimberly hesitated, not knowing what to say, but he continued.

"When you agreed to come and meet me, I wanted you to come. Even though we aren't officially engaged, I have been making plans to marry you."

"I know," Kimberly responded quietly.

"For this relationship to work, we can't have any secrets between us. There needs to be honesty."

"I know," Kimberly said again.

"Are you hiding something?"

Kimberly turned to him and grasped his hands. "I will admit that I am hiding something, something I can't tell you at this time. I came here to meet you and to see if things will work with us, to see if I can be happy living on a ranch."

"And can you?" Patrick held his breath, suddenly overcome with the thought that she might leave him. He hadn't realized how much she had come to mean to him until this moment.

"I think so. You gave me your total trust when Keegan was injured. I need to ask you to trust me again. There are some things I can't tell you about myself, but I can make you a promise. I will tell you before the 30 days are up. Can you trust me one more time?"

Patrick looked at her intently. She looked back at him, doing her best to let him know she was sincere in her request. He finally nodded. "I will give you my trust one more time."

Kimberly felt relief at his words. She didn't know what she would have told him if he hadn't agreed. She suddenly realized she was falling in love with him more and more each day. She watched as he slowly bent his head towards hers and touched her lips with his own. Then he pulled away. In that one instant, the world stopped, and it seemed that nothing else mattered. She could feel the warmth from their first kiss spread to her fingers and her toes, and smiled. Even though it was brief, she had never had such a powerful kiss before.

Chapter 16

Nicky pulled into the driveway of Mrs. Hilton's Victorian home. She grabbed her small pack she had filled with snacks and water bottles. She was prepared to stay the entire day if she needed to in order to talk to Mrs. Hilton. She wasn't going to leave until she had some answers about Kimberly's whereabouts. She even had thrown a sleeping bag in her car just in case she needed to spend the night.

After knocking a few times on the front door with no answer, she set her belongings on a nearby porch swing and started to slowly look around, trying to figure out how this home had been occupied a few weeks ago, and now looked dusty and empty. As far as she could tell, the house was still in good shape. The paint wasn't chipping and the roof was intact. The lawn, while not perfectly manicured, also looked like it had been cared for recently.

She started to walk to a window to see if it was unlocked when she saw a neighbor pull into their driveway across the street. She headed over to talk to the woman who was pulling a screaming toddler out of the back of her car.

As Nicky approached, the little boy stopped screaming and clung to his mother. "Hi there, little man. Are you having a tough day?"

The boy pouted and hid in his mothers' shoulder. The mother looked tired, but tried to answer the question with a little smile. "He didn't want to leave the park, but little boys still need a nap every now and then."

Nicky smiled at the mother and turned back to the boy. "Do you like lions?"

The boy perked up and nodded his head enthusiastically.

"Want to know a secret? Lions sleep almost all day long! That's why they can run so fast!" Nicky lowered her voice conspiratorially. "I bet, if you take a really long nap, when you wake up, you will be able to run just as fast! Do you think you could do that?" The boy nodded his head again with a big smile on his face.

"That's a good idea, isn't it Spencer?" The mother smiled and then turned back to Nicky. "Thank you. He is so afraid he will miss something spectacular if he falls asleep. Are you new to the neighborhood?"

Nicky had to think fast. It would probably make the woman nervous to know what was really going on. "Oh, no. But I am interested in that house that's across the street. It's beautiful! Do you know who lives there?"

"Goodness, no one has lived there for years." The little boy started squirming in her arms. "A man does show up every now and then to make sure the house is in good condition, but I have never talked to him."

Nicky couldn't believe what she was hearing. She tried not to look too disappointed. "Oh, well thanks anyway. I'll let you get your little 'lion' in bed." She winked at the boy, who smiled shyly.

The woman wished her well, then turned to go into her home. Nicky walked across the street, back towards the house, and started walking around again. As naturally as she could, she checked a couple windows, and looked for any other clues she could find. She hoped the woman she had just talked to, or any other neighbors for that matter, wouldn't notice what she was doing. She didn't want anyone to become concerned that she was poking around. She discovered that there were two other doors in the back of the house and she quickly found out that both of them were also locked. She looked in a few windows and could see that all the furniture was covered with sheets. There was a layer of dust all over everything letting Nicky know that the place had been empty for at least a few months.

After she walked around the entire house, she sat down on the porch swing. It had been almost two weeks since Kimberly left and Nicky hadn't heard anything from her friend. It was almost as if she had dropped off the face of the earth. She was very worried about Kimberly and also a little angry. Didn't Kimberly realize how difficult this would be for her? How could she not at least call to let her know she was ok? She was glad that school had ended and she had all summer to find her friend.

Suddenly, she saw movement in the corner of her eye. She turned and saw Mrs. Hilton's butler coming around the corner of the house. Where had he come from? She had searched the entire property as thoroughly as she could and hadn't seen signs of anyone.

"May I help you?" The butler asked. Nicky noticed that he didn't look surprised to see her.

"Yes, I would like to speak with Mrs. Hilton," Nicky requested, trying not to sound angry or frustrated. She was upset at Mrs. Hilton, not her butler.

"She isn't available at the moment. May I help you?" he asked again.

"What was your name?" Nicky asked. She couldn't remember his name, although she did remember that he acted very formal, like the old-fashioned English butlers used to act.

"I am Collins, miss...?" He ended his words with a question, as if asking for her name.

"I am Nicky, Kimberly's friend. I am looking for her. Do you know how I can get a hold of her? Is there any way I can talk to Mrs. Hilton?" She wanted to demand that he take her to Mrs. Hilton immediately, but knew if she did her best to be polite, he might be more willing to do what she asked.

"Mrs. Hilton does know where Kimberly is. It isn't possible to talk to her at this time, but I can promise that..."

"What do you mean, I can't talk to her?" Nicky interrupted him, forgetting her decision to be polite. "She has been gone for two weeks! I didn't even know she was leaving. She just left a letter. She didn't take any of her belongings with her. The Kimberly I know would have never done that on her own." She was so angry and scared for her friend, she suddenly found herself holding back tears, which made her more frustrated.

"If you will calm down and allow me to explain..." Collins requested, his voice staying calm and formal.

Nicky bit her tongue to keep herself from saying anything else and nodded her head. If Collins really knew how Kimberly was doing, it would be best if she didn't antagonize him. She nodded her head at Collins, letting him know she would listen and he could continue.

"Your friend agreed to meet with the man she had been writing and stay where he lives for 30 days."

"I didn't even know she was writing anyone," Nicky muttered under her breath.

"How do you know this man doesn't have plans to hurt her?"

"I promise you that she is well and happy," Collins continued.

"So you have seen her?" Nicky asked eagerly. "Just give me this man's phone number and I will call her."

Collins hesitated. "I'm afraid that isn't possible."

"Why?" Nicky was suspicious. "I just want to make sure she is okay." She knew if she could just talk to Kimberly, she would be able to tell if her friend really was hurt or not. "I promise I won't try to talk her into coming home."

"You need to trust my words. Kimberly is fine."

Nicky sighed in frustration. It seemed like there had been roadblocks every step of the way in finding Kimberly. The police hadn't been any help. She had been calling almost daily and she knew they were getting very tired of hearing from her. They still insisted if she left a note, there was no crime involved.

Justin was concerned, but Nicky knew he still blamed her for some of this. Nicky knew she sometimes came across as bossy and overbearing, but it usually was because she cared so much.

And now she was here, looking for Mrs. Hilton, and her butler was keeping her from Kimberly.

"When can I talk with her?" Nicky finally asked.

Collins hesitated again. "If you would like to write her a letter, I can get it to her," he finally said, but Nicky could tell he was reluctant to promise even that much.

Nicky sighed again. Then she remembered what started this entire mess. Kimberly had filled out an application to be a mail-order bride. What if she did the same? She really wouldn't become one, of course. She would just pretend that she was interested so she could find Kimberly. The last thing she wanted to do was marry someone she hadn't even met.

"I would like to fill out an application to become a mail-order bride, just like Kimberly," she announced, trying to sound convincing that she really meant it.

"That will not be possible at this time." Mr. Collins didn't seem to buy it.

"Why not?" she asked with exacerbation in her voice. "Isn't that what Kimberly did? Isn't she a mail-order bride to this Patrick guy?"

"Yes, she is," Collins confirmed. "But Mrs. Hilton has made the decision to not accept any more applications at this time, for your time. She is putting this part of her business on hold for the moment."

Nicky was flabbergasted. Another road block. "Until when?" she finally asked.

"Mrs. Hilton hasn't made that decision yet."

Nicky sat down on the porch swing and did her best to not break down in tears. Should she continue with her plans to stay here on the porch until she actually talked to Mrs. Hilton? Maybe if she talked to her, woman to woman, she would be able to convince her and allow her to talk to Kimberly.

Collins seemed to read her mind. "Kimberly is safe and happy. Please believe me. You don't need to worry about her."

"I think I will take you up on your offer to give her a letter from me," Nicky finally told him. She waited to see if Collins would say anything else, but he just nodded in his formal way.

Nicky opened her pack and pulled out a pad of paper and a pen. As she started to write, Collins said, "I have something I need to do. I will return when you have finished your letter."

Nicky just nodded, being careful to not say what she really wanted to say. It looked like she really didn't have any choice. Kimberly was an adult and she had made her own decision to meet Patrick. It looked like Nicky was going to have to accept that, for now. She watched as Collins disappeared around the corner of the house. She started to write.

Dear Kimberly,

I was very surprised to find your letter. I really hope you did leave because you wanted to and not because someone forced you to. I am very concerned because it was been two weeks since you have left and I haven't heard from you. I noticed that you didn't take any of your clothing or your cell phone. I have just talked to Collins and he assures me you are happy and safe. I hope he is telling me the truth.

I am asking you to please contact me as soon as you can. I just want to know that you are okay.

Love,

Nicky

P.S. You have gotten a few phone calls from some hospitals for the jobs you applied for. I am sure if you come home, you will be able to find another job.

Nicky didn't know what else to say. As she wrote the letter, she realized she was a little bit hurt. If Kimberly really was safe and happy, that meant that she was falling for this Patrick guy. Why didn't Kimberly want to talk to her about the man she loved? They were like sisters, they always shared everything. Kimberly should be sharing this part of her life, too.

As she put the letter into an envelope, Collins came around the corner of the house. It was like he knew she had finished and he had just been waiting for her.

"I guess I have to trust you and that this letter will really get to Kimberly," Nicky told him as she handed him the letter.

"I promise that it will get to her in a timely manner," Collins vowed. He looked at Nicky directly in her eyes and something inside her knew she could trust him, even if she didn't want to.

She quickly gathered her things and told Collins goodbye. She hurried to her car. As she pulled out away from the house, she looked in her rearview mirror and noticed Collins was still standing where she had left him, watching her. It was if he wanted to make sure she was really going to leave.

As she drove away, she started to think about the conversation she just had with Collins. She remembered some of his words. What did he mean, that Mrs. Hilton was putting her mail-order bride business on hold "for her time?"

Chapter 17

Victoria sat in a nook off the kitchen enjoying some pastries with her morning coffee. She had a book at her side that she was trying to read, but she couldn't concentrate on the story. She was really waiting for Collins return from the future.

For the last few days, she had known that Kimberly's friend, Nicky, had been showing great concern for the whereabouts of her friend. Kimberly had been the first woman who had shown any interest in the mail-order bride ad she had placed in the paper from the future. Victoria had felt good about the idea of sending Kimberly back in time to Patrick, but she was starting to realize that she needed to figure out a better way to send people from the future to her time without worrying their relatives and friends needlessly.

She hadn't realized how connected the people who lived in the future were to each other. In her time, when someone left their home, the only way to contact each other was through letters, and it would be days or weeks before each letter was received. She had planned on Kimberly writing her friends a letter if she made the decision to stay in

Patrick's time. Otherwise, it wouldn't have mattered because Kimberly would have just returned to her time.

When she realized that Nicky was planning on camping out on her porch until she talked to someone, Victoria had asked Collins to use the key, go forward in time, and reassure the girl. Victoria was reluctant to go herself because she wanted to cut back her time travel trips. They were starting to exhaust her. Sometimes she would come home sick and it would take her days to recover. She could tell that time travel was starting to be demanding on her body. Besides, she really didn't like traveling to the future. It was very fast paced. The people who lived in the future seemed to be always in a hurry and very busy. She didn't like their main modes of travel, the automobiles and planes, even though they also fascinated her; how fast they went, and how quickly people were able to get from one place to another. It seemed almost like magic to her. She had almost gotten hit by one of their automobiles, so she was very fearful of them.

Luckily, Collins agreed to travel to talk to Nicky, even though he avoided using the key unless he absolutely had to. Victoria took another sip of her now lukewarm coffee. She heard some footsteps and looked up to see Collins coming into the kitchen. She smiled at him in welcome. He came to her side and stood at attention like usual. She wished he would relax around her. After all, they lived in America now, and had for many years, and in the west besides. There was no reason for him to be so formal all the time.

When she looked at him, she saw something in his eyes that she had never noticed before. He looked down at her kindly and not in his usual formal way. It was if he was trying to tell her something that she didn't understand.

"I am glad you returned safely. Were you able to talk with Kimberly's friend?" she asked him.

"Yes, ma'am," he answered the affirmative.

"Would you please sit down?" she requested as she gestured towards a chair near her own. "It makes my neck ache to look up at you all the time. You do know you don't need to be so formal, especially when there is no one else around."

Collins hesitated, then sat down rigidly across from her. She noticed that he was still looking at her with that strange look in his eyes, even if he hadn't relaxed as she had asked.

"Well, what happened? Were you able to reassure Nicky?"

"Yes, ma'am. I explained that Kimberly is safe and happy and she did not need to worry about her. I did feel I should allow her to write a letter to Kimberly. Maybe if she can at least communicate with her friend in letters, she will be satisfied."

Victoria smiled at Collins. "That is a great idea. Did she accept your suggestion?"

Collins seemed relieved, as if he wasn't sure she would approve of his choice to let the two communicate. He pulled a letter out of his coat pocket and handed it to her. "She did, eventually."

Victoria held the letter in her hands. "I am not sure when we will see Kimberly again. Patrick came a week ago, but I am not sure when he is planning on visiting again, or if he will before they both are ready to marry." In her mind, Kimberly was going to make the decision to stay in the 1890s. When Patrick visited her, she could tell that he already cared for Kimberly and there was a good chance he was starting to feel love towards her. She knew they would be perfect for each other, even though Kimberly was from the future. It was just a matter of time.

"I will deliver it to her," Collins offered. Victoria knew that he would use the key to take the letter to Kimberly, and she was grateful, knowing he didn't enjoy traveling with the key.

"Just make sure that only Kimberly sees you," Victoria nodded her agreement.

"I will, ma'am."

Victoria sighed but smiled at Collins. She had known him for so many years. He had followed Charles and herself when they left their homeland of England to America. He had been a great help and support to Charles as he started his new business in Boston. Collins had become a dear friend to her, especially in the years since Charles had died.

"I wish you wouldn't feel you need to be so formal with me," she told Collins. "You don't need to call me ma'am all the time. It makes me feel old." She smiled at him to soften her words. She wondered what his reaction would be to what she had just said.

She had never expressed her feelings about his formality before.

Collins looked at her in surprise. He opened his mouth as if he wanted to say something, but then closed it again.

"What were you going to say?" she asked him when he stayed silent.

"I am in your employ."

"Yes, you have been a wonderful butler, and also a great friend to Charles, and now to me."

"When shall I take this letter to Kimberly?" he asked her, deliberately changing the subject.

Victoria sighed to herself. She knew he wasn't going to ever relax around her. "I think it can wait until tomorrow or the next day. Time travel can be tiring. Go ahead and rest if you need to."

Collins nodded in his stiff way and stood up from his chair. "Will that be all, ma'am?"

"Yes, Collins." She smiled at him to let him know there were no hard feelings. If a man didn't want to change, there was nothing a woman could do. She watched as he started to walk away, but paused at the doorway to the kitchen. He turned and looked at her. Again, she saw the strange look in his eyes. She had the distinct impression that he was trying to tell her something, but what was it?

Chapter 18

Kimberly just finished her breakfast, noticing again that she was the last one at the table. She had always been a slow eater, but she was realizing that meals didn't last very long around the ranch. The men ate as quickly as they could so they could get back to work. There was always something that needed to be done. Bridget would eat a few bites while she made sure everyone else had the food they wanted, jumping up and down from her chair frequently. At first, Kimberly had tried to help Bridget, but she soon learned it was best to just stay out of Bridget's way. Even Colleen finished eating before Kimberly did.

She gave her empty plate to Colleen because it was her turn to wash the dishes that morning. She then headed outside. Kimberly had started a new habit where she would walk around the ranch for about 30 minutes every morning after breakfast. She enjoyed the time to herself and loved how the ranch calmed her. She recognized that she had never felt this calm in her own time. Everyone was so busy and it seemed hardly anyone slowed down and enjoyed life. Patrick and his siblings were always busy on the ranch, but she never felt they were rushing to get things done. They always enjoyed their work and joked quite a bit with each other throughout the day.

She had been on the ranch for three weeks now, and she was starting to make a pros and cons list in her head about whether she wanted to stay in Patrick's time or go home to her own. The list for staying was growing longer every day. She loved the ranch and enjoyed getting to know Bridget, Colleen, and Keegan. She hadn't been able to really talk to Shaun very much, but she could tell he was a good father to Colleen, and he was very patient with his horses.

She thought of a few days ago when Colleen celebrated her ninth birthday. Shaun had formally presented her the horse he had promised her and Kimberly watched how patient he was with Colleen as he helped her with her horse. Colleen was thrilled that she was old enough to own her own horse. The horse she was given was a beautiful dark brown in color. It was smaller than the horse Kimberly had ridden from Denver to the ranch.

Colleen had taken her time trying to pick a name for the horse. Kimberly could tell she took this decision very seriously. She finally decided to name the horse *Spirit*. Colleen explained it was because the horse was more in tune with nature than other horses. She had learned about it from a woman in a nearby Indian tribe. "Every living thing has a spirit. And this horse knows it." She said in her matter-of-fact tone.

Thinking about that horse Kimberly had ridden, Honey, made her think of Patrick. He had asked her a few days ago if she was ready for riding lessons. She had given him a vague answer. For some reason, she was reluctant to agree to learn to ride until she made the decision to stay. Even though the four-hour ride to Denver was difficult for her, she knew she would enjoy learning to ride, especially if she had her own horse. Kimberly knew Patrick was disappointed in her answer, but he hadn't asked her again.

When Kimberly took her walk around the ranch, she always ended up at the puppy enclosure. Daisy would always come bounding up to her, and Kimberly was growing fonder of her every day. However, she tried not to get too attached because she knew that it was just a matter of time when Patrick would sell her to another rancher or farmer around the Denver area.

She felt someone walk up behind her and turned to see Patrick approaching her. She watched as he vaulted himself over the fence and soon he was standing next to her.

"Are you enjoying your walk?" Patrick asked her with a smile. She nodded at him, noticing that her heart jumped when she saw him. He was one of the most handsome men she had ever seen, with his wavy auburn hair that almost touched his shirt collar. He had removed his cowboy hat and hooked it on a nail on the fence. She could see the tell-tale signs of the band of his cowboy hat around his head. His light green eyes seemed to sparkle at her.

"What do you have there?" he asked, indicating the puppy in her arms.

"This is…" she stopped herself before she told him she had named the dog. "Just one of the puppies I like to hold."

Patrick lifted the dog from her arms and held her at arm's length as if looking her over. "This is the runt of Summer's litter."

"She might be small, but she is very sweet." Kimberly defended the small dog.

"She won't be a good cattle or farm dog. She probably won't even be a good guard dog. She's too calm. She's what I would call a pet dog. I usually give these type of dogs away. In fact, I'm surprised she survived. Most runts don't."

Kimberly didn't know what to say. She knew these cattle dogs were part of the ranch business and he saw them as such, but she wished she could convince him that Daisy had potential, even though she was small.

"Would you like to keep her for your own?" Patrick asked with a grin as he handed the puppy back to her.

"You mean, you won't sell her? She'd stay here on the ranch?" Kimberly wanted to make sure she understood what he was offering.

"Sure." He shrugged his shoulders. "We used to have a dog that was a pet, but he died a year or so ago. I think it's time for a new one."

"I would love to keep her," Kimberly told him with a smile. "Thank you so much." She threw her arms around Patrick's neck to give him a hug. The puppy was still between them and she started wiggling around in excitement. Kimberly set her down and watched the puppy bounce around the two of them. "I've always wanted my own dog."

"Well, now you have one. I can help you train her if you want, so she can go into the cabin. She needs to be able to come when you call her and…" Patrick stopped talking when Kimberly didn't remove her arms around his neck. He pushed her away slightly and looked into her eyes.

Instantly, his eyes darkened and he bent as if he wanted to kiss her. He paused and Kimberly wanted to pull his face to her own, to hurry things along. But something in his eyes stopped her. There was a closeness developing between them and she could tell he felt it, too. He touched her cheek with his hand and then kissed her lightly and tenderly. He deepened the kiss when she responded, but then pulled away. She knew he was trying to keep himself under control.

Kimberly smiled at him, letting him know she enjoyed being with him, then stepped away to give Daisy one last hug. As they left the enclosure, Patrick took her hand, and they walked slowly towards his cabin. "What are you going to name her?"

Kimberly grinned at him. "Her name is Daisy."

"And how long has she been Daisy?" he asked, grinning back at her.

"For a few days now." She continued to smile at him. "I know I shouldn't have named her, but I couldn't help it. She looks like a Daisy and she is so sweet."

"When you name an animal, it becomes yours," Patrick told her as he squeezed her hand.

****

Later that morning, Kimberly helped Bridget in the garden. Colleen also helped for about an hour, but Kimberly could tell she really wanted to go ride her horse. She smiled when Bridget finally told her she had helped enough and gave her permission to go find Shaun.

"Pa told me he'd help me with Spirit," she told Kimberly and Bridget as she ran off.

"She is a sweet girl," Kimberly commented as she pulled another weed from the ground. "I was wondering, where is her mother?"

Bridget glanced at her sharply and at first, Kimberly thought she wasn't going to answer her. "Her mother is dead."

"Oh, I'm sorry," Kimberly wished she hadn't asked. "Colleen must look like her. Her hair is much darker than Shaun's."

"You might as well know. Shaun isn't her father."

"Oh," Kimberly didn't know what to say, but she was curious about Colleen's past and was glad when Bridget continued.

"Colleen's mother was an Indian. She was from a tribe that lives deep in the mountains about ten miles from here, although they are only there for the summer months. They travel south for the winter.

"Colleen's father was a mountain man who got her mother pregnant and then left her. We have no idea who he was. Her mother never told us.

"When Colleen was a few months old, her mother died in some type of accident. We are actually not sure what happened. Her brother brought Colleen to Shaun, telling him that his sister had requested Shaun raise her daughter if anything happened to her."

Kimberly was amazed at what she was hearing. "Why didn't her uncle want her?" she wondered.

"She's half Indian, half white. I guess he figured she would fit in our world better than theirs. Their tribe doesn't treat children like her very kindly. She would have had a hard life if she stayed with them, especially with her mother gone."

"Does her uncle ever visit her?"

Bridget nodded her head slowly. "Sometimes, but not very often. It might seem strange to us, but their ways aren't our ways. Shaun gladly took over her care."

"Can I ask why her mother choose Shaun instead of...?"

"Instead of a woman?" Bridget grinned at her. "Shaun always got along with the Indians. He has a very good reputation with them. He was very good friends with Colleen's mother, as well as her family and her brother."
"Colleen seems very happy."

"Of course, she's happy," Bridget said matter-of-factly. "She is Shaun's daughter. She is my niece. She is a part of this family."

Bridget stood straight and rubbed her back with her hand. "I need to get started on the noon meal."

"I'll keep weeding, if you would like," Kimberly offered. She hoped that the little that she could do helped Bridget a bit. She knew if she decided to stay, she would insist on learning all she could about this time of Patrick's.

As Kimberly kept weeding, she thought over Bridget's story and about Colleen. She knew that children who had an Indian parent and a white parent in the 1890s were often called half-breeds. They weren't really accepted in the white or Indian culture. She wondered what Colleen's future held. She was safe and protected here on this ranch, far away from the nearest city, but would it stay that way, especially as she grew older?

She admired Shaun for taking over the care of Colleen and for the entire family to accept her as their own. Kimberly kept at her job, but was starting to feel very hot, and was glad when Bridget rang the bell signaling the noon meal was ready. She brushed her hands on her apron as she walked towards the cabin, admitting again that she hadn't gotten used to the dresses, and probably never would. She wished she could wear a pair of her favorite jeans she had left behind, just for a few hours.

Chapter 19

The next day Kimberly was taking her daily walk, only this time she had taken Daisy out of the enclosure and was walking the puppy with her. She was trying to teach her to stay near her side when suddenly she heard her name being called.

"Kimberly," someone called her in a loud whisper. Kimberly looked around but didn't see anyone. She almost had decided she had been hearing things when she heard her name again.

"Kimberly, over here." She looked towards the edge of the puppy enclosure. She was surprised to see Collins, Mrs. Hilton's butler, standing there. What was he doing here? Was something wrong? She hurried towards him, leaving Daisy to follow, tumbling over her paws as the puppy ran alongside her.

"Hi, Collins, what are you doing here?" she asked him.

"Shh," he held a finger up to his mouth. "I don't want anyone to see me."

"Okay," Kimberly thought he was acting strange, but nodded her agreement to be quiet and to keep his arrival a secret. "Is something wrong?"

"Your friend, Nicky, and her brother have been very worried about your disappearance. She has been frantically looking for you."

"But I left her a note," Kimberly tried to explain.

Collins interrupted. "Yes, but either she doesn't believe what you wrote or she just wants you to come home. She has contacted the police a few times and…"

"The police!" Kimberly exclaimed. What kind of trouble was she going to be in if the police were involved and looking for her?

Collins held out a hand to silence her. "The police are not actively involved at this time. They feel since you left a note, that you left by your own choice."

"Well, I did."

Collins reached into his jacket and pulled an envelope out of his pocket. "I traveled to your time yesterday and found Nicky on Mrs. Hilton's porch, preparing to stay there until she found out where you were. I tried to reassure her that you are fine and you are safe and happy, but she didn't believe me. I finally told her that she could write you a letter and I would deliver it for her." He gave her the envelope.

Kimberly accepted it, feeling eager to read it right then. The only people she missed from her time were Nicky, Justin, and Garrett. She wished that there was a reliable way to keep in touch with Nicky.

Nicky had always been a great friend since they first met when they were both 16 years old. Nicky tended to be dramatic and bossy, but Kimberly loved her like a sister and did miss her.

"I will wait over there, by that grove of trees, for you to read your letter and respond if you would like. I will make sure she gets it," Collins offered.

Kimberly looked Collins straight in his eyes. "I am probably going to stay with Patrick if he still wants me to after he finds out I am from the future." She wanted Collins to know she had made her decision and she wanted him to let Victoria know.

Collins nodded his head in his usual formal way, but Kimberly could tell that he looked pleased with her choice. He turned and disappeared into the clump of trees. Kimberly quickly put Daisy back with the other dogs and then hurried to her cabin. Once inside, she sat down on her bed and ripped open the envelope. The letter Nicky had written was short, but panicked.

Reading it, she could tell that Nicky was upset and very worried about her. Nicky thought something had happened to her and that she had disappeared by force. Nicky wanted to know if she was okay.

Kimberly quickly pulled out her drawing pad. She picked a page that she had drawn of Nicky a year ago, of her sitting in a park watching children play on the swings. She hoped Nicky would remember that day. They had taken Garrett to the park and while they watched him play with the other children, they had talked about what it would be like once both of them met someone who they could love and would want to spend the rest of their lives with. They had promised each other that if one of them met a man they wanted to marry, that they wouldn't let their friendship interfere with the marriage. Kimberly turned the drawing over and started to write.

Dear Nicky,

I am so sorry that you have been so worried about me. The way I left couldn't be helped. I have traveled to meet Patrick and have fallen in love with him. I plan to stay and marry him. I don't know when, or if, I will be able to come back home.

Patrick is a wonderful man and he has a great family. They are good to me. Please know that what Collins told you is true, that I am safe and I am happy. Please be happy for me.

I will write again if I get a chance. Say hello to Justin and Garrett for me, and give Garrett that stuffed dog that is in my room. I know he is probably too old for it, but I would still like him to have it.

Love,

Kimberly

She paused, then grew teary as she scribbled, *I miss you*, at the bottom of the page. She wished she could write more, but didn't dare because she knew Collins was waiting for her, and she didn't want him to be accidentally seen. Right now, both Patrick and Shaun were working on the far end of the ranch, and she knew that Bridget and Colleen were in the cabin working on a new dress. Keegan still couldn't get around very quickly yet because of his injury. She assumed he was studying at the kitchen table.

She wiped her eyes, quickly folded the letter and slipped it into the envelope Nicky had used for her letter. She crossed off her own name and replaced it with Nicky's. She hoped that Nicky would be satisfied with what she had said. She hoped her friend would understand what she was saying by giving her the drawing she had made that day at the park.

She left her cabin quickly, not realizing she left her door partially open. She half walked and half ran towards the forest where she had left Collins. When she arrived, he came out from behind a large tree, took her letter, and then disappeared without a sound.

****

Keegan pushed himself out of the kitchen chair and sighed. He was tired of not being able to work on the ranch. He had always loved to study and learn, but at the moment he wished he could go round up some cows or something.

"I'm going to walk around a bit," Keegan called to Bridget who was in their living room sewing with Colleen. "My leg is getting a bit stiff. I need to move around."

"Okay," he heard Bridget call back. "Don't push it; you know your wound started to bleed last time you walked too much." He nodded his head, even though last time his wound bled was about a week ago. Bridget was known to mother everybody since she was the only woman around the house. Keegan had never minded it, but hoped it might change now that there was another woman around. He smiled when he heard Colleen giggle at something Bridget said to her.

Keegan left the cabin and started to walk around. As he moved, his leg started to loosen up, and soon he was walking almost without a limp. It definitely was getting better, thanks to Kimberly.

Where was Kimberly? He wondered. He hadn't seen her all morning. He knew she liked to go for a walk around the ranch after breakfast every morning, but she was normally back by now. She usually would come into the cabin and ask him about what he was learning. Sometimes if he was carving, she would sit and watch him for a few minutes.

He sat down on a chair that had been placed on the porch. He suddenly saw Kimberly run into her cabin and close the door.

That's strange. Kimberly is usually so calm and never runs around like that. He noticed that a few minutes later she left the cabin, only this time she seemed to be in such a hurry, she forgot to shut her door all the way. He watched as Kimberly quickly left the cabin, running towards the edge of the ranch near the forest.

I might as well walk over there and shut the door, he muttered to himself. *No reason to leave a door open and let the wildlife in.* He headed that direction, but when he reached the half-open door, he couldn't resist a look inside. He wondered if she had any interesting books from when she went to school to be a nurse. He saw the trunk open with some clothes spilling out of it. He looked towards her bed and saw an open book on the colorful quilt. He knew he shouldn't go inside, but curiosity got the better of him and he slipped into the small cabin. He held his breath, thinking he had really lucked out. He could tell it was larger in size than the books he usually read. This would distract him from his leg for hours. His heart dropped when he saw the cover of the book; it had no indication that it was a medical book. His eyes started to wander again.

He liked Kimberly and he was fine if Patrick wanted to marry her, but there was something weird about her, something he couldn't put his finger on. He felt she knew way too much about how to heal his injury. She sometimes used words he had never heard of before. There was something about her that puzzled him. He just didn't know what. He remembered that Patrick talked about some of the medical equipment he had seen that Kimberly had used to help heal his leg. He mentioned to Keegan that she kept it in some type of white box that had a large red cross on it. She had gotten the box from her cabin. He looked around the cabin trying to find the unusual box, but couldn't see anything.

His leg was starting to hurt a bit, so he sat down on Kimberly's bed. He picked up the book and realized it wasn't a book at all, but a bunch of blank papers that had been somehow tied into a book with a spiral wire. He turned to the first page and what he saw amazed him. There were many drawings, some in color and some in black and white. To his artistic eye, the drawings were very good. Evidently Kimberly was an artist. He saw a colorful drawing of a squirrel in a pine tree and a black and white of an interesting rock structure with a river nearby. When he turned the next page, he was confused at what he saw. It was some type of machine, with big wheels. It was a very bright red, brighter than anything he had seen before. It was also extremely shiny with strange, long divots in it. He thought of a small silver candlestick in the kitchen that Bridget would shine for hours before a special occasion, but it never got as shiny as this. A person that looked like Kimberly was inside. He wondered what this machine was used for.

The next one was one of a large space with a lot of people walking. The people were wearing strange clothes that showed a lot of skin. None of the women were wearing dresses, and almost none of them had their hair done up at all. He knew the area was outdoors because there were clouds and a sky, but there wasn't any dirt or bushes anywhere. More machines like the one in the previous picture were in the distance. This is so strange. Keegan couldn't make sense of it. He kept flipping through the book, more and more confused with every drawing. *What are these things? I know Kimberly is from the city, but I can't imagine it is that different from our lives here.*

The last one was what looked like a young boy in strange clothing sitting on a large soft looking chair. He had some type of device in his hands. The device was small and fit into his hands perfectly. There was a small box in front of the boy and he was staring at it intently, as if expecting it to change. He had his forefinger and thumb manipulated in a strange way and Keegan wondered why the boy didn't relax his hands.

Keegan slammed the book shut. He needed to get out of the cabin before Kimberly came back. She would be mad if she thought he was snooping. He would think about what he had seen in the book later. As he walked to the door, he looked out the window and noticed Kimberly in the distance. He stopped to watch her. He stared in amazement as he saw a man in a black suit step out from behind the trees. Kimberly gave him something which he tucked into his coat pocket. Then the man disappeared!

Keegan turned and quickly left the cabin, his head pounding. He had to think about what he saw. He knew he would need to talk to Patrick the first chance he got. He hoped his brother would believe him when he told him what he had seen just now.

Chapter 20

Victoria glanced up from the financial papers she was looking over to see Collins walk into the room. She usually didn't need to make many changes to her finances; her husband, Charles, had made sure she was taken care of in that area before he had passed. Even still, she felt it necessary to review the numbers now and then to make sure everything was on track.

"Were you able to successfully deliver the letter to Kimberly?" she asked Collins, hoping the letter would help ease Nicky's concern for her friend.

"Yes, Ma'am. I have a response from her to Nicky as well. I will travel to her time as soon as possible to give it to her." Collins responded in his formal manner; however, there was something in his voice that caught Victoria's attention. He sounded tired, his words wavered slightly.

Victoria was taken aback. Collins had always performed his duties so perfectly, sometimes she forgot that he was a few years older than she was. Traveling with the key was surely as hard on him as it was on her, although he was doing his best to hide the fact.

"That can wait a few days Collins. In fact, I think it would benefit both of us to take a day or two to recover. It has been quite busy here this week."

Normally, Collins would have listed things he had wanted to accomplish or insist a break was not necessary. Instead, he thought for a moment and replied with some relief in his voice. "I think that would be wise, Ma'am."

He looked directly in her eyes to convey his appreciation. For the first time since she had met Collins, there was a softness in his features; a tenderness that she had never seen before. Then, as soon as she recognized the emotion, it was gone. "Is there anything else I can do for you?" he said in his normal formal way.

"No, thank you, Collins," Victoria replied softly. "You may go rest."

She watched him stiffly turn and leave the room and sighed to herself. Even after they all they had been through together, he couldn't relax around her.

She tried to finish reviewing her finances, but couldn't seem to focus. Collins had been the same professional man for as long as she had known him. He must be very weary if he had let down his guard like he had a moment ago. She remembered feeling just as exhausted after her last trip through time.

She held the key, running her fingers over the familiar grooves. Maybe it is time to find someone better suited to take over the care of these keys.

****

A few days after Collin's visit, Kimberly ran out of the cabin with tears streaming down her cheeks. She had asked Bridget that morning to let her cook the entire noon meal by herself. She wanted to prove to herself, as well as to Patrick, that she could cook a meal. Patrick didn't seem to mind that she hadn't learned to cook; however, in Kimberly's mind this was something that was important to learn to do, especially now that she was in the 1890s and living on a ranch.

It took her all morning to cook the meal. She planned to serve fried pork chops, along with mashed potatoes and some spinach greens from the garden. She also wanted to make some rolls and a cobbler for dessert. She had watched and helped Bridget make these dishes multiple times in the last few weeks. She had felt that she was ready to make a complete meal on her own.

There were so many things to remember. She needed to make sure the water was boiling for the spinach right before they were to eat. The rolls needed to be put in the oven about 20 minutes before the men were due for the meal, so they would be hot and ready. The pork chops and potatoes could be cooked at the same time, but they each needed to be watched carefully so as not to burn them. The cobbler could be baking while they ate the rest of the meal. She knew it needed to be done when they finished, so the men could immediately have a serving before going back to the ranch.

The entire meal was a total disaster. She fried the pork chops too long and they were completely black on one side. While she was frying the pork chops, she forgot about the boiling potatoes. The water had boiled dry, scorching the potatoes on the bottom. She mashed them anyway, hoping no one would be able to tell, but they had tasted burnt. The spinach was soggy. And the rolls were harder than a rock. No one could even bite into them.

Kimberly left the cabin in the middle of the meal and stood on the porch with her head in her hands. She heard a chair scrape and Bridget say, "Let her be." Patrick must have been trying to come after her. Wanting to avoid a conversation with him, she took off at a run. She was so embarrassed that she had failed so miserably at cooking what seemed to her a simple meal. Was she kidding herself, thinking she could fit in this time period?

She admitted to herself that Patrick didn't seem too concerned that she couldn't cook, probably because Bridget was around to do it. But it was important to her that she would be able to do something to contribute on the ranch if she stayed.

She had learned over the last few weeks that she had a knack for growing things. She loved working in the garden and Bridget told her that their produce was growing the best it ever had in years. Bridget seemed relieved that she didn't need to work in the garden as much. She liked being indoors, cooking, cleaning and making things.

Kimberly thought of the dress Bridget had made Colleen and the braided rug she was working on. Kimberly had discovered that Bridget had made all the braided rugs that were in the large cabin as well as in the small cabin she was sleeping in. They were beautiful.

Kimberly also wanted to help Patrick train his dogs. She had been working with Daisy and found that she loved it. She hadn't dared ask him, though. What if he said no?

As she lectured herself for the damage she had done to the meal, she wasn't paying attention to where she was walking. She soon found herself quite a way from the ranch, walking along the river that ran from somewhere deep in the mountains. She slowed down when she saw the river and started to feel calmer. Hearing the running water always seemed to do that to her.

Kimberly promised herself to not offer to make another meal by herself again, at least for the immediate future. There was no reason to throw away good food. She hoped the family was able to get something to eat for their noon meal. She knew she should turn around and go back, but she didn't want to, not yet. Maybe, if she walked a bit more, the men would be finished, and back at work. That way, she would only have to face Bridget. She saw a large rock near the river and decided to sit on it for a few more minutes. As she headed towards the rock, she heard some rustling of brush and strange noises nearby, so she decided to investigate.

What she saw thrilled and scared her at the same time. She saw two small bear cubs wrestling with each other. They rolled over each other until one got bored and tried to climb a nearby tree. It fell when the other one climbed up after its sibling and tackled it. She laughed at their antics, but then sobered when she remembered Patrick's warning about the mother bear. Kimberly looked around but didn't see her.

She breathed a sigh of relief when she didn't see the mother bear. Maybe it was off eating or something like that. She decided she would watch the cubs for a few more minutes and then head back to the ranch. She noticed that the two cubs looked different from each other. One was totally black, but the other had a white spot on its belly. She laughed silently again as they continued their wrestling with each other, oblivious to Kimberly's presence.

Suddenly, she heard a loud low growl that made her heart clench in fear. It came from behind her. She slowly turned and sure enough, there was the mother bear. It growled again, showing intense anger that Kimberly was so close to her cubs. Kimberly was frozen to the spot that she stood. She didn't know what she should do. Should she run? She faintly remembered reading that if someone was being threatened by a bear, that they should curl up into a ball and pretend that they were dead. Would that really work?

She slowly started to back away from the mother bear. In doing so, she inadvertently backed closer to the cubs, who had seen their mother and came running towards her. The mother growled loudly again and stood on her hind legs. She was huge and Kimberly knew that there was nothing she could do. She was going to die, and in 1892, no less.

The mother bear dropped to all fours and started to lumber towards her. Then Kimberly heard a large bang. It sounded like a gunshot. The mother bear turned towards the sound and Kimberly followed her gaze. She could see Patrick nearby, pointing a shotgun to the sky. The mother bear looked at Patrick and then back at Kimberly as if trying to decide who she should attack first. Patrick fired his gun again, this time shooting a tree trunk that was close to the bear, splintering some of the wood.

The mother bear turned and clumsily ran into the forest, her cubs following. Soon they were out of sight. Kimberly was still frozen to the spot she was standing in, afraid that if she moved the bear might come back.

Patrick ran towards her. "Are you nuts, Kimberly? Don't you remember that we specifically told everyone to not leave the ranch boundaries? That the bears were still nearby?" he shouted at her. He walked right up to her and she wasn't sure if he was going to shake her or hug her. Instead, he quickly cleaned his gun and reloaded it. He gave her a lecture the entire time about bears and the dangers that were around them and how she needed to listen to his instructions. Kimberly was still in shock, and her ears rang from the gunshots, so she barely heard what he was saying.

Chapter 21

Patrick stopped talking, mainly because he could tell Kimberly wasn't listening. He quickly finished reloading his gun, sighed heavily, and tried not to mumble to himself. She was from the city after all. He should have known she wouldn't understand the danger. He went through the actions of reloading his gun as if it was second nature. He wanted to make sure he was prepared if the bears came back, but he figured they were long gone. He was glad he didn't have to shoot the mother bear, but he would have if she had gotten any closer to Kimberly. He hoped he scared them away and they would continue to head deeper into the mountains, away from his land.

After he finished with his gun, he leaned it against a nearby tree and looked at Kimberly. She was still standing as if frozen in the same spot. Every so often she would make a small sound that threatened to break through his resolve to lecture her some more. Tears were running down her face. He groaned and gathered her into his arms. At first, she held herself stiffly, as if she didn't know he was holding her. Eventually, she started to relax and soon she put her arms around him. He sighed and closed his eyes as he held her. At that moment, he realized he loved her, and he didn't know what he would have done if he lost her.

Again, he reminded himself that she grew up in the city. She obviously had no idea what threats there were in the mountains. He would need to do a better job explaining them to her, making her understand that she should never go off on her own, for any reason.

"I'm sorry," Kimberly whispered to him and her words shot straight to his heart. "I know it was stupid of me to leave like I did."

"Why did you leave?" he asked as he pulled her away from him so he could see her face.

"I ruined the meal."

Patrick waited for her to continue, and when she didn't, he felt puzzled. She was upset because she burned a few things?

"I really wanted to show everyone that I could cook a meal all by myself. I have had a hard time learning how to cook on that wood stove. It is so much harder to use than the stove I cooked on back home. I had been watching Bridget very carefully all week so I could make sure I would get it right. Even Colleen knows how to cook better than I. I ruined everything. I wasted a lot of food."

Patrick shrugged. "We were able to eat some of it and Bridget made beef sandwiches. We didn't starve."

"I want you to know I can cook a meal, especially if..." Kimberly hesitated, looking down at the ground.

"Especially if what, Kimberly?" Patrick felt his heart start to pound. Was she starting to seriously consider staying?

"Especially if I decide to stay," she whispered softly.

Patrick broke into a grin, thrilled that she seemed to be making plans to be a permanent part of his life. "So you would like to stay? I think you are doing great. Bridget is very happy you enjoy working in the garden. You don't have to learn to cook if you don't want to, or at least if you want to learn, you can learn a bit slower. If you stay, you have all the time in the world."

Kimberly smiled at him through her tears. "Are you sure? I thought it would be important that I know how to cook."

"It is only important if you want to learn. Bridget loves to cook. I am sure she won't mind if she keeps doing that."

"Well, if she enjoys it, I won't push so hard to cook. I would still like to learn, though. What I would really enjoy is to help with..." Kimberly started to talk and then stopped.

"Tell me," Patrick encouraged her. "What do you want to help with?"

"I would like to help you train your dogs," Kimberly said the words quickly, as if she was afraid he would dismiss her desire.

"That's a great idea," Patrick wished he had thought of it on his own. "You have done great with Daisy, just teaching her the few commands I have taught you."

"I don't know if I could help train them around the cattle, but I could help train them in obedience."

"I would like that," Patrick loved the idea. In the few days since he had given her Daisy, he had noticed that she was a natural around dogs. And it would give them a chance to spend more time together. "After you get more comfortable around the livestock, you may want to help the train the dogs around the cattle, too."

Kimberly smiled at him, the earlier stress and fear visibly draining from her face. Patrick saw her look at his lips and lick her own, as if silently telling him she wanted him to kiss her. He happily obliged, leaning forward and capturing her lips with his own, cupping her face with one of his calloused hands as he did so. The other hand automatically intertwined with one of her own in such a strong way that seemed to hold them together.

When he pulled away, he kept her in his arms, and held her for a moment. He enjoyed the peace they felt together, but knew that he needed to address the bear issue. "We need to talk about what could have happened with the bears, Kimberly." She just nodded into his chest. "Please, don't ever go off alone like that again. I also would like to teach you to shoot a gun."

Kimberly pulled back and looked a little panicked at his words. "I'm not sure I can do that."

"Everyone knows how to shoot, even Bridget. It is the way of life out here. You never know what you are going to run into." He moved away from her but kept his hand in hers. "Let me show you something."

He showed her how to observe her surroundings. He showed her the bear tracks and scat that she had passed on the way to the river. If she had known and recognized what they were, she would have known bears were nearby. He showed her how they were probably attracted to some bushes near the river that were full of small red berries. He was determined to show her all he knew, teach her all he knew, in order to protect her.

****

As Patrick talked about the bear tracks and showed her how some of the bushes had been trampled by the bears, Kimberly realized that she had fallen in love with him. Nothing could stop the feelings that swelled from her heart. And she knew judging from the kiss they had just shared, that he felt something for her, too.

She had been so scared that she had gone into some sort of shock when the bears had run off and Patrick had started yelling at her. Then she felt him gather her into his arms and she instantly knew at that moment that she would be staying here, in 1892. She wasn't going to be going back to her time. She wanted to stay with Patrick. She couldn't believe how understanding he had been about her cooking disaster, and had felt very relieved when he told her he didn't care if she didn't know how to cook. A part of her couldn't believe someone cared about her, maybe even loved her, like she had always wished for. Someone who wanted her love in return.

But how was she going to tell him about her secret, now that she had made the decision to stay? And when she told him, would he believe her? In her time, it was easy to find time travel stories and movies, even though they were considered fiction. But in Patrick's time, had he even heard about the concept?

Kimberly was silent on the way back to the ranch. Patrick kept her hand in his and just before they left the protection of the forest, he again pulled her into his arms and just held her. She wanted to tell him right then that she had decided to stay, but something held her back. She knew she needed to think of the best way to tell him, but one thing was for sure, she wanted to tell him as soon as possible.

When they walked by the field where some of the horses were kept, Kimberly saw the light colored horse she had ridden from Denver in the distance. She thought of one way she could let him know she was thinking of staying.

"Patrick, I think I am ready for you to teach me to ride," Kimberly told him. She was glad she had brought up the subject, for a huge grin broke out over his face.

"That's great," he told her. "I was afraid I had scared you too bad when I made you ride a horse for over four hours when you first came here, but there was no other way to get here."

"No, you didn't scare me," Kimberly tried to explain. "I guess I just needed some time."

There was a pause, as Patrick turned solemn. "And your secret?" Patrick asked, stopping her and turning to face her, a serious look on his face.

"Soon," Kimberly reached a hand up and touched his face. She tried to show him of her honesty through her eyes. "Soon, I promise."

Chapter 22

Nicky heard a knock on her front door and she wondered who it was. She had just gotten off the phone with the principal of her school. He had called to tell her that one of the teachers who was teaching summer school had just broken her leg, and he was wondering if she could fill in for the six-week program. Normally, she would have declined, for she loved having her summers free. She usually spent the months hiking, fishing, and rock climbing with Justin, or with some of her other friends. She also would take a short vacation with Kimberly. But now that Kimberly was gone, she wasn't looking forward to the summer months, and she agreed to take the place of the teacher for the next six weeks.

Whoever was on the other side of her door knocked again and she got up to answer it. To her surprise, it was Collins.

"Come in," she invited him and stepped aside so he could enter. She was surprised to see him so soon. Had he been able to deliver the letter she wrote so quickly? It had been barely a day since she had been at Mrs. Hilton's home, fully prepared to camp out in the yard until she talked to someone who knew where Kimberly was.

Collins shook his head at her invitation. "I have delivered your letter and Kimberly has written a reply." He handed her the same envelope she had sent. She noticed that Kimberly's name had been crossed out on the envelope and her name had been replaced, written in Kimberly's handwriting.

"Are you sure you don't want to come in?" Nicky asked as she accepted the letter.

Collins shook his head. "I must go. I have been away too long."

"But," Nicky wanted to argue, but Collins had already turned away.

"Have a good day," he called to her formally as he walked down the sidewalk.

"Thank you for bringing the letter," Nicky called back, then shut the door. She had noticed that there wasn't a car parked in front of her townhome and she wondered why he hadn't driven a car to her house. She opened her door to offer him a ride back to Mrs. Hilton's home. When she did, she couldn't see him anywhere.

"That's strange," she said to herself. "How could he have disappeared so quickly?" She shrugged her shoulders and quickly opened the letter.

She could tell it really was from Kimberly. When she saw the drawing of herself, Nicky remembered when her friend had drawn it. She also remembered their conversation they'd had about marriage to future men. She knew Kimberly was giving her a message.

After she read Kimberly's words, she knew her friend really was happy. She still didn't understand why she couldn't just talk to her, but she would respect Kimberly's wishes, and quit looking for her so intensely. She just hoped Kimberly would invite her to her wedding. That is, if she wasn't married already. If she was honest with herself, part of her was envious of Kimberly. She had found someone to love, even if it was in an unconventional way.

Feeling better than she had since Kimberly left, she decided it was time to clean her townhouse and pay the bills. She went into her kitchen and was appalled at how dirty it was. When was the last time she did the dishes? She couldn't remember, but it was obvious it had been at least a week. Dishes were something Kimberly had taken care of regularly. She saw a stack of mail and newspapers on the corner of the table, which was getting larger and larger by the day.

I might as well take care of the bills first, she thought to herself. She started to go through the stack, placing the mail she needed to keep in one pile and made another pile for junk mail and newspapers that she would recycle. It took her awhile since there was such a large stack. As she got down to the last of the newspapers, she realized she was holding a copy of the paper which Kimberly had found the ad in: *The Denver Rocky Mountain Gazette.*

I wonder if the ad will still be in there, she thought to herself. She noticed that the newspaper was dated a few days after Kimberly had left. She quickly turned to the classified section and started to scan through the ads. Sure enough. The ad was there. It looked exactly like the ad Kimberly had shown her, the same ad that Nicky had dared Kimberly to answer as a joke. The ad that eventually took Kimberly away from her.

She remembered that Collins had told her that Mrs. Hilton had decided to put the mail-order bride business on hold "for her time." What did that mean?

Instantly, she made a decision. She was going to answer the ad, just like Kimberly did. She didn't really want to be a mail-order bride. She didn't understand why someone would want to marry a man they had never met. How could they marry when they hadn't spent months getting to know each other? Nicky had dated quite a bit, but she hadn't found someone she wanted to spend her entire life with. She firmly believed when she dated someone, she need to see them in all sorts of situations before making the commitment to marriage; holidays, sports games, interaction with children, and everything else life could throw at them. She felt that she would need to date someone for at least a year before she would be able to see that person in all the situations that would be possible. Then, there would be no surprises.

Nevertheless, she was going to answer this ad. She was going to test Mrs. Hilton. If the woman thought Nicky was sincere in her request to be a mail-order bride, maybe she would match her to someone close to Kimberly. Then she could make sure Kimberly was happy.

I am also going to send Kimberly another letter through Mrs. Hilton, she said to herself as she quickly opened her laptop and started a new word document. Even if Mrs. Hilton doesn't match me with someone, maybe she would at least make sure Kimberly got this second letter. She quickly started to type before she changed her mind.

Dear Mrs. Hilton,

I am writing in response to your ad that was placed in the Denver Rocky Mountain Gazette a few months ago. I would like to send in an application to be a mail-order bride.

Your butler, Collins, did tell me that you have decided to close part of your business "for my time," whatever that means. But I am asking you to consider me as an applicant anyway and send me the same information you sent to Kimberly.

I have found my time without Kimberly as my roommate to be rather lonely. There is a hole in my life that I have been hiding from, and now with Kimberly gone, I feel I must address the issue, and find myself a companion.

I am also enclosing another letter to Kimberly. If you really are going to shut down your business "for my time," please at least make sure Kimberly gets this letter. She is my best friend and is like a sister to me. I don't want to lose contact with her.

Thank you,

Nicky Foster

Nicky wasn't sure why she wrote about feeling lonely, but hoped it would convince Mrs. Hilton that she was being sincere. While she didn't feel like she needed to marry, she realized as she wrote the words, there may be more truth behind them than she was willing to admit.

After printing the letter, Nicky found an envelope and slid the paper inside. She quickly found a stamp, addressed the envelope, and walked to the nearby mailbox to mail it. Whatever happened was now in Mrs. Hilton's hands.

****

"Patrick, I need to talk to you," Keegan said to his brother. They were both taking care of the animals that were in the barn.

"What about?"

"I saw something strange the other day, about Kimberly," Keegan said. Patrick looked at his youngest brother sharply. He had tried to talk about this to Patrick before now, but there had never been a good time.

"I don't want to hear anything negative about her," he said flatly. He could tell by the look on his brother's face that it wasn't going to be good. First Shaun had gotten off on a bad foot with Kimberly, and now Keegan thought she was strange. Why couldn't his brothers just accept his choice of a bride?

"This really isn't negative, just strange."

"Okay then. What is it?"

"I saw Kimberly meet with a man in a black suit near the forest behind the barn."

Patrick looked at his brother again and could tell that he was serious. "Okay. You better explain. We haven't had any visitors recently." They had visitors so rarely, that when someone did come, everyone knew about it.

"I have to tell you something else first. You're probably going to be mad at me, but you should know everything."

"Just tell me, Keegan."

"Yesterday, I was studying for a long time and needed a break, so I went outside. I saw Kimberly going into her cabin. She seemed to be in a hurry. She was inside for only a few minutes and when she left, she forgot to shut the door.

"I was curious about what she has in her cabin. I like Kimberly, I really do. But you have to admit there is something strange about her. I wanted to see that box with the red cross on it that you told me about when she worked on my leg. So I went inside her cabin."

Keegan paused, grimacing as if waiting for Patrick to get angry. Patrick bit his lip to keep from lecturing his brother about the privacy of others, especially Kimberly. He wanted to hear what Keegan had to say.

"Go on," Patrick said gruffly.

"Well, I couldn't find the box, but she had a book that was open on her bed, so I went to look at it. It wasn't a book to read. It was a pad of paper that was tied together with some type of wire. There were drawings in it. I think Kimberly drew them."

"Well, that's not so strange. Lots of people like to draw," Patrick felt relieved. If that was what Kimberly's secret was, he didn't have a problem with it, although he knew many people felt drawing was a waste of valuable time. Maybe that was why she hid it, because other people gave her a hard time.

"I looked through the book. Some of the drawings were strange. There was one of what looked like a weird machine with large wheels. She had drawn herself inside it. There was another one of a boy who was looking at a small box in his hands, but not like any box I've ever seen before. The boy was dressed weird.

"Anyway, I decided I better leave just in case she came back, so I put the book down. Then I looked out the window and that's when I saw him."

"The man in the black suit?"

"Yes. Kimberly gave him something, a paper I think. Then he just.... disappeared." He stopped, and stared right into Patrick's eyes, as if he was frightened. "He vanished into thin air."

Patrick felt frustrated with his brother. When Keegan was small, he would tell stories all the time about people who were around the ranch that really weren't there. Keegan hadn't told these type of stories for a few years now. Was Keegan starting to make up stories again?

"I know what you're thinking," Keegan rushed on to say. "But I swear I saw that man. Ask Kimberly if you don't believe me. She was talking to him and then he disappeared."

"What did Kimberly do after the man.... disappeared?" Patrick decided not to brush Keegan off, if only to figure out why Keegan would make up such an outrageous story.

"I don't know. I left the cabin as quickly as I could. I figured she'd come back and I didn't want her to see me there."

Patrick was silent as he thought about what Keegan had just told him. He weighed the possibility of Keegan's story being true.

Keegan hadn't made up a story for a while and had grown into an honest young man. Patrick had also noticed a bond between the two ever since Kimberly had saved his life.

He was sure Keegan had mistakenly seen the man disappear. Clearly, it must have been a trick to his eyes. The drawings sounded strange, but maybe Kimberly just had a strong imagination. Then there was the man Keegan saw. All of this left him thinking, what should he do about it? He knew his feelings for Kimberly were real. But what if she wasn't who she said she was? When he held and kissed her after the bear scare, he thought she had strong feelings for him. But why would she be meeting up with another man? What was going on?

"Don't worry about this, Keegan," Patrick finally said to his brother who was waiting anxiously for his response. "Don't say anything to Shaun or Bridget. I will talk to Kimberly and get to the bottom of this." *It is time for her to tell me her secret,* he thought.

Keegan nodded his head. Patrick could tell he was relieved that he believed his story. "Why don't you make sure the horses in the first field have enough water?" Patrick suggested and sighed when Keegan left the barn, limping a bit as he went. The limp reminded Patrick how Kimberly had helped Keegan. He had trusted Kimberly with his brother. But could he continue to trust her?

Yes, it's time for her to tell me her secret, Patrick whispered to himself.

Chapter 23

Dinner was finally over and Kimberly sighed with relief as she dried and put away the last dish. Patrick had been giving her strange looks all through the meal and hadn't talked to her at all. He had come in late for dinner and hadn't sat next to her like he usually did. She knew it was time to tell him. She said a prayer that he would listen to what she had to say and that he would accept where she was from. She didn't want to go back to her time. She liked it here with Patrick and his family. She wanted to marry him as soon as the 30 days were up, which was in less than a week.

Patrick had left the cabin as soon as the meal was over and Kimberly hoped she would be able to find him in the barn and that he would be alone. She let Bridget know she was leaving and walked quickly to find him. Just as she hoped, he was in the barn brushing his favorite horse, Apache. Patrick hadn't heard her come in, so Kimberly stood and watched him for a moment. He ran the brush over Apache's back and murmured something. The horse nickered back and shook his head as if responding to Patrick's words.

Kimberly then studied the man. His cowboy hat was on his head as usual, which shaded his face. She could see his auburn hair touching the collar of his shirt. His hair was getting long and she remembered Bridget mentioning to her brothers at dinner that she would cut their hair the next day if they wished. Both Shaun and Keegan kept their hair short, but Patrick's was long and Kimberly liked it that way.

She saw his muscles tighten through his shirt as he brushed the horse and something stirred inside her heart. She prayed again that this conversation she was going to have with Patrick would go well. She was so nervous. How did someone tell another that they were from the future? She took a deep breath, portraying her nervousness, and Patrick turned at the sound.

He looked at her intently for a moment, but did not smile like he usually did when he saw her. He patted Apache on his neck and then stepped out of the stall, walking towards her.

"I would like to talk to you," Kimberly told him, trying not to stammer. "Is now a good time?"

Patrick was silent as he put the horse brush away, but then he turned to her. "I think it is time you tell me your secret."

Kimberly nodded at his words. She started to feel even more nervous because he seemed so serious and solemn. What if it was too late? A few weeks ago, she had asked him to trust her. She promised she would tell him her secret when the time was right. What if she had waited too long?

"Can we walk?" Kimberly requested. It might be easier to talk to him if she didn't have to look at him. He nodded his agreement and then held out his hand. Her heart swelled with happiness and she slid her hand into his. He still wanted to touch her. Maybe this wouldn't be so bad.

They left the barn and walked towards the river. Kimberly was silent for a few minutes, trying to calm her nerves. She tried to let herself enjoy the dusk as it settled across the ranch and the twinkling stars that were starting to appear. She took a deep breath again.

"Just tell me," Patrick said in the still of the coming night. She could hear frustration laced in his words. "I think I need to know what you need to tell me if our relationship is going to go any further."

"Yes, I agree. I just don't know where to start or how to tell you."

"Start at the beginning."

"Before I start, I would like to ask you to not say anything. Please don't ask any questions until I am done. Will that be okay? I might say some things that will not make sense to you. I will answer any questions you may have when I am done."

Patrick scowled but nodded his agreement at her request.

She waited for a moment, scared of what could happen if Patrick did not believe her. Deciding that the longer she took to tell him, the worse it would get, she took a breath, and started talking.

"Around the middle of April, I saw an ad in a newspaper. I live with my best friend, Nicky, and she was collecting newspapers to use in her classroom. She is a school teacher. I saw the ad for a mail order bride from Mrs. Hilton. It intrigued me and I decided to send away for more information.

"I really didn't think I would hear back from her, but I received a response about a week later. She had sent me some information about how to become a mail-order bride, as well as a questionnaire to fill out and send back to her. I filled out the papers she sent and took them to her house. She looked them over and then gave me your introductory letter.

I wrote my first letter to you that day, in her library. I enjoyed each letter I received from you over the next few weeks. I decided I wanted to meet you and so I told Mrs. Hilton. She made the arrangements for me to come.

I was working at a hospital in the ER department as a trauma nurse. I love taking care of people, but I hated my job. My supervisor didn't like me and she was doing everything she could to make work miserable. I think she wanted me to quit, which I did right before I decided to come meet you.

"When I told Mrs. Hilton that I wanted to come, she was very pleased. She felt we could be good together."

Kimberly could tell that Patrick was starting to look confused, but was doing his best to not ask any questions. She realized she had used a few words that must not recognize and knew she had better hurry with her story.

"She told me something that was strange to me, something that she also said I couldn't tell you unless I decided to marry you when the 30 days were up.

"She told me she lived in 1892, and so did you."

"Why is that so strange?" Patrick couldn't resist responding incredulously.

Kimberly hesitated, and then she said as quickly as she could. "Because I live in 2005. I am from the future."

There was a long silence. "Did I just hear you say that you were from the future?"

"Yes."

"That's impossible. Listen if you don't want to tell me what you're hiding, then I think…"

"You promised not to ask questions until I was done," Kimberly said firmly. "I'm not finished."

Patrick clamped his lips shut and nodded at her to continue.

"Mrs. Hilton showed me two keys. She told me that they were magic keys. When a person held one of the keys in their hand and pictured a place and time where they wanted to be, the key would transport them to that time." She cringed when he sighed, and looked away, clearly still thinking she was making this story up.

"She told me that if I wanted to meet you, I would need to use one of the keys to come from my time, 2005, to her time. To your time, 1892.

"At first, I didn't believe her. I had heard about time travel, but just in stories. It wasn't supposed to be real. But she showed me proof. She held one of the keys and disappeared right before my eyes. She came right back, but she was gone for a few seconds."

When she said that, Patrick whipped his head around, and stared at her. She continued on, glad to have his full attention again.

"I wasn't sure what to do. Did I really want to leave my time? There would be a lot of things I would miss, especially Nicky and her family. Then I realized I didn't have a job. Besides Nicky, I didn't have anything or anyone to hold me to my time. I loved your letters and I wanted to meet you. So I agreed to leave my time and go to yours.

"Mrs. Hilton helped me get ready. She has this room full of things she has collected over the years as she used the keys. I guess she has been going back in time and into the future on a regular basis. She gave me the carpet bag and some dresses from your time."

Patrick looked away and started to walk towards some trees. She could tell he was angry with her.

"Patrick, wait! I'm not done yet!" Kimberly called and tried to catch up to him. The skirts of her dress wrapped around her legs, so she couldn't move as fast as he was moving. She almost fell to the ground as she tried to follow him. She still hadn't gotten used to those darn skirts.

He turned around and faced her, an angry look on his face. "Couldn't you come up with a better story than that? Traveling from the future to my time using a key? That's ridiculous!"

"You have to believe me." Kimberly reached out to grab his arm, but he shrugged her hand away. "I wouldn't make something like this up. I can prove to you that I am from the future."

"I think your secret is that you have actually met someone else. Keegan saw you meet a man in the forest. I have no idea how he got here, but Keegan told me how you left your cabin and ran to meet this man. You gave him a paper. Are you going to deny that?"

Kimberly shook her head. "I did meet a man yesterday. It was Collins, Mrs. Hilton's butler."

Patrick looked confused. "If he came to visit, why didn't he just come to the cabin? He would have been welcome. Why didn't he stay? It's a long ride from Denver." He then looked suspiciously at her. "Why did he come to see you?"

"He came to give me a letter Nicky had written. What Keegan probably saw was me giving him a letter I had written to Nicky, so he could deliver it to her. Nicky has been very worried that I left like I did. In the future, we have these devices that…"

Patrick interrupted again. "I don't understand why he didn't just wait until we went to Denver again. Our 30 days are up in a week and…" He paused as if he realized what he just said. Kimberly wondered if he was rethinking what he wanted now. Maybe he wasn't sure he wanted to marry her.

The thought of Patrick changing his mind devastated her; however, she knew that if she did marry him, she would want him to know all about her previous life. She definitely would not want to hide where she was from.

****

Patrick was angry at Kimberly. Why would she make up such a ridiculous story? But Keegan had told him that he had seen the man Kimberly had met with disappear. What did that mean? And somehow, it coincided with the story Kimberly told. How could it be?

And what about the box Kimberly had used to help Keegan? Was that why the box had so many things in it that he hadn't ever seen before? He thought about some of the different words Kimberly had used. He had never heard words like them before; *online, ER, trauma nurse,* and just now she used the word *device.*

He shook his head in disgust. Was he really thinking her story could be real? Time travel?

He turned and looked at Kimberly. She had wandered away from him and was sitting on a rock near the river. Her head was bowed and she had tears running down her face. Seeing her tears made him want to gather her into his arms, and he had to harden his heart to keep himself from doing just that. Then he realized that they had walked to the exact area where he had saved her from the bear and he hadn't brought his gun with him.

"We'd better head back, Kimberly," he told her gruffly. "We are too far from the ranch and I don't have my gun." He didn't know if the bears were nearby, but he didn't want to take that chance.

Kimberly nodded and tried to stand up, but she got tangled in her dress. He had noticed that this happened quite often with her. She seemed to have a hard time with her skirts. Was this another sign that her time travel story was true? What kind of clothing would people wear in the future? Bridget never seemed to have problems controlling her skirts. He reached down and took her hand to help her up.

When he pulled her to her feet, she looked at him deeply. He suddenly wanted to kiss her, like he had before. Even though he didn't believe her story, he was still attracted to her. What was he going to do? Her eyes looked straight at him and seemed to be pleading with him to believe her. He could tell that she really believed her story.

"I will need to think about what you told me," Patrick finally told her. He stepped back and dropped her hand after she had gotten to her feet.

"I would like to make one request," Kimberly told him.

"What is it?"

"Can we travel to Denver and talk to Mrs. Hilton, before you make any decision about us?"

Patrick hesitated and then nodded. It was a fair request. He would make arrangements for them to travel to Denver in a few days. In fact, he felt the entire family should go. It would be a nice break for everyone. He would ride into the mountains and ask Running Deer, Colleen's uncle who lived in the Indian village, if he would watch over the ranch for a few days.

Chapter 24

The next morning, Kimberly watched as Patrick rode off on Apache into the mountains. He hadn't told her where he was going, but she knew that Shaun was aware of why he was leaving. She did her best to keep the tears from her eyes. She knew his reaction to her story was normal. Wouldn't she have reacted in much the same way if the situation was reversed?

She was glad he agreed to the trip to visit Mrs. Hilton. She hoped he would be able to keep an open mind until he could talk to her. She turned to Bridget and tried to smile. She didn't want Bridget to know something was wrong.

"I would love it if you could show me how to make those braided rugs," she requested of Bridget. If things weren't going to work out between her and Patrick, she wanted to bring back one new skill to 2005. She wanted to be able to make a braided rug for her room.

Bridget seemed pleased that she asked. "Sure. Today is a good day. We are caught up on the weeding in the garden, the house chores, and the laundry. I think we can take a few hours so I can teach you."

They were soon sitting at the kitchen table, with a large pile of scrap fabric between them. Colleen stayed with them for a while, chattering in her usual fashion until Bridget sent her outside. Kimberly loved having the child around, but she was glad Bridget found her something else to do. She was having a hard time following the conversation with the child.

"Colleen, why don't you go find your father?" Bridget suggested. "He mentioned he was going to work with one of the new colts."

"Really?" Colleen jumped from the table. "I know he will want my help." She dashed outside.

Bridget showed Kimberly how to take the fabric and tear them into thin strips. She then sewed the end of each strip together until she had a large pile of strips all sewn together.

"When we get enough, we will braid them together as tight as we can," Bridget told her.

The women worked quietly for a few minutes and Kimberly couldn't help but let her mind drift to Patrick and their talk the evening before.

Bridget finally broke the silence. "A few days ago, you and Patrick seemed to be getting along great. Now, you two will barely look at each other. What happened?"

Kimberly didn't know what to say. She knew she couldn't tell Bridget about herself. She also knew that all three of Patrick's siblings suspected she was hiding something, especially since Keegan had seen Collins disappear. She wondered if Keegan had mentioned what he had seen to Shaun or Bridget.

"I told Patrick something about my past and where I am from. He is having a hard time with it." Kimberly finally felt it was safe to say. "I'm sure we will work things out." She hoped the last sentence was true.

Bridget stopped her sewing and laid a hand on top of Kimberly's. "Do you love Patrick?"

Kimberly immediately nodded her head. "Yes, I do love him. I didn't expect to fall in love with him so quickly, but he is a good man."

"I can tell he loves you, too. He has been different since you came. He is happier, more willing to laugh and have fun with us. He doesn't work so much. He used to always be working. The only time I would see him was at meal times and even then, he would eat as fast as he could, and then leave to work some more."

"I can tell your ranch is doing well," Kimberly commented.

"It isn't my ranch. Although Shaun, Keegan, and I live here, the ranch will never be ours. It is Patrick's. He is the oldest son."

Kimberly was surprised at Bridget's words. Why couldn't the ranch belong to all four of them?

"Does that bother you?" she finally asked. Bridget worked just as hard as Patrick did around the ranch.

Bridget shook her head. "It's the way it has always been in our family. Patrick will never make any of us feel we have to leave, but someday we will. Shaun is saving his money he earns from training his horses to buy his own land. Keegan will likely never want to own land. I wouldn't be surprised if he becomes a doctor. And I will marry someday, leave, and start my own family."

Kimberly felt surprised there were no hard feelings about Patrick inheriting the family ranch. "Tell me about how your family was able to purchase this land." This was one of the subjects she was very curious about. Why did they have land in the middle of the mountains, so far away from the nearest city?

"My grandfather and grandmother lived in Ireland during the potato famine. They lived in a small cottage and were forced to work for a rich man. They barely made enough to feed their children. Then there was the potato famine. It lasted for five years. By the time it was over, they had lost all of their children, except for my father. He was ten years old.

"They decided they wanted to move to America. They had a set of china dishes that had been passed down to my grandmother. She was smart enough to bury the dishes in their small garden, so their landlord didn't know they had them. If he had, he would have insisted they give them to him as part of their payment they had to pay him every year."

Kimberly watched as Bridget looked off into the distance, as if she was remembering her father telling the story. "Pa helped dig them up. They left their little village in the middle of the night and were able to sell the dishes for enough money to send them to America. They settled in Boston. Grandfather spent the rest of his life here in America working two jobs just to get by, but they were able to educate our dad. When he was old enough, he took advantage of the Homesteading Act. And here we are. It meant a lot to our dad to be able to own his own land, so he could grow whatever he wanted and raise whatever animals he wished, to live where he wished. Patrick has made our father's dream into his own."

"You have a wonderful family history," Kimberly commented softly. She thought about her own family and how her parents were killed by a drunk driver when she was 15. She didn't have any grandparents or other family members to take her in after their deaths. She thought it was wonderful Patrick had such strong family ties.

"We're proud of it," Bridget told her with a smile. "And now Patrick is ready to settle down. That's why he brought you here."

"I haven't been here very long, but I love the ranch. I love the mountains."

"Do you think you could really live here in the mountains, on this ranch, when it's so far away from a city? After all, you grew up in one."

"Yes," Kimberly was able to tell Bridget her answer firmly and decisively. "I have never liked the city. I have a lot to learn, but I will have no trouble living here."

"Well, I wasn't sure how this was going to work out. After all, how strange is it to bring a woman here, someone Patrick had never met before? But I have been watching and I think you are perfect for him."

"Thank you," Kimberly told her. Now, if only Patrick could feel the same.

Chapter 25

Kimberly left her small cabin dressed in her split riding pants. The entire family was going to Denver on this trip, which was a rare occurrence. She was glad Patrick had given her some riding lessons over the last few days since she would be required to ride a horse for at least four hours to get to Denver.

She was worried about how things were going to turn out in Denver. Patrick hadn't been exactly avoiding her, but he hadn't been seeking her out either. She wished she could insist on talking with him about her being from the future, but in the end, she decided it would be best to let him take the lead. It was obvious he needed time to think about things. She hoped when they arrived in Denver, he would be willing to talk to Mrs. Hilton about how the keys worked. He hadn't even asked to see the key she had. Part of her was tempted to get the key out of its hiding place from the bottom of the trunk in her cabin and show him how it worked, just like Mrs. Hilton had done with her, but something stopped her from that plan. What if something went terribly wrong? What if she wasn't able to return to her time? What if she wasn't able to return back to Patrick's time? No, it would be best if she waited until they arrived in Denver to help him understand.

She sat on the back of Honey, the horse she had been learning to ride on the ranch, and listened to the chatter of Colleen to her father, Shaun. The child was so excited she was going to get to go to Denver. The family was planning on spending at least a few days there. Patrick had asked an Indian friend, who was also Colleen's uncle, to take care of the ranch while they were gone.

"Let's go," Patrick hollered. Kimberly watched as he and his two younger brothers, Shaun and Keegan, mounted their own horses. Shaun took the lead with Keegan, Colleen, and Bridget following. Kimberly waited until Patrick moved his horse next to her own before instructing Honey to move. She hoped she would be able to handle the four-hour ride to Denver. Even though Patrick had given her lessons, she wasn't sure how the trip was going to go. She remembered how difficult the trip to the ranch was for her, almost 30 days ago.

She noticed that Patrick let the others get quite a bit ahead of them, as if he wanted them out of hearing range. She hoped he would be willing to talk while they rode.

Patrick finally did start to talk. "I want you to know that I still don't know how I feel about what you told me. I just can't imagine how you could really be from the future. Keegan told me that he found a book with drawings in it, in your cabin."

"Yes, he saw my sketchbook. I like to draw things that are around me. Would you like to see it? I have drawings from my time that I could show you." She had brought all her belongings with her, just in case she wouldn't be returning to the ranch, although she hadn't let Patrick know that. Her heart fell when he shook his head.

"I'm not sure I'm ready for that. To be honest with you, I am having a very hard time with this. I sent away for a bride with the idea that it was going to work, that I would be married in 30 days. I am wondering if I can really trust you or Mrs. Hilton."

"I understand." Her heart dropped at his words. This was what she was afraid of, that he wouldn't be willing to give her a chance to prove her story. But at the same time, she knew that if he didn't want to believe her, she didn't want to marry him. The only way she would marry him was if he accepted her the way she was, including the fact that she was from the future.

"Tell me about your family," Patrick invited.

Kimberly turned in her saddle and faced him. She realized he hadn't asked her very many personal questions over the last 30 days. Was it because she was always vague with her answers? She was glad he asked. Now she could tell him without being afraid to use terminology that was from the future. She didn't have to hide anymore.

"My parents both died when I was 16 years old," Kimberly started to say.

"Wow, both of them at the same time? What happened?" Patrick asked with sympathy.

"They were killed in a car crash by a drunk driver."

Patrick looked at her with confusion. "You keep using words that don't make sense. What is a car crash and a drunk driver?"

"Cars are something that we use to get around in my time to different places. The best way to explain it is it's like a large buggy that runs by itself instead of with horses. It runs on a liquid called gasoline. It can go very fast. In fact, if we were riding in one now, from your ranch to Denver, it would only take about an hour to get there." She could see the astonishment on his face and she wondered what he would say if she described planes to him.

"You either have a great imagination or…"

"Or I am telling you the truth." Kimberly finished for him. "Sometimes, people will drink a lot of alcohol and then drive their car. Alcohol in my time does the same thing to people in your time. It makes them so they can't make wise decisions if they drink too much. A man who had been drinking heavily drove his car straight into my parent's car. My mom was killed instantly. My dad died about a day later." She stopped talking, thinking back to that awful day when a social worker and policeman had come to her school with the news.

"Even though what you are saying doesn't make sense to me, I'm sorry you lost your parents that way," Patrick told her. "What happened to you after your parents died?"

"I don't have any living relatives, so I was put into the foster care system."

"And a foster care system is...?"

"Sort of like an orphanage, I guess. I went to live in other people's homes. They were paid by the government to care for me."

"How long were you in this foster care?"

"I was actually in three different homes before I was sent to Nicky's home, my best friend. I have told you about her. I was able to stay there until I graduated from high school," Kimberly explained. She was starting to see that she was going to need to explain quite a bit to Patrick if he ever decided to believe her and she stayed in his time.

"What do you mean, you graduated from high school? Is that where you learned how to be a nurse?" Patrick asked. Kimberly could tell that Patrick was really wanting to know and wasn't just asking the questions out of politeness.

"No. In my time, kids go to school until they are 18. Then they graduate. I went to college to become a nurse."

"Didn't you tell me once that Nicky's family became like your own?"

"Yes. In a lot of ways, they did. They try to include me in their family get-togethers. Nicky has an older brother, Justin, who is like a brother to me. That's why Nicky has been so worried because I just disappeared. I left a note, but that wasn't good enough for her."

"So that's why Collins came to our ranch. He was delivering a letter from your friend because you couldn't mail her a letter? Our ranch is too far away?"

"Mailing her a letter wouldn't have done any good," Kimberly reminded him.

"That's right. Because you are from the future. Don't you have some type of mail service that goes between time periods?"

Kimberly could tell Patrick was being sarcastic. "So you still don't believe me?"

Patrick stopped his horse and looked at her. Honey obediently stopped beside him. "I'm not sure, Kimberly. What you are saying doesn't make sense to me. But I am starting to want to believe."

"You do?" For the first time since she had told him about her secret, Kimberly felt some hope. Was Patrick going to give her another chance? One of the things she had discovered in the last month was that she loved living in Patrick's time period: 1892. As much as she missed Nicky and Justin, she had no desire to return to her time.

Patrick moved his horse close to hers and reached his hand out. She placed her hand in his. "I want to believe, Kimberly. When I met with Mrs. Hilton and started the process for a mail-order bride, she said something strange, something that I just ignored because I didn't understand what she meant. But I think I do now."

"What did she tell you?" Kimberly asked curiously.

"She said to me, 'I hope that you can give Kimberly a chance. She will be a bit different from what you might be expecting. But remember that she is sincere and is willing to travel a great distance to see if a marriage with you will work.' She must have meant you traveling from the future."

"Yes, she did," Kimberly agreed. She was glad Mrs. Hilton had said what she did to Patrick. It planted a seed.

Patrick continued. "I have enjoyed getting to know you, both through our letters to each other, and the time we have spent together since you arrived at my ranch. You get along with my family. I know Bridget enjoys having another woman around. You saved Keegan's life. I made the decision to send for a mail-order bride with the idea that we marry. That was the ultimate goal- is the ultimate goal." He looked at her very intently. "Is marriage still possible? Can a person from the future marry someone from the past? Won't it change history?"

"I guess we can ask Victoria or Collins about that. I am sure we can marry, as long as we both still want to," Kimberly replied. "I still want to, as long as you are able to accept me for who I am."

Patrick started to say something, but then noticed the rest of his family had disappeared around a bend and they couldn't see them anymore. "We need to catch up to everyone. We will talk more about this later." He clicked his tongue at his horse and Patrick took off down the trail, Kimberly's horse following close behind.

Kimberly sighed. She felt a little better about the situation, and the conversation she just had with Patrick went well. But she still wasn't sure if her future was going to include him in her life.

Chapter 26

Nicky used her key to open her front door. Today had been the first day of her summer school and she was exhausted. She loved to teach, but when she had days like today, she wished she could have a longer break instead of just a few hours in the evening before the next school day.

Justin was coming over for dinner, so she quickly threw a few frozen pizzas in the oven since she knew his son, Garrett, would enjoy them. She went into her room, shed her clothes, and took a quick shower, hoping she'd be done before her brother showed up.

When she stepped out of the shower, she could hear the TV blaring. She knew that Justin had let himself in and he and Garrett had made themselves at home. She quickly dressed and went out to the living room.

"Hi, Justin. Hi, Garrett," she greeted them both. Garrett grunted his answer. He was busy trying to beat some aliens on the game he was playing.

Justin stood and gave her a hug. "Hi, sis. How was work today?"

"Exhausting," she told him with a grin. She could smell that the pizza was done. "How about we eat? Are you guy's hungry?"

"We sure are, aren't we Garrett?" The boy grunted again but ended the game when Justin insisted. They soon were sitting around the table eating their dinner.

"Where's Kimberly?" Garrett asked between bites of pizza. "I miss her. When is she coming home?"

Nicky looked at her brother. She knew that Justin hadn't told Garrett that Kimberly might not be coming back.

"I'll let you know when I know, how's that, bud?" she asked him with a ruffle of his hair.

"Sure, I guess," Garrett said as he put another piece of pizza on his plate. "Can I take this piece into the living room, Dad? I really want to beat that level. At summer school, Mike bragged today that he beat it two weeks ago."

Justin laughed. "Sure. You only have 30 minutes of game playing left today, though."

Nicky knew that even though Justin wrote video games for a living, he did his best to keep Garrett grounded in the real world, and only let him play video games an hour a day.

After Garret left the kitchen, Nicky set her pizza down on her plate. She wasn't hungry anymore and she stood up to clear the table, but sat back down when Justin pulled on her arm.

"Any news from Kimberly?" Justin asked her.

"Yes, in fact, I have received a letter from her. I went over to Victoria's home again last Saturday. Collins was there. He told me that Kimberly was happy and safe. He told me I could write a letter to her, which I did. Yesterday, he came again, this time to my apartment. He gave me a letter from Kimberly."

"Well that's good, I guess. I'm glad you have heard from her. I just don't understand why you aren't able to at least call her."

Nicky shook her head. "I don't understand either. But at least I know she is okay."

"Yes, I'm glad she is okay. Did she say when she was going to be back?"

Nicky hesitated. "I'm not sure she will be back. She loves Patrick. I think she is going to marry him."

"So soon? Doesn't she want to spend more time getting to know him, first?"

Nicky had nothing to say to that, especially since she agreed with her brother.

"Well, I wish her luck," Justin said as he finished the last of his pizza. "Do you want to go see a movie tonight? It would have to be a kid's show, of course, since Garrett would be with us."

Nicky considered his offer for a moment and then shook her head. "No. I have to work tomorrow, and I'm tired."

"All right," Justin said, accepting her decision. "I think we'll go now." He stood up to get Garrett but then turned back. "You okay?"

"Sure, I'm okay," Nicky smiled to reassure her brother. "I'm relieved that I finally heard from Kimberly. I guess I just miss her."

"She's been a big part of our lives for a long time. Let me know if you hear from her again, okay?"

****

Victoria picked up the last envelope that had arrived with the afternoon mail. Her mail-order bride business was picking up nicely. She received many applications weekly from men and women around the western states.

She started to slice open the envelope when she realized that it looked different. She quickly read the address and realized that the envelope was from the future. Why would she still be getting letters? She thought she had stopped the ad. She and Collins had made the decision to not accept any more applications from the future. Kimberly had been the first one. Soon after, they both realized that they needed to find a solution so the woman's family and friends didn't worry about her. Kimberly's best friend, Nicky, had started to do some drastic things in order to try to find out where Kimberly was.

Victoria opened the letter and quickly read it. Surprisingly, it was from Nicky.

Evidently, she also wanted to be considered as a mail-order bride, like Kimberly had, and she was writing for more information.

"Collins," she called out, knowing that her butler was close by. Sure enough, the tall distinguished man came into her office a few second later.

"Yes, ma'am," Collins said in his usual formal voice.

"Look what I just received," Victoria said as she handed him the letter. She watched as Collins quickly read the letter. She noticed that he didn't look surprised that Nicky had written.

"I wonder why she is suddenly interested in being a mail-order bride," Victoria wondered out loud.

"I don't think she is, ma'am."

"What do you mean?" Victoria was curious as to how Collins knew this.

"When I traveled into the future to talk with her last week, she told me she was interested. I was suspicious."

Victoria looked at him in surprise. "Suspicious about what?"

"I think she is expressing interest because she wants to see Kimberly. I don't think she really wants to be a mail-order bride."

"Oh," Victoria waved her hand at his words. "I need to take her at her word. Although I really didn't want to have another bride from the future, at least at this time."

Collins took a few steps away from her. "I don't think it would be wise to encourage her interest, but the choice is yours. There is something I must finish." Collins quickly left, without waiting for Victoria to dismiss him.

Victoria didn't understand what had just happened. She thought they were both discussing a fairly simple matter, and she wanted to make sure Nicky wasn't dismissed because of past actions. When she thought back on the last few sentences said between Collins and her, she realized she hadn't even considered his opinion.

She regretted the action. She had noticed a bond starting to grow between them; one they hadn't ever experienced during his entire employment. He was starting to become her friend. She cherished it. Since her husband had passed, she had started to grow lonely. She always had her staff around, but they never relaxed around her. When Collins had started to treat her more kindly, and less formally, it had started to fill a hole in her life. She hoped that this past conversation wouldn't push him back to his formal ways.

Victoria made a mental note to talk to Collins about it later and put the letter aside. She noticed there was another piece of paper in the envelope Nicky had sent. When she removed it, she saw that it was a sealed letter addressed to Kimberly. Maybe Collins was right. Did Nicky mail her a letter, pretending to answer the ad when she really just wanted to get another letter to Kimberly?

Chapter 27

The ride to Denver wasn't as bad as the trip she took to the ranch almost a month before. They stopped and rested twice. Patrick told her the stops were for Colleen, but Kimberly was grateful for the breaks just the same. She loved riding the trail along the river. The sound of the stream had become a rhythmic comfort to her. It helped ease the stress of what she and Patrick were going through. The brush started out fairly thick, but eventually evened out as it became evident the trail was used more frequently. If she kept her eyes open, she could also see various types of wildlife. The deer were majestic and calm, the squirrels and rabbits were busy, and never held still. Both would scurry away as soon as they heard Colleen's constant chatter. Eventually, the trail left the river as it headed towards the city. Soon they left the forest and the mountains and were riding down one of the main streets of Denver.

Patrick sent Shaun to the nearest hotel to reserve two rooms for the family. Then he and Kimberly went to Victoria's home. Kimberly silently wished he had given her a minute to freshen up; she felt a layer of grit and dirt covering her face and arms from the ride to Denver. But, she was also glad he was so anxious to get Victoria's opinion.

Kimberly was amazed that Victoria's home looked just like it did in her time, although there were a few differences. The paint was just a slightly different shade; it was a fresher coat of paint, so it was a bit more vibrant. It was clear the tools they used to upkeep the lawn could not trim the lawn as evenly as the mowers they had in her time, and the grass was not edged, giving it a rougher look than grass back in 2005 normally was. She could see that Victoria's home would probably be considered a historical home in her time.

Patrick tied both of their horses to a nearby post and knocked on the door. Collins answered, looking surprised that they were there standing on the porch. "Hello," he greeted them. "Would you like to come in?"

Kimberly and Patrick stepped into the entryway. Kimberly saw the same marble table she had seen in her time with an arrangement of flowers on top of it. They heard footsteps and she turned, seeing Victoria walking towards them. She was dressed exactly the way she had been when she first met her in her time. It was good to see her. It was nice to be around someone who had known her in her own time.

"Welcome, Kimberly and Patrick," Victoria greeted them. "I was just thinking today that the 30 days were up. I am assuming since you are both here, that you have good news to tell me?"

Kimberly looked at Patrick. "Well..."

Victoria interrupted them. "We can talk about it in a few minutes. How long will you be in Denver?"

"My entire family is here," Patrick explained.

"They are? Well, invite them in, Collins," Victoria said, turning to the butler who was standing nearby.

"They went to get rooms at a hotel," Patrick said.

"Oh, you don't need to do that," Victoria argued. "I have plenty of room in this house. Why don't you and your family stay here?"

Kimberly expected Patrick to turn down Victoria's request, but he smiled as if in relief.

"I think I will take you up on your offer." He turned to Kimberly. "I am going to go catch up with Shaun before he pays for the rooms at the hotel."

Kimberly nodded her agreement and watched as Patrick left the room. Her heart skipped a beat as he left. It was if she was noticing him for the first time. She had dated a few men in her time, but she had never been attracted to anyone like she was to Patrick. He carried himself like a man; but also showed some grace when he walked. It was obvious to anyone who saw him that he took pride in his lifestyle. He was always wearing his riding pants, and a neatly pressed, sturdy button-up shirt. He kept his long hair combed out of his face, showing a hint of ruggedness without being sloppy. Somehow, while carrying all of that masculinity, he was still able to be perfectly courteous and gentlemanly.

She felt someone touch her sleeve and noticed that Victoria was standing close to her. She smiled at the woman almost sheepishly. She must have been standing there staring at the doorway that Patrick had just gone through for at least a few seconds.

"I am assuming that you and Patrick are going to marry," Victoria said as she guided Kimberly to a nearby sofa.

Kimberly glanced around the room and noticed that Collins had left. She was alone with Victoria and she was glad. She desperately needed to talk to someone who was aware of what was going on. She shook her head at Victoria's words.

She quickly brought Victoria up-to-date about the last 30 days. She explained to the older woman how she loved living on the ranch and enjoyed getting to know Patrick and his family. She talked about Daisy and how she learned to ride a horse. She explained that when Collins had come to deliver the letter from Nicky, Keegan had accidentally witnessed her giving Collins a paper and then the man disappeared, which raised a number of questions.

"By then, I had already decided I wanted to stay and marry Patrick. I just hadn't told him about my past yet. So I told him a few days ago." Kimberly paused as tears formed in her eyes.

"And…?" Victoria questioned, softly encouraging her to continue.

"He is having a hard time believing that time travel is possible. I really think he would want us to marry immediately as soon as the 30 days were up. That is, if I was from his time. Things were going well between us."

"I can understand his concerns," Victoria told her. "After all, as far as I know, no one in my time period has even heard about the possibility of traveling from one time to another. My dear husband, Charles, couldn't accept that it could happen. When he was alive, I was very careful to only use the keys when he was on a business trip."

"What do you think I should do?" Kimberly asked, desperately needing advice at this time. "I would like to stay. I have fallen in love with him. I believe he loves me. But I don't want us to marry unless he can accept where I am from."

Victoria thought for a moment, then took one of Kimberly's hands in a motherly gesture. "Maybe one of his concerns is that you might change your mind, that you might someday long for your own time, and wish to return."

Kimberly was silent as she thought about this possibility. Would she miss her time? She knew she would miss many of the conveniences that her time offered. Wearing pants and t-shirts were a big one, as well as hot showers, air conditioning, and the ability to travel in a comfortable, timely manner. Most of all, she would miss Nicky and Justin. But she knew that she was willing to give all that up to be with Patrick.

"Have you shown him the key?" Victoria asked.

Kimberly shook her head. "He hasn't asked. I have something else to tell you, something that happened the first week I was at the ranch." She confessed to Victoria that even though she wasn't supposed to, she did bring a few items from 2005 with her. She explained how Keegan had become injured when he was cutting wood and how she was able to help him using her first-aid kit and knowledge because she was a trauma nurse. She also confessed to Victoria that she had brought her sketch pad and some pencils, feeling a bit sheepish at deliberately ignoring one of Victoria's rules.

"Keegan saw my sketch pad. I have drawings in it of things from my time. I offered to show it to Patrick, but he refused to look at it." She turned hopeful eyes to Victoria. "Could you use the key and disappear? Like you did when you first told me about how it works?"

Victoria hesitated, then shook her head. "Using the keys are starting to affect my health. I don't dare use them again, at least for a while. After you left your time, I used the second key to come back here, and it took me days to recover. I don't think I will be using the keys anytime soon."

Kimberly nodded her understanding, but then asked, "How can I convince him, then?"

Victoria took her hand into her own and squeezed it in reassurance.

"Patrick is a good man. I am willing to talk to him and I am sure Collins will, too. I think eventually he will believe you."

"I have already decided I don't want to stay if he can't accept where I am from, who I am. I don't want to have a marriage filled with mistrust."

Victoria nodded. "I think that is a wise decision, but I don't think you will need to worry about that. I really feel that in the end, Patrick will understand."

"I also feel we should let his family know when Patrick believes me. I don't want to live on the ranch trying to keep such a big secret from them. It has been difficult to not use words from the future around them," Kimberly explained.

The older woman thought about it, then nodded her head again. "I am okay with Patrick's family knowing about the keys, as long as they understand they are not to tell anyone else. When the man gave me the first key, he warned me that only one other person should know about it. At first, I obeyed his wishes. I only told Charles and he didn't believe me. Because I had already told him, I didn't dare tell anyone else. I finally told Collins after Charles' death."

"How long did it take for Collins to believe you?" Kimberly asked.

"He believed me right away. I think there were a few times when I had used a key and was gone for awhile. He would look for me and couldn't find me. Then suddenly, there I was. I think he suspected something. In fact, when he first held the keys, he felt the vibration from them. Charles never felt that."

"Well, both Patrick and I know about the keys and if we tell his family, more people will know about them. Aren't you worried about this?" Kimberly was concerned that it might be dangerous if more people knew about them.

"It can't be helped. We will just need to be very careful."

"What about Nicky?" Kimberly asked about her friend.

"She isn't aware that Collins has been traveling back and forth from my time to yours, although I think she suspects something."

"Nicky is very aware of her surroundings. I wouldn't be surprised that she suspects something."

Victoria stood and walked to her desk and picked up an envelope. "In fact, Nicky sent this to me." She handed the envelope to Kimberly.

Kimberly quickly opened it. Inside was a sheet of paper and another smaller envelope with her name on it. She quickly read the paper and could see that Nicky had asked for information about being a mail-order bride. She smiled to herself. Nicky was doing what she could to make sure she was okay.

"Are you going to let her be a mail-order bride?" Kimberly asked.

Victoria shrugged her shoulders. "I'm not sure. Before this arrived, I had made the decision to not have any more brides come from your time. Nicky's behavior has shown me that I should have planned better before sending you to my time. I don't think I was fully aware of the amount of contact your society has with each other."

Kimberly nodded. "Yes, we can talk or communicate with each other basically whenever we want, no matter what the distance is. Nicky wouldn't have understood why I couldn't talk to her."

"I will need to think about it. Collins seems to think Nicky is not sincere in wanting to be a bride."

Kimberly smiled. "Well, she originally thought this entire plan was a scam. I agree with Collins. I think she is just trying to find me. I wish there was a way I could stay in contact with her, even though I am here and she is there."

"We'll have to think about a solution to that, won't we?" Victoria asked with a smile.

Kimberly heard voices coming towards them and knew that Patrick and his family had arrived.

Chapter 28

Patrick entered the cool house with his siblings and Colleen. When they had arrived, a man was standing in the yard as if waiting for them. He offered to take care of the horses and Patrick gratefully accepted. He wanted to get his family settled and then find Collins. He wanted some answers that he felt only Collins could give.

"This house is big," Colleen said with awe in her voice. She looked around, turning in a circle as she did so, her eyes wide at what she saw.

"It is a big house, isn't it?"

Patrick heard a voice and turned. Victoria was coming towards them with Kimberly behind him. He wondered what they talked about while he was gone.

"Much too big for an old woman like myself. I am glad you agreed to stay here. You are all welcome. Please use this house as you would your own," Victoria came up to them and smiled down at Colleen.

"You're beautiful," Colleen said with the same awe in her voice she had when she first walked into the house.

"Thank you," Victoria took the compliment in stride. "You are quite pretty yourself." She turned to Collins. "Could you show them to the rooms they will use?"

Collins nodded stiffly, yet pleasantly. "If you will follow me."

Very quickly, they were all settled into their rooms. Patrick shared a room with Shaun and Keegan while the women and Colleen shared a room across the hall. The rooms were large, almost as large as their cabin was on the ranch. There was plenty of room for them all. Both rooms had a large bed adorned with many pillows at one end, and a small table near a fireplace at the other. The table had a couple of chairs and a fancy sofa for seating. There were two large windows with beautiful beige curtains that hung close to the ceiling and fell all the way to the floor. A large rug covered most of the floor, providing comfort to those who walked across it.

After they were settled and had cleaned up from their trip to Denver, Victoria served them a delicious lunch. Then Kimberly left with Bridget and Colleen to do some shopping. When Patrick learned of their plans, he pulled Kimberly aside. He handed her some money.

"I assume you might need some things. Go ahead and use this to get what you need."

Kimberly looked at him in question, as if wondering why he would give her money if it wasn't certain they would be marrying yet. But she accepted the bills.

"Thank you," Kimberly told him. "I promise I will only get what I need."

Patrick wasn't worried that she would over spend. "You should buy some more riding britches." He was giving her a message. He wanted her to stay. He still wasn't sure about this time travel issue, but he felt they would be able to work it out.

"Really?" Kimberly's face broke into a beautiful smile. He smiled back and knew she had understood the message hidden in his words.

After the women left, Victoria going with them, Patrick immediately went to seek out

Collins. He found him sitting in Victoria's office looking through a stack of papers.

"Can we talk?" Patrick asked frankly. The older man nodded his agreement and indicated with his hand that Patrick should sit.

"I should let you know that Kimberly has told me she is from the future. I think she said from 2005." Patrick decided to just jump into the conversation.

"Did she now?" Collins asked him with a slight smile on his face. "What do you think of that?"

"I'm not sure what to think. She just told me a few days ago. I did think there was something strange about her. She would sometimes use words that didn't make sense, words I had never heard before. The week she arrived Keegan was gravely injured. Kimberly used her nursing skills and some items from a box to help him. I think she saved his life."

"She brought something with her from her time?" Collins usual formal face looked a little disapproving.

Patrick nodded. "Evidently, she brought some type of drawing book with her, too."

Collins didn't say anything, but Patrick could tell he wasn't pleased to hear this.

"To be honest, I'm glad she had the medical things she needed to help Keegan. If Kimberly hadn't been around, we would have needed to take him into Denver. I don't know if he would have survived the trip."

"I'm glad she was able to help then," Collins said to him.

"I need to ask, is what Kimberly telling me- that she is from so many years in the future- is this true?"

Collins didn't say anything for a few minutes. He stood up and started to pace the room as if thinking, his hands clasped behind his back. Even though Patrick wanted his question answered, he kept quiet.

"What do you think?" the man finally asked. "Do you think she is telling you the truth?"

Patrick was surprised at the man's questions. Why couldn't he just answer him? But then, if Collins said, yes, that Kimberly really was from the future, would he immediately believe him?

"I don't know what to think," Patrick admitted.

"Forget about the time travel for a moment," Collins advised. "How do you feel about Kimberly?"

"I asked for a mail-order bride for a reason. I want to marry and start a family. My ranch is so far away from other people. I knew it would be hard to court a woman properly. I figured this was the best option for me. I trusted Victoria to find the woman who would be best for me."

"And do you feel Kimberly is the best one for you?"

Patrick nodded. "Before she started to talk about being from the future, I did feel she was who I wanted to marry. I have fallen in love with her. She is a wonderful woman. She has done her best to learn how to live on the ranch. She has tried hard to learn how to cook. She loves working in the garden. I gave her one of my puppies and she fell in love with her." He caught himself smiling fondly while talking about her.

"So I will ask again, if she wasn't from the future, you would want to marry her?"

"Yes," Patrick said firmly. "She says she wants to stay. She wants to marry me."

Collins nodded his head. "She was told that she could only tell you about her time travel under one circumstance; if she decided to stay with you."

"The crazy thing is, I am starting to believe her."

"Why is that so crazy? There are many things in life, in our world, that aren't always what they seem."

"I need to tell you, my brother Keegan saw you when you came to visit Kimberly. He saw you disappear."

Collins looked at him in surprise and then shook his head. "And I was so careful. I guess I wasn't careful enough."

Patrick smiled at the man. "You should have just stayed and had a good visit with us. We don't get many visitors. We would have been happy to see you."

Collins stood and walked to Victoria's large desk. He opened a drawer and pulled out a small wooden box. He carried this box over to where Patrick was sitting and handed him the box.

"Open it," Collins instructed him.

Patrick looked at the man with a question in his eyes but did as he was asked. Inside was nestled a beautiful gold key. It was clearly old and well used; the gold was worn in places. The handle of the key was extremely intricate. On the other end, the notch had a simple but beautiful design as well. He picked it up and immediately could feel a vibration run through his hand into his body. He dropped it in surprise.

Collins looked at him as if with satisfaction. "Victoria has two keys that are used for time travel. Kimberly has the other one right now. You felt its power. Not many do."

"I felt... something," Patrick said, not sure what to say.

"This key and the key Kimberly has in her possession, can take a person back in time, forward into the future, or somewhere else in our time. I would demonstrate for you, but time travel is tiring and I don't want to be out of sorts for the rest of the day."

Patrick set the key back into the box. Something strange had happened when he was holding the key while Collins explained how it worked. Collins had started to fade away. It was if the key was ready to take him to another place. The last thing he wanted was to test the key. He wanted to stay right where he was, in his time.

"When Kimberly and I marry, what will happen to her key?" Patrick asked him, not realizing how he had worded his question. He had said when, not if.

But Collins picked up on it. "Kimberly will not keep it. She is to give the key back to Victoria. By giving it back, she is making a commitment to you -and to Victoria- that she will stay here in 1892."

"And what if she changes her mind?" Patrick voiced what he was really worried about. What if, as time went on, she wished she could go back to her time?

"That is something you will need to talk to her about," Collins told him.
"You need to find out what her wishes are. Before you marry her."

Chapter 29

Kimberly enjoyed shopping with Bridget and Victoria. She could tell Victoria was well liked and well known. Many people greeted her and stopped to talk to her. She would introduce Kimberly as part of Patrick's family, and she could tell that some people were aware of Patrick's ranch deep in the mountains. What would these people think about her if she was able to stay and marry him?

In the store, she noticed that there was one young woman, whom Bridget introduced as Lucy, who looked at her with suspicion. Right after the introductions, she rudely turned her back and started to whisper to an older woman who was behind the counter.

"Don't worry about Lucy," Bridget said softly to Kimberly as they walked towards the clothing. "She has always wanted to marry Patrick and my brother was never interested in her."

Kimberly felt a gladness in her heart that Patrick had chosen her, but why would he? There were so many beautiful women in

Denver, including Lucy. Why would he choose to send away for a bride?

Bridget started to look at some ready-made dresses, but Kimberly went to the shelf that held riding britches. She was still wearing her riding pants that she had worn for the trip to Denver. They were much more comfortable than the long skirts. She could walk more freely and they didn't get tangled up around her legs like skirts did. She immediately made the decision to buy a few more, like Patrick had suggested. She was going to wear these riding pants from now on, when she could.

After choosing two pairs in her size, she walked around the store, looking at what was available. There was clothing for men, women, and children, as well as fabric for those who wanted to sew their own clothes. She walked a little farther and browsed the bookshelf she had seen on her first trip to this store. She had helped Bridget pick out some new books for Keegan. She kept browsing until she reached the back of the store.

There was a simple collection of jewelry. She could tell none of it would be too expensive. Nonetheless, she blushed when she saw the rings, thinking about how close she was to her own marriage. She quickly walked back to the front of the store to find Bridget.

"So, you are visiting Patrick's family," she heard a voice and turned around. It was Lucy with a haughty expression on her face. "If you think you are going to marry him, you better think again."

"Why would you say that?" Kimberly asked. She couldn't believe how rude this woman was.

"Everyone knows he's going to marry me, it's just a matter of time," Lucy said with her nose in the air. "Where did Bridget say you were from?"

"I don't think I did," Bridget said, walking up to them. "We are ready to purchase our items." She looked at Kimberly who felt relief that Bridget rescued her.

Kimberly followed Bridget to the front counter. The woman who Lucy had whispered to was behind it, writing down on a piece of paper all the things they were buying. In addition to the two pairs of riding pants Kimberly was purchasing, Colleen had added a few books and her own pair of riding pants.

Bridget was buying a few more books for Keegan.

After the woman told Bridget the amount owed and everything was paid for, she spoke.

"How long will your family be in town this time?"

"Only for a few days, Mrs. MacKay," Bridget said politely.

"We will be having a nice gathering at our house this evening," the woman continued. "I will send an invitation to the hotel for your family."

Bridget shook her head. "We won't be able to attend, but thank you for inviting us." She quickly walked away, but the woman wasn't done.

"You shouldn't be answering for your brothers. I will send the invitation and they can decide for themselves."

Bridget looked back at the woman and nodded her head once, then they left the store. Kimberly noticed that Bridget didn't bother to explain that they weren't staying at the hotel.

"Wow," Kimberly breathed, slightly amused. "I guess your brothers are quite popular around here."

Bridget grinned. "Lucy has been after Patrick since she first moved to Denver five years ago. I think if Patrick was at all interested in her, he would have done something about it before now."

I guess there are "Lucy's" in all time periods, Kimberly thought to herself. She remembered a woman she went to college with named Carlee. She would brag about her test scores, even though Kimberly generally scored better than she did. Once Carlee had realized that, she had made it a point to interrupt Kimberly if she was answering a question the teacher had asked, and she always had to sit in front of Kimberly during class. It had always astounded Kimberly how some people still acted like they were teenagers, even when they were adults.

"Don't worry about Lucy, dear," Victoria told her with a squeeze on her arm. "I can tell Patrick is quite taken with you."

Kimberly wasn't worried. She knew Victoria was right. If Patrick was at all interested in Lucy, or any other woman in

Denver, he wouldn't have sent away for a bride. He wouldn't have ever met her.

The women went into a few more shops, but they did more window shopping than anything else, just enjoying the time together. Kimberly remembered that this was one of Nicky's favorite past-times. She remembered the letter Victoria had given her, and she suddenly missed her friend very much.

****

That evening, after dinner had been served and cleaned up, and Colleen put to bed for the night, the rest of the family gathered in Victoria's parlor. For a while, everyone kept to themselves. Keegan had found Victoria's library and was busy reading a new book. Shaun was writing down something on paper, and every once in a while, he'd scribble something out and write something new. Bridget and Victoria were sewing. Kimberly had a book in her hands, but she wasn't reading it. She wished she had brought her sketchbook down from her room. In her time on evenings like this, she would spend her time drawing. She looked at Patrick who was watching his youngest brother read the book he had.

Kimberly wondered what he was thinking, when he turned his attention to her. He reached up and lightly touched her face, then took her hand into his own.

"I guess it's time to look for other options for Keegan's education," Patrick said quietly to her.

Kimberly was glad he was willing for Keegan to go to school and started to say so when Victoria looked up from her sewing.

"I have noticed that Keegan really likes to learn," Victoria commented. Kimberly knew she had noticed that Bridget had bought new books for him that day.

"Yes, he seems to always have a book in his hands," Patrick replied.

Kimberly looked at Keegan who was still reading and seemed to not be following the conversation around him.

"What are your plans for him?" Victoria asked as she set her sewing aside.

"Well, I guess we will need to find a place for him to board this fall, so he can attend school here in Denver. Maybe I will look into his options while we are here."

"Keegan?" Victoria called to him and the young man finally lifted his eyes from his book.

"Yes, Mrs. Hilton?" He asked politely.

"If you were to get the schooling you want, do you have an idea what you would study?"

"Well, ma'am, I would like to be a doctor someday," Keegan told her almost shyly.

"That's a good goal to have," the woman told him. She was quiet for a few minutes as if thinking about something else, although Kimberly noticed that she didn't pick up her sewing again.

"I have a proposition for you," Victoria said, turning to Patrick. "Why don't you allow Keegan to board here this winter? There is a school just down the street he could attend."

"Well, I'm not sure…" Patrick started to say, but Victoria continued talking as if she didn't hear him.

"One of my gardeners quit just last week. Keegan could work in the gardens for me in exchange for room and board. He could work for a few hours after school and on Saturdays. That way he could have the evenings to study."

"Are you sure?" Patrick asked her. "What about the winter months when it snows? Can I pay you the room and board then?"

"Don't be ridiculous. He can shovel my walks and keep the icicles off my roof."

"I'm sure he will do his best to help, but he is only fifteen. He might not be the employee you're looking for."

Victoria said firmly, "It is so quiet in this large house. It would be nice to have someone else around."

Patrick looked at Shaun and Kimberly could see that both brothers communicated something to each other. He then looked at Keegan who was looking at him hopefully.

"What do you think, Keegan?" Patrick asked him. "Would you like to live here with Mrs. Hilton this winter and attend school?"

Keegan nodded his head eagerly. "I would like that." He turned to Victoria. "I promise to be a big help and work hard."

"I'm sure you will," Victoria told him with a smile. "I can keep you pretty busy in the gardens, but your school work would need to come first."

Everyone seemed to hold their breath as they looked at Patrick. Kimberly could tell that even though everyone liked the idea, the final decision would be Patrick's.

"Okay, we'll give it a go," Patrick said and Keegan let out a whoop, raising his fist in the air with a grin. "But you have to promise you'll do your best with school and with helping Mrs. Hilton," Patrick told his brother.

"I will, I promise," Keegan said. He looked at Victoria. "Thanks, Mrs. Hilton. I promise you won't regret it."

Victoria smiled at him, looking pleased that she was going to have company for the winter.

"I'll bring him down the end of August, will that work?" Patrick asked Victoria. "I would want him to come home next spring when school is out for the summer."

"That's fine," the woman agreed.

Patrick turned to Keegan. "You will need to plan on being here in Denver the entire school year, even during Christmas. You know that we might not be able to come visit during the winter months because of the snow. It might be months before we see you."

Keegan grinned at him. "I'm fine with that. I'll miss you all, but I really want to go to school."

Kimberly noticed that Bridget discretely wiped a tear away from her face. She knew Bridget was happy for Keegan but would also miss her brother.

Chapter 30

Kimberly spent the next day in Victoria's home. She helped Victoria and Bridget get a room ready for Keegan. Victoria wanted Keegan in a room closer to hers, so they cleaned out a room that was smaller than the guest rooms they had been given for this trip, but it was still larger than the cabin she had been staying in. After a few hours, with Collins help, they had a room ready for Keegan when he returned in a few months. While it was a simple layout with a bed, desk, and dresser, everything was very nice, and suited Keegan well. By the end of the day, he had a grin from ear to ear that couldn't be wiped off his face.

Patrick had left for the day with Shaun. They planned on purchasing items they would need for the summer on the ranch.

Kimberly saw the door to the room which she knew held many items Victoria had collected from the traveling to different time periods. She tried to open the door, but it was locked.

The day passed quickly. That afternoon Bridget took Colleen on a walk to a nearby park because the girl was having a hard time being inside for so long. During this time, Kimberly was able to read her letter from Nicky.

The letter was short. Nicky expressed that she was glad Kimberly was okay and happy. She mentioned a few things that were happening in their time, including the job Nicky had taken, to teach summer school for six weeks. She gave updates on Justin and his son, Garrett.

The last paragraph made Kimberly smile. Nicky mentioned she was interested in maybe being a mail-order bride too, and she hoped that she would be able to see her soon. Kimberly knew that Nicky was using Victoria's business as an excuse to come visit. She couldn't picture Nicky being willing to meet a man, sight unseen, and make a commitment to marry him before spending months with him beforehand.

She did wonder what would happen if Victoria took her seriously and sent her the paperwork. How far would Nicky go?

****

That afternoon, Patrick sought Kimberly out. He had returned from purchasing what he needed for the ranch and he was ready to talk to Kimberly and to make a final decision about their future. He found her sitting on a bench in Victoria's gardens. The bench was down a fairly long path with plenty of trees to provide shade. There were yellow and white flowers lining either side of the path, along with shrubs directly behind them. The air smelled so fresh and clean next to all the plants, and Kimberly was feeling quite relaxed.

Kimberly smiled as he approached and she rose to greet him.

"Have you had a good day so far?" he asked her as he helped her sit down beside him on the bench.

Kimberly nodded. "Bridget and I helped Victoria get a room ready for Keegan to use when he comes this fall."

"That's good. I'm glad this has worked out for him. I was a bit worried having him board with a family I didn't know."

Kimberly nodded. "What about you? Were you able to purchase everything you needed?"

"Yes." Patrick took notice of what Kimberly was wearing. He hadn't asked her what she had purchased the day before, but Bridget had informed him that she had bought a few more riding pants, and he noticed that she was wearing a pair.

"Do you want to go riding? Is that why you have riding breeches on?" he asked her.

Kimberly smiled slightly. "No. I'm wearing them because they are more comfortable than skirts. I'm really not used to wearing dresses so much."

Patrick felt confused at her words, but then realized she was talking about her time. "What did you usually wear in… 2005? Don't women wear dresses?" he asked, trying to get used to the idea of saying her time.

"Women do wear dresses sometimes, but they are shorter and have less fabric. I usually wore pants most of the time," Kimberly explained. She almost started describing her outfits more in detail but stopped after seeing the confusion on his face. She realized she would have to take this slow.

Patrick couldn't picture what she was describing. To him, it sounded like women in the future wore too little clothing.

"I want to talk to you about the time travel," Patrick told her. "I think we need to make a decision. I need to know if you really are willing to stay here, in 1892."

Kimberly smiled and nodded her head firmly. "Yes. I like your time period. I love your ranch and your family. I would like to stay here."

"What if I decide I don't want to deal with the situation that you are from the future? What would you do?" Patrick asked curiously, although he wasn't considering it.

He was surprised to see tears form in Kimberly's eyes and she quickly looked away as if to hide her face from him. "Kimberly?"

"I would have to go back to my time, I guess," she whispered.

He took his hand and lifted her face so he could see her eyes. What he saw moved him. He could see her feelings for him. He could tell that she desperately wanted to stay with him. At that moment, he knew he was making the right decision in believing her and her story.

"I'm going to make this official." Patrick stood up, then knelt down in front of her, keeping her hands in his own. "Kimberly, will you marry me?"

He watched as her eyes teared up some more and he wondered at the source, but then he saw a smile spread over her face. "Really? Do you believe me? You do want to marry me?" she asked shakily.

Patrick nodded. "I had a talk with Collins and he helped me understand a few things. I do believe you, although it is still hard to picture how those keys work."

"Yes, I will marry you," Kimberly threw herself into his arms.

As Patrick held her, he felt a strong bond growing between them. He cupped her face with his callused hands and pressed his lips to hers. The kiss became the beginning of a link that would hold them together throughout all time.

"I do have one question," Patrick told her after their kiss. "What if someday you change your mind? From what I've gathered, living in the future is much easier than now."

Kimberly reached and touched his face with her hand. His heart pounded when she did this. He realized she always did this when she had something important to say to him.

"I promise, Patrick, I will not leave you. I am committed to staying in this time and I am committed to you. I don't want to go back to my time."

"What about your friends?" He asked, speaking of Nicky and Justin.

"I admit, I will miss them, but I have been able to write Nicky a few letters. I think I will be able to stay in touch with them through Victoria and Collins, but even if that ends, your family has become my family, your ranch has become my home. I will never regret my decision to stay here with you."

Patrick gathered her into his arms again, and this time, he just held her against him. He felt so blessed that this woman had chosen him to be her husband. She was so beautiful, he figured she could have picked whoever she wanted from her time, and she chose him instead.

"Why did you decide to be a mail-order bride, to come from your time to mine?"

She chuckled at the memory, and explained, "I first answered the ad on a dare from Nicky. But after I read your first letter, I felt a peace in my heart. I knew this was the direction I should go."

Patrick felt a stirring in his soul at her words. He realized that he had felt the same thing when he had read her first response. They were meant to be together, even though Kimberly had to travel so far to make that happen.

"When would you like to marry?" Patrick asked her.

"I would like to marry you now, if possible. I would like to go back to your ranch as your wife."

A huge grin broke out on Patrick's face. "Then, that is what we will do."

****

After Colleen had been put to bed, the rest of the family, along with Victoria and

Collins, again gathered in the parlor. Kimberly had told Victoria that afternoon that she and Patrick were officially engaged and wanted to marry before they returned to the ranch. Victoria was very happy to hear the news and was glad that she had been able to work things out with Patrick.

"I knew you two were meant to be together," Victoria had told her with a hug.

Bridget had also been delighted with the news. She immediately started to make plans for the small wedding, which was to be held in two days' time. Colleen asked if she could wear a new dress. Keegan was thrilled to be gaining another sister and promised her a wedding gift when they returned to the ranch.

The only person who did not seem delighted with the news was Shaun. Kimberly knew he didn't trust easily and he treated her with suspicion. He was always polite to her, especially after Keegan recovered from his injury so quickly, but he was reserved with her. She knew he had questions about her and also knew that the entire family needed to be told about her history.

Luckily, Victoria and Collins had agreed, and they planned to tell Patrick's family that evening.

They had agreed that Collins would be the one to explain everything about the keys and time travel. Kimberly got the idea that Collins volunteered to do this to protect Victoria from any backlash or negative comments that might be said.

When Collins started to talk, Kimberly watched Shaun, Keegan, and Bridget carefully, wanting to make sure they understood, wanting to know what they thought of what was being said. Collins started the conversation by explaining how Victoria had come into possession of both keys and the way she learned how they worked. Victoria explained a few of her early trips with time travel, visiting her family home in England and going back further in time to Ireland where she met her grandmother and found the second key.

Not surprisingly, Shaun's face grew more and more tense with the story. Bridget, on the other hand, looked fascinated with what Collins described.

"I knew there was something odd about you," Shaun accused as he looked at Kimberly. "Time travel just can't happen. I can't believe you would just make this all up so you can marry Patrick."

Kimberly opened her mouth to defend herself when she felt an arm slide around her shoulders. "Be careful what you say, brother. You don't know what you are talking about."

Keegan's eyes lit up with interest during Collins' story and he immediately wanted to see the keys. "Can I try them out? I promise I will come right back," he asked with a grin.

Bridget was a little more reserved with her response, but in the end, she said, "Patrick, you have never given me a reason to doubt you, in all our growing up and adult years. Everything you have ever told me was truth. I have no reason to doubt you now. If you say time travel can happen, and you believe Kimberly is from the future, then I believe it, too. Although I'm not sure I'm as eager as Keegan to try them."

"At this time, no one will be trying them," Victoria told everyone with firmness in her voice. "I need to ask everyone in this room to not talk about the keys in public or tell anyone else about them. For your safety, this needs to be kept secret. We are telling you about them for Kimberly's sake, because she and Patrick are to be married, and we feel it will be easier for everyone if the truth is known, but no one else should know."

Chapter 31

The next day was very busy. Kimberly spent the morning with Bridget and Victoria getting ready for her wedding. Victoria had brought out her wedding dress and asked Kimberly if she would like to wear it. Kimberly instantly fell in love with the gown, even though it was a bit yellow with age. It had a wide neck, showing off her neck with elegance. There was a lace overlay that covered the entire gown and extended behind the skirt to form a small train. There was a curved "V" just above her hips. Kimberly couldn't imagine finding a dress more suited for the occasion. Bridget agreed to help Kimberly with her hair and Colleen wanted to help choose flowers for the bouquet.

At one point, Victoria pulled her aside. "I would like to give you a wedding gift. Is there anything you might need?"

Kimberly shook her head. "I have everything I need. I just wish..."

"What do you wish?" Victoria asked when Kimberly stopped talking.

"I wish Nicky could be here. A long time ago we promised we would attend each other's weddings. I know it isn't possible, but I do wish she could be here."

Victoria didn't comment and changed the subject, but she remained thoughtful after their conversation.

****

Victoria sent Kimberly out to choose the flowers she wanted for some vases and then went to find Collins. She understood Kimberly's desire to have her best friend at her wedding and wanted to see if there was a way they could make it happen.

She found Collins in the kitchen. When she entered, she saw Collins look up and smile. For the first time, Victoria had seen Collins' true feelings when he looked at her. She had suspected for some time that Collins had feelings for her, but he was always so formal and reserved around her. She always wondered if he would ever be able to relax around her. It seemed that having Kimberly, Patrick, and his family around made Collins a bit less formal.

He stood when she walked up to him and she indicated that he could sit back down.

"Is there something you needed, ma'am?" Collins asked her.

"Yes, I was wondering what you thought about bringing Nicky here for Kimberly and Patrick's wedding," Victoria said. She knew that he would need to agree because he would be the one to go get her and bring her to 1892. She also wanted his opinion on the matter. She had learned to trust his instincts, that they were usually right.

Collins didn't answer at first and Victoria started to wonder if he didn't think it was a good idea but didn't want to say anything. Finally, he spoke. "I think it would be good for Kimberly to have someone she knows here at her wedding, but are you sure this is the right thing to do? Patrick knows the truth, and now his siblings all know. The more people who know about this, the more dangerous it could be."

Victoria hadn't thought of that. She had just been thinking about Kimberly's desire to have her friend attend her wedding. "I guess it isn't a good idea."

"I didn't say that. How about this. Ask Kimberly to write Nicky another letter and I will deliver it to her. I will feel Nicky out, see if she will be receptive to the idea. If she is, I will explain to her about the keys and where Kimberly is. If she wants to come, I will bring her. If she doesn't believe me, most likely she will decide I am just an old man with an old man's ramblings, and I will leave quietly."

"You aren't an old man," Victoria smiled at him. For if he was an old man, then she was an old woman.

So the plan was put in place. Victoria asked Kimberly to write her friend the letter, which Kimberly did with excitement. She was glad for the opportunity to at least let Nicky know of her wedding and how happy she was with Patrick. Victoria also asked Kimberly for the key she had kept hidden for the last month. She watched Kimberly's face carefully as she placed the key in her hand, making sure the young woman didn't show any regrets in giving up the last link to her time, but there was none. Kimberly happily returned the key. Kimberly had no idea what Victoria and Collins were planning.

That evening after dinner was over, Collins quietly left. Using the second key, he pictured the townhouse where Kimberly had lived with Nicky and just that quickly, he was there.

****

Nicky was getting ready for bed when she heard a knock on the door. Justin had just left with Garrett and she figured they had forgotten something, so she opened the door without looking to see who it was. She was surprised to see Collins standing stiffly on her porch.

"Hi, again," Nicky greeted him. She wondered why he was here so soon after his last visit. Maybe he had another letter from Kimberly. If he did, maybe that meant that Kimberly was living closer than she thought. Maybe she was still in Denver.

"Hello, May I come in?" Collins asked, and Nicky stepped aside so he could enter. She invited him to sit down, which he did after she sat down on the couch.

"So, how is Kimberly?" Nicky asked him.

"I have another letter from her." He reached into his pocket and pulled out an envelope. He also took something else out. It looked to be an old-fashioned gold key.

Nicky accepted the letter but didn't open it, wishing to read it privately.

"I have been sent to tell you that Kimberly and Patrick are going to marry on the morrow."

"That's great, I guess," Nicky told him. She was surprised for a moment at the short time frame, but relaxed when she remembered how taken Kimberly had sounded when she talked about Patrick in the last letter. Even though she was happy for her friend, she felt a distinct disappointment that she didn't get to be at the wedding, or even meet Patrick. She had always imagined Kimberly asking for her opinion of a man before committing to marry him.

"I have a story to tell you, if you have the time to listen," Collins said.

"Okay, yes, I have time," Nicky responded.

"Kimberly is not as far away from you as you think she is. She is just in another time." Collins seemed to watch her carefully. "She has time traveled to 1892, using a key similar to this one," Collins held out the key in his hand to show her.

"Time travel?" Nicky asked with confusion. "There is such a thing as time travel? It's real?"

"Yes. Victoria owns another key like this one. Both of them have the power to take the person holding them back in time, forward in time, or to another place in the same time period."

"Wow," Nicky breathed. "Seriously?" It was starting to make sense that she wasn't able to find out where Kimberly was. She had always wondered about time travel, if it could be true. The only time she had heard about time travel was in movies and books, but she always believed in the back of her mind that sometimes movies and books could have some truth to them, even though they portrayed the truth as fiction.

"Yes." Collins continued to watch her and she realized he was waiting to see if she believed him or not.

"Okay, so let me see if I understand this. She answered that mail-order ad and started to write Patrick through Victoria. She decided she wanted to meet him, but she had to travel through time, back to 1892, in order to meet him?"

"Yes. Does this seem strange to you?"

"It probably should, shouldn't it? After all, time travel has never been proven. But to answer your question, no, it doesn't seem strange. I know Kimberly well enough to know she wouldn't have done something that she didn't feel good about."

Collins smiled at her, and Nicky noticed when he smiled he looked very handsome and distinguished, not at all formal and stuffy liked he seemed to portray himself.

"So, what time is Victoria from? What time are you from?"

"We are both from Patrick's time, from 1892."

Nicky sat back and looked closely at Collins. "Why are you telling me this?"

"Because Kimberly would like you to attend her wedding. Victoria and I felt it would be appropriate for you to come if you believed my story."

"Really?" Nicky jumped up from the sofa. "I can go to Kimberly's wedding? Can we go now? I want to see her. I've missed her."

"Yes, we can go now if you desire. I have been sent to fetch you."

"I have to do a few things first, if you would be willing to wait," Nicky said.

"I will wait. I just ask that you don't tell anyone you are leaving. You should be back before anyone misses you."

"Okay, I won't tell anyone," Nicky assured him. *Not that anyone would believe me anyway*, she thought to herself.

She picked up her cellphone and dialed the man who was over her summer class. She was glad he didn't answer, and she quickly left a message that she wouldn't be in to teach for a few days. Then she went into her room to pack a few things.

Once she was inside her room, she did a little celebration jig. She felt so excited that she was going to be able to see Kimberly, and that she was going to be able to experience time travel. What would it be like? Well, she would know soon enough. She pulled a small suitcase out from under her bed and quickly put a change of clothes and some toiletries inside it. She took her favorite dress off of its hanger and carefully folded it. It would be the dress she would wear to Kimberly's wedding.

What else would she need? She looked around, but couldn't see anything. The last thing she did was leave her cell phone on her dresser. She wouldn't need it while she was gone and she didn't want anything to happen to it.

"I'm ready," she announced as she walked back into her small living room. Collins was standing near her TV and entertainment center as if trying to figure out what everything was for and how they worked.

He turned around at her words. "Good. Now, we will be traveling together, using this one key. We will need to hold hands and we cannot let go of each other no matter what."

Nicky gave a nervous sigh. "What would happen if we did?"

"I'm not sure, as it has never happened, but I don't want to find out, do you?"

"No," Nicky denied. She would make sure she hung onto him with everything she had.

"I will take your bag for you," Collins held out his hand for her suitcase and she gave it to him. She then grasped his other hand lightly. The golden key was wedged between their two hands. She saw Collins close his eyes, so she did the same. She felt a tingling sensation that started in her toes, then spread inward. It grew to feel almost like the pins and needles she would feel if she had fallen asleep on a limb. When it got so strong and it was almost unbearable, it suddenly stopped.

Just like that, they were whisked back in time.

Chapter 32

Patrick went to find Shaun. He knew he had some damage control to do with his brother. Shaun tended to just see things in black and white. He wanted his brother's support. He knew he needed to help Shaun see that marrying Kimberly was what he wanted and that the time travel issue didn't matter. He loved Kimberly. Sometimes love can travel through time.

"Let's take a walk, brother," Patrick suggested to Shaun when he found him in the library, pacing up and down the length of the room in agitation.

"I'm fine with your marriage to Kimberly, Patrick," Shaun insisted. "We don't need to talk about it."

"If we are going to live on the ranch together, we do," Patrick insisted.

Shaun hesitated as if he was going to argue again, but in the end, he followed Patrick outside into the night. They started to walk down the street in silence.

"Tell me what your concerns are about me marrying Kimberly," Patrick invited his brother.

"How about time traveling from, what was the year? 2005? To our time? Do you really believe that? I have never heard of such a thing." Shaun said scornfully.

"Just because we haven't heard of something doesn't make it not true," Patrick argued. "For your information, I do believe it. There is too much about Kimberly that is different. I can't not believe it."

"Yes, like the way she knew exactly what to do to help Keegan," Shaun stated.

"Yes, like that. What if she hadn't been around? You know Keegan very likely wouldn't have made it."

"I am glad she was able to help Keegan, but that doesn't mean you need to marry her," Shaun told him.

While they were talking, neither of them realized they were being followed. This person did his best to stay in the shadows so he wasn't seen, but he stayed close enough to be able to hear every word the two brothers were saying.

"I'm marrying her because I love her," Patrick told him.

Shaun scoffed again.

"Look, Shaun. Like I've said before, not all girls are like Delia. You seem to judge every woman by what happened with her. I don't think it's very fair."

"I know all girls aren't like her, but I still think you need to be cautious. Let's say I do believe this story that she is from the future. What's going to stop her from finding one of the keys Victoria has and send herself back to her time when she gets tired of this one?"

"She has told me she won't do that. She likes our time period. She likes living on the ranch."

"And you believe her?"

"Of course, I believe her. She traveled a long distance to take a chance with me. How can I not believe her?"

Shaun just shook his head and abruptly turned to head back to the house.

The man who had been following them quickly hid behind a large tree. Shaun didn't seem to notice him, but Patrick thought he saw some movement in the corner of his eye and turned his head to look, but didn't see anything in the darkness. He turned his attention again to his brother.

"Look, all I'm asking is that we have your blessing. If you are so against our marriage, it is going to be hard to live together."

"Okay, if that is what you want, you have my blessing. I will do my best to be polite to her. She is the one you chose and I respect your decision. Just don't ask me to believe in this time travel business."

"Thank you," Patrick told his brother with relief. "I would like to ask you to be my best man."

For the first time, Shaun turned to him and smiled. "Sure, I guess I can do that."

When they returned to the house, it was in a small uproar. Patrick could see Kimberly laughing and crying at the same time as she hugged a woman dressed in strange clothes. The shirt was a bright blue, and seemed to be cut like a men's shirt, the only difference being that it was more form fitting, and the sleeves were quite short. The pants looked like riding pants, but were also more form fitting, and were made out of denim, which was also normally worn by men. Patrick found it odd that the clothes were men's clothes, yet somehow more revealing.

"Nicky, I'm so glad you came," Kimberly told the woman she was hugging. He watched as Kimberly then hugged Collins. "Thanks for bringing her for my wedding. This means so much to me."

Collins patted her back awkwardly as if he wasn't used to hugs from a woman. "It is my pleasure."

Kimberly noticed that Patrick and Shaun had come into the room. She ran up to Patrick, pulling the strangely dressed woman behind her.

"Patrick, this is my best friend, Nicky. Collins traveled to my time to bring her back for our wedding." She turned to the woman who hadn't said a word. She looked around her in amazement of what she was seeing. "Nicky, this is Patrick."

Patrick watched with amusement as Nicky focused on him and then smiled. She held out a hand. "It's nice to finally meet you."

"I'm glad you were able to come," Patrick said. From what he could gather, Collins must have taken a trip to the future to retrieve Nicky. He would have liked to hear the conversation Collins must have had with Nicky to try to convince her to travel in time. Unless, time travel was more accepted in the future?

****

The man watched as Patrick and his brother entered Victoria's home. He smiled to himself. He finally found the location of two other keys. Now he just needed to get them for himself.

He had been looking for them for years. He almost had one of them when Victoria had bought it from her grandmother in Ireland before he could get to it. She had left so quickly, going back to her own time, and he couldn't follow her. It had taken a long time to figure out what exact year Victoria was from and where she lived. But now he finally knew.

Now, he would need to figure out a plan to steal the keys. He didn't know how he would accomplish it, but he would have them in his possession, soon. Then he would be able to put his other plans into place.

The man laughed under his breath quietly and then pulled a key of his own out of his pocket. He disappeared with a smirk on his face.

Chapter 33

It was late before everyone finally went to their rooms for the night. Kimberly made some tea and then settled in the parlor with Nicky, both of them ready for a long talk.

"I can't believe you're here," Kimberly told Nicky. "I was so surprised to see you with Collins."

"I can't believe I'm here either," Nicky told her. "Kimberly, I need to tell you, I've been very worried about you. You just... up and disappeared. I know, you left a letter and money to cover expenses, but it scared me. You didn't even take your cell phone."

"Well, I left it because I don't exactly need it here," Kimberly said with a smile.

"I wished you had just been honest with me. I had no idea you were writing Patrick."

Kimberly looked down in her lap. "I didn't tell you because you thought the entire idea of being a mail-order bride was stupid. I didn't want you to try to talk me out of it." She scooted closer to her friend and squeezed her hand. "I'm sorry I disappeared the way I did. I didn't mean to worry you. I just wanted to meet Patrick. I really thought I'd be back before the month was up."

"But you fell in love instead," Nicky said with a smile.

"Yes, I did," Kimberly said. "Patrick is wonderful. I am glad I came to meet Patrick and I get to stay. Nicky, I love it here."

"I can tell. You are happier, more peaceful. If you want to marry Patrick, then you have my blessing. I just hope we will be able to keep in touch after the wedding, when I have to return to our time."

"I'm sure we will be able to, although it wouldn't be through the usual ways," Kimberly told her friend with a grin.

"Obviously, Patrick is incredibly attractive, so I've got to congratulate you on that! What else do you like about him? Tell me more about Patrick," Nicky encouraged Kimberly.

For the next hour, Kimberly happily told her friend everything that had happened in the last month. She told about Keegan getting hurt and how she had been able to help. She told her about Daisy and the run-in with the mother bear and her two cubs. She talked about each of Patrick's siblings and noticed that Nicky showed quite a bit of interest when she talked about Shaun.

"Shaun is a good guy. He hasn't been all that warm to me, but I think he just has a hard time trusting. He is a good father to Colleen."

"I'm glad Patrick's family has accepted you," Nicky told her. Nicky then caught her up with the events happening with their time, including what Justin was doing. Evidently, he was starting a new computer game and was very busy getting his crew together to start writing it. Garrett was glad school was out for the summer and was enjoying his summer program.

"I'm so glad you are here," Kimberly told her again. "We probably should think about going to bed, but I have one more question. Are you really okay with the time travel?"

"Sure," Nicky waved her hand. "There was always something strange about Victoria's house, you have to admit. When I was looking for you, I went to her house. It was this house, only in our time. It looked the same, only quite a bit older, you know? No one was home. When I looked into the windows, everything was covered with sheets, as if the house had been empty for years. Dust was all over everything. The grounds were well cared for, though. It was all very strange.

"When I talked to Collins, all three times, it was almost like he just appeared. Time travel isn't a new idea. It isn't considered a true idea, but movies were good at telling stories, making fiction look real. I think sometimes the movies in our time portrays something as fiction, when it really is real."

"Well, I'm glad you believed him."

"For some reason, Collins isn't hard to believe."

****

The next day turned out to be one of the happiest days of Kimberly's life. She was marrying Patrick, the man she traveled so far to meet. She was very excited to start her life with him.

She had learned to love Patrick's family. Bridget was quickly becoming like a sister to her, as well as Keegan a younger brother. She couldn't say the same about Shaun, but he hadn't glared at her since Nicky had arrived. In fact, it seemed he was fascinated by her friend. He hadn't said anything, but he couldn't keep his eyes off her. Kimberly found it amusing and wondered what he was thinking. She knew that it was just a matter of time before Shaun accepted her as family.

The wedding was scheduled for early that afternoon. Kimberly had risen early that morning even though it had been late when she had finally fallen asleep. She had risen early, wanting to enjoy every moment of her wedding day.

She headed towards the kitchen, but heard voices coming from the parlor, so she went that direction. She thought she was the first one up, so she was surprised to hear others were up.

She found Colleen in the room, Nicky sitting next to her.

"You wear funny clothes," Colleen was saying. Kimberly stayed in the doorway, watching Nicky interact with the child. Nicky loved children and they always responded to her.

"I do, don't I?" Nicky smiled at her. "I guess I better change into clothes like what you wear, don't you think?"

Kimberly noticed that Nicky wore a pair of jeans and t-shirt, just like what she would have worn at home.

"Yes, you should wear a dress. Women should wear dresses, not boy pants."

Kimberly wondered how Nicky was going to explain her jeans, but she just changed the subject.

"Tell me about the ranch you live on," Nicky invited the child.

Colleen's eyes lit up. "I just turned nine. Pa gave me a horse for my birthday."

"Really? That sounds like a great birthday gift. What is your horse's name?"

"I named her Spirit," Colleen told her, leaning against Nicky as she talked. "She is beautiful. She's mostly brown but has some white spots. Pa calls her an Indian pony."

"Spirit is a beautiful name for a horse."

"You should come see her. Can you come visit after Patrick marries Kimberly? Then I can show her to you."

"I think I will have to go back home after the wedding, but thanks for inviting me."

As Kimberly watched Nicky talk with Colleen, she felt a presence behind her. It was Shaun. He must have been looking for his daughter and stopped beside her in the doorway to watch Nicky talk with Colleen.

"Colleen is fine with Nicky. She's a school teacher and loves kids," Kimberly quickly explained to Shaun. "In fact…"

"I know she is fine," Shaun smiled slightly at her. "I've been watching for a while." He turned his attention to his daughter. Kimberly decided to go to the kitchen for some coffee, so she started to turn away but felt a hand on her arm.

"We should talk," Shaun told her in a half-whisper.

Kimberly hesitated, but then nodded. She hoped she would be able to say something to reassure Shaun to her presence in Patrick's life. She followed Shaun down the hall and into the library.

When they were both settled on the couch, Shaun started to talk. "I just want to let you know that I am supporting Patrick's decision to marry you."

"I'm glad," Kimberly smiled. "I want you to know that I love him very much."

"I have to admit I'm afraid you might change your mind in the future. After all, I am sure our time is very different from your time. You might come to miss it."

"I'll admit, there are things that I will miss," Kimberly told him, thinking about the nice stoves, the ease of communication between people, and the art supplies she had to leave behind. "But Patrick means more to me than things."

"And other people? Are there friends you will regret never seeing again?"

"Nicky and her brother are the only ones I will miss," Kimberly admitted. "I am hoping I can stay in touch with them, in some way."

"But if you can't?" Shaun asked.

"I am marrying Patrick. He comes first in my life, Shaun."

Shaun looked at her intently, and Kimberly let him scrutinize her, wanting him to feel comfortable with her marriage to Patrick.

"I have one more question," Shaun told her. "Do you really wear clothes like Nicky has on in the future?"

Kimberly smiled. She knew that she had passed some type of test with Shaun. "Yes, we dress like that. I guess I had better find her a dress from this time."

Chapter 34

About an hour before the wedding, Bridget, Nicky, and Colleen were in Victoria's bedroom helping her prepare for Kimberly's wedding. The wedding dress Victoria lent her fit almost perfectly.

Victoria gave a dress to Nicky when she found out that her friend had brought a dress from the future to wear, a dress that wouldn't have been appropriate to wear in 1892.

"How did you get used to wearing long dresses?" Nicky asked as she tried to keep the skirt smooth as she walked.

"I really haven't," Kimberly admitted. "I trip over them quite a bit."

"I've noticed that, "Bridget said. "I wondered why you had such a hard time with dresses. I guess it all makes sense now."

Kimberly looked at Colleen who was standing in front of a large mirror, brushing her long black hair with Victoria's hairbrush. She didn't want Colleen to know about the time travel until she was older. She felt it was too hard for a child to keep something like that a secret. But it didn't seem that Colleen thought anything was weird about their conversation.

Bridget caught her glance at the child. "I'm sure you will soon be great at wearing dresses."

"I really like those riding pants I wear when I ride Honey. I bought a few more when we first arrived in Denver, remember? I think I might be wearing those more than skirts from now on."

Bridget nodded her understanding. "I guess that would be okay. Just make sure you wear dresses when we go to Denver. There are quite a few people who won't understand about a woman wearing pants all the time."

****

Collins walked Kimberly into the parlor. She had asked him to give her away and she could tell he was honored. She could see the reverend standing against one wall of the room. Patrick was standing next to the reverend and he smiled when he first saw her. All of the furniture had been moved out of the room except for a few chairs where the women were sitting. Kimberly noticed that Colleen sat on Nicky's lap. Shaun and Keegan stood off to the side.

Kimberly stood in front of Patrick and he took her hand in his. He looked down at her and Kimberly's heart skipped a beat, just like it always seemed to do when he looked in her eyes.

Very quickly, the ceremony was over, the reverend telling Patrick he could kiss the bride. He cradled her face with one hand and reached the other back to touch her neck. He bent and carefully placed his lips to hers, and held them there for just a moment. When he pulled back, Kimberly had to blink away tears in order to see him. She was surprised to see he had small pools of tears in his own eyes. Not enough for anyone else to notice; these tears were meant for only her. They radiated joy to each other for a moment until everyone started moving toward them with smiles on their own faces.

Kimberly kept her hand in his as everyone surrounded and congratulated them. Patrick had made arrangements for them to spend the night at a nearby hotel. They were soon on their way to spend their first night together as man and wife.

****

Nicky enjoyed her time in 1892. It was the morning after the wedding and she felt a little sad that she was going to need to return to her time. She would miss Kimberly, but she was so grateful that she had been able to spend time with her. She knew that Kimberly was going to be happy with Patrick and his family. She felt comfortable knowing that she was leaving her friend in good hands.

She didn't want to leave until she said goodbye to Kimberly though. She put her jeans and tee-shirt back on and packed up her things in the small suitcase so she would be ready to go when it was time.

Nicky wandered around Victoria's large home. She wanted to go outside but knew she couldn't because of her clothes. She ended up in the library and spent some time looking at the books on the shelves. She soon had company; Colleen came in.

"I found you,'" the child said with glee. "I have been looking all over for you."

"You have?" Nicky asked her with a smile. "Well, here I am."

"I wanted to see your clothes again."

Nicky knew that Colleen was fascinated with her clothes being so different than her own.

Colleen walked over to her side and reached out a hand to touch her jeans.

"Colleen," Shaun came into the library. "Why don't you go outside for a while? I would like to talk to your new friend."

"Ah, Pa, do I have to? Nicky is going to leave soon."

"Yes, please do as I say. You'll get to say goodbye, I promise."

Colleen left the room very slowly showing her reluctance at Shaun's request. Soon Nicky was alone with Shaun. What did he want to talk to her about?

"You are good with children. Colleen really likes you."

"I'm a school teacher to children a little older than her in my time," Nicky explained.

"Yes, Kimberly told me," Shaun explained. "Can we sit for a moment?" he gestured towards a nearby sofa.

"Sure," Nicky agreed and sat down. Shaun sat down next to her.

"Are you okay with Kimberly marrying my brother?" Shaun asked her.

"Sure. I'll admit I was concerned when I didn't hear from her after she disappeared so quickly. But now that I know the circumstances, I'm fine with it. I can see Patrick loves her."

"He does. He has wanted to marry and start a family for quite some time."

"Is that what you wanted to talk to me about, Kimberly and Patrick's marriage?"

Shaun was starting to see that women from the future were much more straightforward than the women he knew. He found it refreshing. She was blunt enough that you never had to wonder if she was hiding anything.

"I…I was wondering if you wouldn't mind if we wrote each other when you went back to your time."

"Really?" Nicky sounded surprised at his question. "Why would you want to write me?"

"I just would like to get to know you better. I figured you will be writing Kimberly. Maybe we could write, too."

Nicky was silent for a few minutes and Shaun started to sweat. Maybe she wasn't interested in someone from the past. Maybe she already had a boyfriend in her time.

"I guess I could write you. It would be fun to get to know you," Nicky agreed with a smile.

Shaun breathed a sigh of relief. When he watched Nicky with Colleen that morning before breakfast, he had realized he wanted to get to know her better. He could tell she was great with children and she didn't seem to have a problem with Colleen's dark hair and skin.

"I have to admit, though, I am surprised you would want anything to do with me. You didn't seem to approve of Kimberly at first, especially when you found out about the time travel," Nicky confessed.

"No, I didn't," he admitted. "But as I got to know her, I started to realize she is a good person. Patrick loves her and that is what matters. And you have to admit, this time travel thing is strange."

Nicky smiled at him. "It is weird. But I think it's cool. It makes me wonder how many other people have traveled through time and we have no idea. So how will this work? Us writing?"

"I'm not sure what Victoria and Collins will say, but I'm guessing when Collins picks up letters for Kimberly, he'll take yours. Just know that you might not get letters from me too often, especially during the winter time. It takes four hours to get to Denver and we don't make the trip that often."

"Oh, I think Collins can help us with that," Nicky said with a grin.

****

Kimberly and Patrick arrived at the house at lunchtime looking happy and well rested.

Soon after they arrived, Collins announced that it was time for him to take Nicky back to her time.

Kimberly was happy to hear that Nicky and Shaun wanted to keep in touch, although she was also surprised, given that Shaun had been so against her at first and especially when he heard about her past.

"I think his daughter likes me," Nicky whispered to her when Kimberly looked at her in surprise.

Goodbyes were said by everyone. Collins led Nicky out of the back door, and then she was gone.

Kimberly felt arms come around her and turned into Patrick's embrace. "I'm going to miss her, but I am so glad she came," she said into his chest, trying not to sob.

"I have a feeling that we will be seeing a lot of Nicky in the future," Patrick told her.

He kept his arms around her and Kimberly treasured the feeling. She was going to miss Nicky, but she didn't regret her decision to marry Patrick. She had found a love that she had always wanted, a once-in-a-lifetime love.

This is the first book of the Mail-Order Brides/Time Travel Series. Please go to *http://www.zoematthewsromances.com* for more information about this series. You can also go to the next page to get information about 2 FREE books.

Get Zoe Matthews' Starter Library FOR FREE

If you sign up to my mailing list, I will send you two ebooks!

Plus, you will be the first to know when a new book is available!

You can get these books **FOR FREE** by signing up at

www.zoematthewsromances.com/

Also by Zoe Matthews

Have you read these books?

The Orphan Train Romance Series

In the late 1800s, many orphans were sent to different states in the western United States in order to provide stable and loving homes. This series features fictitious orphans who traveled to Texas, the families they found homes with, and finding love when they were adults.

An Unexpected Family

The Promise of a Family

Anna

Serena

Katrina

Orphan Train Romances Series: Five Books in One!

Westward Promises

Westward Skies

Majestic Mountain Ranch Romance Series

Six siblings come together at their family ranch after their father's death. They work together to convert their ranch into a dude ranch. Along the way, each of them finds true love.

Colorado Dreams

Colorado Secrets

Mail-Order Brides of America Series

After the death of their infant daughter, Mary, Elizabeth and Thomas decide to open their large plantation home to orphan girls who need a second chance. They name their new home "Mary's Home for Girls." Each book features one of these girls, how they came to Mary's Home, and the decision they make as adults to become a mail-order bride. Each book is set in a different state.

Mail-Order Brides/Time Travel Romance Series

Written by Zoe Matthews and Jade Jensen, a mother/daughter team

This series is based in modern times, as well as in the late 1800s. Nicki and her friends find themselves swept up in the past when Nicki reads an ad in her local newspaper, advertising for a mail-order bride. Curious, she answers the ad and is soon sent back in time to meet Patrick, a man who owns a large ranch deep in the Rocky Mountains, and his siblings. Nicki's friends soon become involved and what happens next changes their lives forever.

Touched by Time

River of Time

Winds of Time

Secrets of Time

The Xoralia Chronicles

A Young Adult Romance Fantasy Series. The first book is about a young woman who becomes the convenient wife of a handsome sorcerer in order to save her village from attack from evil men. She also learns how to become who she was born to be, and that true love can even happen with a sorcerer. The following books are about the lives of the sorcerer's seven sisters.

Kiara's Quest

The Seventh Daughter

Harvey Girls Romance Series

Written by Zoe Matthews and Evelyn Michaels, a mother/daughter team

Follow a large family of men (and one daughter) who live in Arizona near the Grand Canyon at the beginning of the 1900s. This series is Historical fiction about the Harvey Girls, a true event that was started by a man named Fred Harvey. These women helped shaped the West in their own way, just as much as the men did. The first book should be available in August, 2016.

Desert Dreams

Desert Wishes

Desert Bell

ABOUT THE AUTHORS/CONTACT INFORMATION

Zoe started writing as a young teenager and has kept that passion alive throughout her life. At any one time, she can be found relaxing and devouring a good western romance novel or gathering information for one of her own future books.

She loves living in the high mountain deserts of the western United States. Her hobbies include photographing desert landscapes and her adorable grandchildren as well as dabbling in Watercolors.

Her perfect summer days would be spent up at the family cabin writing, painting, hiking and associating with family.

Zoe Matthews is the author of the "Orphan Train", Majestic Mountain Ranch," Mail-Order Brides of America," and Mail-Order Brides/Time Travel" series.

Zoe is excited to start writing this new series with her daughter, Jade.

Jade has loved books her entire life; some of her favorite memories are the 'read-a-thons' she would have with her family as a child. She recently started tunneling that passion into writing.

She also loves oil painting, yoga, and trying new recipes in the kitchen. She enjoys spending the majority of her day with her two young children and visiting family.

She makes her online home at www.zoematthewsromances.com and on facebook. You can also send her an email at irmeloly6@gmail.com if you wish.